MISSING WOMAN

Michael Z. Lewin

"Lewin writes well, uses detail sparingly but effectively to establish the local atmosphere, allows his hero moments of calm introspection as well as of hectic activity, and, like Ross Macdonald, realizes that the causes for human behaviour may not necessarily lie around on the surface, but may be buried deep in the past."

—*Times Literary Supplement*

"The dialogue is authentic, the settings attractive, and the mystery real."

—*The New Republic*

MISSING WOMAN

Michael Z. Lewin

PERENNIAL LIBRARY
Harper & Row, Publishers
New York, Cambridge, Philadelphia, San Francisco
London, Mexico City, São Paulo, Singapore, Sydney

A hardcover edition of this book is published by Alfred A. Knopf, Inc.
It is here reprinted by arrangement with Alfred A. Knopf, Inc.

First PERENNIAL LIBRARY edition published 1984.

Library of Congress Cataloging in Publication Data

Lewin, Michael Z.
    Missing woman.

    Reprint. Originally published: New York : Knopf : distributed by
Random House, 1981.
    I. Title.
PS3562.E929M5 1984   813'.54   83-48955
ISBN 0-06-080709-1 (pbk.)

84 85 86 87 88 10 9 8 7 6 5 4 3 2 1

MISSING WOMAN

She was lovely. Gorgeous. A work of art. The pure realization in the human medium of what any private detective would want to have climb the steps to his office, sit down in his client's chair, fidget with its purse.

She didn't speak at first, looking around from bare wall to desk to cardboard box. I could have watched her forever, the many profiles of client, the many moods of client. I could hardly believe she was there, this incarnation of clienthood. When she was facing the other way, I bit myself to make sure I wasn't dreaming.

Or because I was hungry. I'm not quite sure which.

Then, then, the vision spoke. And the voice, too, was mellifluous, melodic, with tones that carried me to other, better worlds and times.

It was the words she said that I didn't like so much.

"At first I wasn't sure this place was inhabited. Christ, I'm not so sure even now."

"Just a little spring cleaning."

"In June?"

"Why not? It's still spring."

"I suppose so," she said. "Just about."

"I haven't had a chance before," I said. "You know, what with one case and another." Packing cases, mostly.

"Looks more like you're moving."

"Just clearing it for a lick of paint.".

"Oh," she said, without question, but without conviction.

I dusted off my best father-detective smile and put it on my face. I folded my hands on my desk and leaned forward. But before I could relate to her in a strong but gentle way, as it says in *How to Be a Private Eye*, she asked, "You really make a living at this?"

An all too pertinent impertinent question. If I let her go on much longer, I was going to get depressed.

"Not when people come in to jaw instead of asking interesting things like am I free to take on their jobs and what is my *per diem*."

"Your *per diem*? What's your *per diem*?"

That was better. "Eighty-five dollars a day."

"Oh. Your daily charge. I see. So you really are in business here?"

"I am," I said, with my head busy preparing my heart for disappointment.

"And you're the guy on the sign outside?"

"Albert Samson, at your service." Heart's last gesture: I sat up straight in my chair.

"I haven't come for any detective stuff." she said. But the notion caught her fancy. "Do ordinary sorts of   e ever?"

"Less and less," I said.

"Business not so good, huh?"

There must have been something revealing in my voice. But I have my pride. "Business is fine," I said. "I'm just specializing more in multinationals. What can I do for you?"

"I'm collecting," she said.

"I'm afraid all my old clothes go to a charity of my choice already."
Me.

"Oh, I don't want clothes. I want money."

I just stared.

"We're starting a play school, for the neighborhood kids. We figure if downtown is going to be a better place to live, it's gotta start with a little effort from the people who still live here. It's going to be kind of like a Head Start thing before the kids go to school, you know? We've already got temporary premises, in a building on this block just around the corner. They're going to tear it down, but we can have it through the summer. . . ." Her voice trailed off.

I watched her register that mine was one of the buildings that was coming down too.

I said, "I'm a great one for making gestures. I'm going to paint the place before I leave next Monday." This was Thursday, June 12.

"You got someplace else to go?"

My head, through my mouth, said "Sure," but my heart, through my eyes, said "No."

Being a work of art, she could read the heart.

"Thinking of giving it up, huh?"

"I am exploring various options," I confessed. Like the application for food stamps in my desk drawer, underneath my five-dollar bill.

"Not a real good time to come around, huh?"

"Well—" I began.

"It's just I'm hitting everybody. My area, see, and it's a real good cause. It helps the kids and helps us mothers too."

She didn't look old enough to be a mother to me, but I am a little old-fashioned that way.

"Jeez, anything you could afford would help. Honest," she said. She looked around again. "Anything at all."

I opened the desk drawer and gave her the five.

It was just a matter of starting the diet a day early.

"Oh great!" she said. Looking extremely pleased.

"For art," I said, inside. If I'd said it outside, she'd have asked, "Art who?" and it would have kind of spoiled it.

Instead she said, "I can give you a receipt and you can try to deduct it from your income tax."

"That won't be necessary," I said.

I'd fought the eviction, and delayed it quite a while. But the whole business was doing funny things to me.

The worst was making me ask me what I was doing with my life.

It wasn't a question I could answer. And that made me restless, because I don't like unanswered questions hanging around. They pollute the mental atmosphere.

And being restless meant I couldn't settle down to work at anything.

That left me more time to ask myself questions.

What are you doing being forty-two and not knowing one month to the next whether you're going to have the money to pay the bills?

If you're not making money at it, why aren't you at least enjoying it?

If you're not enjoying it, why aren't you doing something else?
What else could you do?
Can you even do this?

The play-school lady left me at about four-thirty and by five I was ready to leave me too.

It's not that I had no work to do. There was a report due Friday. I'd been trying to get around to it all day.

I had just put it off a little while, in favor of packing. And in favor of washing some socks. And in favor of watering my ivies.

And because I was afraid that when I finished it there would never be any more work, ever again.

An irrational fear, I told myself.

But even I don't always listen to me.

At five I decided to go out for a meal. A big steak. Start the diet in style. That way when, later, I dropped in unexpectedly again to spend the evening with my woman and her daughter and my woman asked "Have you fed yourself decently?" I could say "Sure," with head, heart and anything else required.

I might have given away my last five bucks, but I still had a credit card. My romanticism has a practical side.

And something would turn up.

The bill from the credit-card company, if nothing else.

2

I got up at nine to unlock the office door, as if ready for a day of business. Over a light breakfast I applied myself to the report I had to do.

Nothing difficult. I'd been hired for a fixed fee, to check into the background of the girl friend of a businessman's twenty-one-year-old son. The kid was in college and the father, a wheeler-dealer who hadn't finished high school, was eager that his oldest son not be put off his studies.

The businessman's name was Albert Connah. "She looks like a hooker to me," he had said. "Not that I'm going to knock hookers, but they tend to want to get their dough the easy way, you know? How many hookers keep good records and pay taxes like the rest of us?"

Like the rest of who?

"So," he said, "look around. Find where she comes from, what she sees in a dope like my kid except his old man's money."

O.K.

"And on the quiet, right?"

On the quiet. Check.

"If she turns out to be straight—and how do I know, 'cause most of the chicks these days look like hookers to me—then I don't want my kid to know I've been poking around."

Kid not to know. Check.

"Money's a terrible thing, Samson. Makes you suspicious where before maybe you were easygoing. This whole thing makes me feel bad. I mean, what would I have done if my old man had messed in my business? Beat him up, that's what. I ought to be satisfied that my kid even likes girls, the state of the world. But I'm not. There you are. Why, I've even come to you to do this work because I don't want my regular detectives to know I'm so petty. What do you think of that? Eh?"

I didn't think a lot about it one way or the other. The job helped me with my own petty feelings about not having any money in my pocket.

And I hadn't turned up anything that damning. The girl was a secretary in an office at Connah's son's college and she hadn't advertised her background in the ten months she'd worked there. I'd tracked her back to Toledo, where she'd grown up. I'd found a shoplifting conviction and a brother with a pot arrest. Before dropping out into secretarial work, she had done two semesters at Ohio State, but only the most rabid Hoosier would hold that against her. She was living in Indianapolis with an auntie. She was taking catering classes at night.

I figured Papa Connah was going to be disappointed. But not at my work. I'd been thorough and earned the fee.

Which, considering I didn't have it yet, was another problem.

After breakfast I read the newspaper thoroughly.

After the newspaper I put on more coffee.

I got out paper and a carbon.

I cleaned the keys of my typewriter.

I looked out the window.

I dusted the sill.

I found my notebook.

I poured the coffee.

And then, lo and behold, I heard someone come into the office.

It was a new day and such was my refreshed confidence that I didn't even think I was hearing things. Pregnant with optimism, I gathered my notebook and a pen and walked from living quarters to business quarters.

I found a plumpish woman of about thirty in a beige headscarf and a dowdy lightweight gray coat.

"Mr. Samson?"

At least she hadn't come in by mistake.

"Can I help you?"

"I hope so," she said. She sat down, of her own volition, in my client's chair. She took her headscarf off and shook out short dark hair. She looked as if she were staying. My optimism was birthed.

I took the traditional place behind the desk and opened my notebook. I tried to look as if I were searching for a page that was empty. I wrote down the date.

"I'm in a somewhat strange situation," she said measuredly. "I saw your sign last night and I've come in on an impulse."

"I'm happy to hear about it," I said. The happiness was genuine. I was pleased to have someone to talk to. "And I've just made some coffee. Would you like some?"

"Oh? All right. Yes," she said. She thought for a moment. "With cream and two sugars."

Cream, milk. It's only a matter of degree.

When I returned, she said, "My name is Elizabeth Staedtler. I'm in Indianapolis to see about a job. I came in yesterday afternoon and my first appointment is at eleven."

I looked at my watch: just after ten.

"I will probably be here until tomorrow," she said.

I asked, "Where have you come in from?"

"Connecticut. Bridgeport."

"And what do you do, or hope to do?"

"I'm an academic," she said. "I'm considering a post at I.U.P.U.I."

The joint Indiana University and Purdue University campus in Indianapolis.

"So you are, perhaps, Doctor Staedtler?"

"A Ph.D.," she said, with a faint smile. "Yes. But my problem isn't about that."

"What is it about?"

"I have a friend," Dr. Staedtler said, "who lives in Indiana. In Nashville, in Brown County."

"I know it," I said.

"We were at college together, the University of Bridgeport, and we've kept in touch."

"How long is that?"

She thought for a moment. "I graduated in 1975. But she left early. She had a rough year or two and then got married in 1974. We wrote letters once or twice a year since then, and when I found out I was coming to Indianapolis I thought it would be a good chance for us to get together. The trip came up so quickly that it was too risky to write with the mail the way it is, but I phoned after I got settled."

"And what did she say?"

"Well, that's the problem. Her husband answered the phone. I asked for Cilla. He said, 'She's been gone for two months,' and hung up on me. I called back again, just to say who I was and ask where she had gone, but he wouldn't talk to me or help or anything."

"Mmm."

"I don't know what to do. I gather it's not very far, but I'm just not going to have time to go myself."

"It's about an hour's drive to the south."

"There. Two hours, plus not having an idea who to ask what. I just can't do it. I've got to go back East as soon as I'm finished here, but I would hate to leave knowing nothing more than 'She's been gone for two months.' The only thing I could think of was to get somebody to find out what happened for me. If she's left her husband, fine, but maybe someone knows where she is or how to find her. And if I do take this job, and she's around—well, I'd like to have that information. She might even want to come up and share a place with me." Dr. Staedtler sat back. "There it is."

"I have a report to finish this morning," I said, "but I can go down to Nashville in the afternoon."

"Good."

"But it is inevitably going to be pretty expensive for what I am likely to be able to find out."

"You cost what, something like a hundred and twenty-five a day?"

"Eighty-five plus necessary expenses," I said.

"Well, that's worth it to me."

"All right, then," I said, trying to contain a sudden bubbling cheerfulness. "Half a day with some traveling is likely to run about fifty dollars, so twenty-five in advance is fair."

She opened her purse, but seemed to hesitate. "Mr. Samson?"

"Yes?"

"If it takes more than half a day, would you be available to continue on the job?"

"I ought to be able to learn whether she's left her husband and whether she's still around Nashville easily enough," I said.

"But if she's not?"

"Actually finding her would depend entirely on what's happened."

"All I'm saying," she said, "is that if it takes more than half a day, I'm willing to pay for it." She took out a fifty-dollar bill and pushed it toward me across the desk.

I took it but scolded her gently: "That can be an expensive thing to say to someone in a profession which is thought of as badly as mine is."

She seemed surprised. "Oh? You mean you might take advantage of me? You are licensed and bonded and all those things, aren't you?"

"Yes."

"And how long have you been in this business?"

"Since the mid-sixties," I said. And it suddenly sounded like a terrible period of time to work at something and still have to scratch for a living.

"What more can I do?" she asked then, bringing me back.

"Nothing. It was just a facetious comment because private detectives don't exactly have the reputation as professionals that, say, doctors do."

"Doctors can keep their reputations as far as I'm concerned," she said sourly.

We seemed to understand that we were talking about medical doctors and not her kind of doctor.

"May I ask what field you're in?"

"What? Oh. Sociology."

"I see. Interesting."

"Yes," she said.

"Right, then, I'll need a few details."

"Like what?"

"Like your friend's name."

"Oh dear. I'm sorry."

"There's nothing to be sorry about."

"Priscilla Pynne." She spelled it, and pronounced it "pin."

The husband's name was Frank and she gave me the home telephone number and address. "I also have a picture," she said. And she fished it out of her bag. "It's about three years old."

The picture was a lakeside snapshot of an exceptionally pretty girl in a bikini, which might also have been pretty except there wasn't enough of it to tell.

"I'm sorry it's a bit informal for identification," Dr. Staedtler said, "but I happened to have it with me and thought it might help."

"I'm sure anyone who's seen her wandering around like that will be able to identify her." She was a hazel-eyed sandy blonde, mostly thin, with long flowing hair. The only thing which kept it from being a completely attractive picture was the look of mild discomfort on

Priscilla Pynne's face. It was out of sync with what was otherwise, apparently, a relaxed circumstance. I commented on this to Dr. Staedtler.

"She didn't like pictures being taken of her."

"Why not?"

"Well, she's extremely good-looking," Dr. Staedtler said, "and she felt her looks kept people from appreciating her other attributes."

"I had the same problem when I was her age," I said. It was meant as a joke; she took it seriously. I let it pass. "I don't know where your eleven-o'clock appointment is," I said, "but if it's at I.U.P.U.I. you haven't got a lot of time."

"Oh."

"Only two more things."

"Yes?"

"One is a receipt." I wrote it out and gave it to her. "And the other is arrangements for telling you what I've found out. Shall I call you?"

"That's a little difficult. I can call you."

"Which may also be difficult, depending on how things go. What shall we do?"

"I can give you a number I'll be at between eight and eight-fifteen."

"O.K., fine. And if, for some reason, I can't call then?"

"Then I'll call you. Do you have an answering machine? I could leave a message when you could call me again. See, I don't know yet what my schedule is going to be."

"I'm afraid my machine is being repaired." By a pawnbroker. "But I can give you a number where you can leave a message." I wrote the number on the back of her receipt.

"Your home?"

"My mother."

"Oh," she said.

"As you see, I'm moving offices."

"Oh yes. I hadn't noticed."

She put the receipt in her purse and rose. "That's it, then?"

"Yes. I'll get started as soon as I can."

"Good," she said. And left.

. . .

And there I was. Employed again. Rather unusually and by a client whose motives might not be exactly as advertised. But fifty dollars in the pocket go a long way sometimes.

I walked straight back to my typewriter and produced a succinct, articulate report, with accompanying bill and accounting of expenses. I was a model of purposeful, efficient activity.

3

I dropped my report at the offices of Albert Connah Enterprises: ACE, Inc. Then I drove out of Indianapolis on South Meridian Street.

I felt buoyant, as if suddenly freed. Not only did I have a little money, but I was being sent from paint-starved ante-demolition Indianapolis to one of the nicest areas in all of Hoosierland.

Glaciers in the dim and distant past flattened out most of what is now Indiana. But some way south of Indianapolis, the famously flat terrain suddenly sprouts hills. That's where the glaciers stopped, and where Brown County begins.

A forest here is set aside as a state park and although there are other areas protected one way or another, Brown County is the place preferred by flatland Hoosiers when they make their day trek in autumn to see treey hills lush with the colors of dying foliage.

It's nice in June too.

Nashville is the county seat, and center of the county tourist trade. It's known for a flourishing art colony, focused on the attractions of the scenery, that was established around the turn of the century. There are dozens of full- and part-time professional artists in the area and they add a dimension which is not standard American small-town equipment, even in tourist centers.

The antique and curio and craft emporia are as expected and are interlaced with franchise catering outlets, restored historic buildings and associated spin-offs like a John Dillinger Museum. But quaint history provides one earthy feature which I particularly appreciate. This is the Liar's Bench, outside the courthouse in the town square. Not only should every town have one, every courthouse should.

The forty-three miles took me a little more than an hour. I parked within sight of the Old Log Jail and went first to the sheriff's office. This was a carefully rusticized modern building on the west side of the square with a heavily tinted glass door.

Just inside on the left was a counter with a notice proclaiming INFORMATION.

That suited me, so I stood there until the young woman behind the counter finished with a telephone call and turned from her switchboard to attend to me. It was just before one o'clock.

I asked to see the sheriff.

"I'm afraid Sheriff Dunlap is out just now," she said. She had a soft and pleasant voice.

"What time will he be back?" I asked.

"You don't know our sheriff, then?" she asked.

"No."

"Well, you'll find her just across the street partaking of her lunch at the Nashville Inn."

"Her?" I asked. It was involuntary, even though the switchboard operator had set me up.

"That's right, mister," she said, with a grin.

"How many times a day do you get to spring this surprise on culture-cosseted strangers?" I asked.

"Oh, not very often. Mostly strangers don't come in asking for the sheriff."

"I suppose not."

"And Jeanna's pretty well accepted now among all the local folk." With a bit of pride she added, "She's now been in office three years."

"Long may she reign," I said. "You said I could find her across the street. Does that mean she wouldn't mind my interrupting her?"

"Not since it sounds like you've got something on your mind."

"Thank you kindly," I said.

As I crossed the street, I nearly convinced myself that I dimly remembered reading about the election of Indiana's first woman sheriff. If the restaurant had been farther away, I might have succeeded.

I asked the cashier in the restaurant and she called over a waitress, who led me through the dining room to a small window table.

The sheriff was a tall woman, over six feet, and although not remotely beefy, neither was she frail. She wore a uniform shirt and trousers and a gun on her left side. She was somewhere in her thirties and she was finishing what seemed to be a bowl of stew.

"Gentleman's asked for you, Jeanna," the waitress said.

The sheriff wiped her lips as she turned to look at me. "Thanks, Julie," she said, and the waitress left. "Sit down, sit down," she said to me, and turned back to her meal.

I sat down. "Sorry to interrupt."

"You want something to eat?"

"No, thanks. I had a bite in Indianapolis before I came down," I said.

"O.K.," she said. Carefully, she spooned up the final contents of the bowl. She wiped her mouth again, and then lit a cigarette. "I'm Jeanna Dunlap, sheriff of this heavenly county. Who might you be and what can we do for you?"

"I'm a private investigator and I've been asked to get a few details about a local woman who I understand left her husband a couple of months ago. A Priscilla Pynne."

The sheriff leaned an elbow on the table. "Do you mind if I have a look at your ID?"

"Not at all." I gave her my license card.

She studied it and handed it back. "That's who you are," she said. "What makes you think I can help you, Mr. Samson?"

"I don't know that you can. But it's good form for investigators to inform the local law when they come into their jurisdiction."

"And you're feeling in good form today," she said, without cracking a smile.

"I guess I am, Sheriff," I said. "And it also seemed possible that you would know the woman."

"You think she might be known to us, eh?"

"I think she might have been reported as a missing person, even if she wasn't a criminal recidivist."

"I must confess," the sheriff said, "I do know Cilla Pynne. But I'd like to hear a little more of what you're looking for her for, and on whose behalf."

"It's pretty simple," I said. "A college friend of Mrs. Pynne's came to Indianapolis and when she called she was told that Mrs. Pynne left home two months ago. The friend hired me to find out the story, since she doesn't have time to do it herself."

The sheriff thought about this for a moment. "Good friend?"

"I don't know. Sounds like. But she walked into my office this morning and is leaving for the East tomorrow. I'm down finding what I can for her."

"There some way I can check this by phone?"

"I don't have a daytime number for her. She's at a job interview. I'm to phone her tonight."

"Some way I can check on you? Someone who knows you?"

I gave her the name and number of a friend in the Indianapolis Police Department.

"O.K., Mr. Samson," she said, "I sure can tell you Priscilla Pynne left home about two months ago."

I waited. "That's it?" I asked finally.

"There isn't much more. I don't know the date exactly. I got the call early on a Sunday morning. You can get the date from the log over in the office. Or from the local paper. They publish the sheriff's log week by week."

"Who was the call from?"

"Her husband."

"Do you know where she went?"

"Nope. Her whereabouts are unknown. Her husband filed a missing persons on her, and there is also a warrant for her arrest."

"A warrant? What for?"

"On her way out she seems to have picked up about fifty dollars from her husband's wallet."

"That's it?"

"Crime is crime," Sheriff Dunlap said. "The lady also took his wedding ring, some silver cuff links and some loose change off the bureau."

"Sounds like he's lucky they don't put gold in teeth anymore."

"Could well be," the sheriff said. "Although it could also be that her husband thought we'd look harder for her if she was accused of a crime."

"I take it the circumstances of her leaving are not otherwise suspicious?"

"You take it correctly. Mrs. Pynne appears to have departed with a local man by the name of Boyd."

"Oh," I said.

"Springtime," Sheriff Dunlap said. "Sap starts to rise."

"You say 'appears' to have left with him?"

"Nobody's heard from either of them, but they kind of left town in the a.m. of the same morning. Bit coincidental otherwise."

I nodded. "Did Boyd leave family here?"

"Nope, none. He wasn't married, and, in fact, he lost his only relation—his mother—in the beginning of March this year."

"Were he and Mrs. Pynne known to be friendly?"

"No, I'd say they kept that little secret pretty well."

"How did they leave?"

"Don't know that for sure either. We found the Pynnes' car in the Memorial Union parking lot at I.U., over in Bloomington, you know? Billy's car isn't around."

"Billy?"

"Billy Boyd. Just about everybody calls him Billy."

"He's well known here, then?"

"Oh yeah. Billy grew up here. Everybody local knows Billy."

"What does he do?"

She snorted gently. "Billy has interests."

"What are you saying? Business interests?"

"Some. From time to time. Well, look, Billy grew up here and then went away for a while, some years. When he came back, his mother set him up in pretty much whatever he wanted to do. First thing was that he took over a drugstore his father owned and converted the place into an art gallery. He was going to sweep through the art business here. But after a while he seemed to become more interested in the lady artists. In a business way he's dabbled in one thing and another."

"All financed by his mother?"

"Far as I know."

"And since his mother died?"

She shrugged. "He's talked about developing some land his mother left. But I suppose he's carried on pretty much the same."

"Then Mr. Boyd has had quite a number of female friends over the years."

"I would have to say that notching up ladies is the one thing he has devoted himself to with unflagging consistency."

"Has he ever run away with any of them before?"

"Billy ran away with a woman a long time ago. Let me think. He's thirty-six now. That'd be when he was about fifteen, sixteen."

My face showed surprise.

"He was gone several years," she said. "That was the time I mentioned before."

"You know Mr. Boyd fairly well, then, do you, Sheriff?"

"Not these days," she said. "Not for maybe twelve years. Hell, it's no secret. We spent some time together and I kind of thought he liked me. But in the end he was doing it just because he wondered what it would be like for Nashville's littlest man to go with Nashville's biggest woman."

"He's a small man?"

"A short man," the sheriff said carefully. "About five-one, hundred and twenty."

"He sounds like a real romantic, if you don't mind my saying so."

"Oh, Billy's O.K. Apart from being a real bastard, if you take him for what he is, he's O.K."

"And do you know Mrs. Pynne well?"

"Hardly at all. I met her a few times."

"Could you give me the name of someone who knows her better? A friend?"

"You might try Sharon Doans. Lives down the road from the

Pynnes. I understand that Sharon was just about her best friend. Though there was maybe a little trouble between them before Cilla left. You might ask her about it."

"All right. And Mrs. Pynne's husband?"

"Frank? He's something over at I.U."

"Professor?"

"No, no. Something in the administration kind of way. Buying things and something to do with buildings."

"And what does he think about all this?"

"Well, he calls me up most every week to find out whether I've found her or not."

"Every week?"

"Just about."

"So he's eager to have her return?"

"He wants her found. That's not the same thing."

"Why does he call, then?"

"He wants his fifty bucks back."

4

The sheriff and I left the restaurant together.

"I wonder if you could give me some directions," I said.

"Directions are a specialty," she said.

I asked for the local newspaper and for the Pynnes' house.

"You can see the *Democrat* offices from here," she said, and pointed north up Van Buren Street.

I saw them.

"To get to the Pynnes' log cabin, you'll want to go the other way."

"Log cabin?"

"Oh sure. They're all over the place. You only got to look."

I resolved to look.

"Van Buren here runs into State 46. Turn toward Bloomington and head on out over Salt Creek. Just outside of town there's a dirt road on the right. You'll see their mailbox, but the house is way back."

"Fine," I said.

"Sharon Doans' place is the next one along, and if you come to the entrance to the State Park you've gone too far."

In the general offices of the *Brown County Democrat* I asked to see some recent back issues. I half expected to be given specialty directions to the public library, but a grave young man at the advertising desk pointed across the room. There, just inside the photo-filled front windows, a row of newspaper display racks stood holding the previous twenty weekly editions.

I looked first for the sheriff's log entry about Priscilla Pynne's departure.

The sheriff's log was part of a feature called "The Fine Print," which also listed area accidents, arrests, ambulance runs and hospital admissions.

Frank Pynne's call about his wife had come on Sunday, April 13: "7:34 a.m. Man reported his wife left home and took the family car as well as some of his money and personal possessions."

I leafed through that paper and the following week's but could find no further information.

Then I started looking through the preceding weeks to see if I could find any other references to Mrs. Pynne or Mr. Boyd.

In the edition of April 2, I found a headline which read COUNTRY STAR FOR BOYD BIRTHDAY. The previous Saturday, Billy Boyd had had himself a big birthday celebration. The birthday was his thirty-sixth. "I generally don't make a fuss out of this sort of thing," Boyd was quoted as saying. "But in the Orient they have a twelve-year calendar and so they make a big thing out of every twelfth birthday. That sounded like a good idea to me." He had rented the Nashville Theater for a country-music concert open to the public, and then held an après-show party for some two hundred people at his house. There was a head-and-shoulders picture of Boyd shaking hands with a guitar-toting gent whose name I did not recognize. Boyd had dark hair and heavy eyebrows over penetrating eyes. His features otherwise were fine, even delicate, and I would not have guessed him as old as thirty-six.

I thumbed a few weeks farther back and, in the edition of March 5, I found the story of Boyd's mother's death. It was a news story and not an obituary. She had died in an accident, having slipped in her bathroom and hit her head two days before. There was no suggestion of anything suspicious, and most of the short article was the equivalent of an obit. Her husband had died in 1960; she had one child, "a local businessman"; she was a vigorous woman with an active interest in the Brown County Trust and in the Brown County Supernatural Society.

In the same issue I found out what the Brown County Trust was. B.C.T. TAKES ON THE PYRAMID.

The B.C.T. was an environmental group. At their annual general meeting they had voted to fight the plan to use defective limestone blocks to build a huge pyramid in Bedford as a tourist attraction and promotional device for the limestone industry.

The B.C.T.'s "chairman and founder," David Hogue, was quoted as noting that the vote "declared this group's acceptance of its duty to serve as a protective watchdog for the whole of southern Indiana, in the absence of other properly concerned organizations. Bedford may be the limestone capital of the world and may have provided stone for the Pentagon and the Empire State Building, but the proper place to build a pyramid is in Egypt. If they want to do it there, we won't fight it, but anywhere in southern Indiana and they've got a battle on their hands."

The B.C.T. also elected officers at their meeting. Among them, as a "committee member with responsibility for project evaluation," was Frank Pynne.

I got my little panel truck from the parking lot and headed toward Bloomington. Town ended abruptly and I started looking for dirt roads. The first possibility was called to my attention by a red Ford Fiesta turning sharply onto the highway ahead of me from the right. It came out of the road mouth and I saw there a mailbox with large red-orange letters spelling Pynne.

I didn't get much of a look at the driver. The car was filled in the back with cardboard boxes. Nothing seemed to be gained by my chasing it. There aren't many vehicles my van can catch. I turned up the driveway.

After a considerable drive I came to a clearing and the Pynnes' "log cabin." They don't make them like they did in Abe Lincoln's day. Double glazed windows, television antennae, solar panels. This one even had a front door instead of a bearskin flap.

I could see no cars and suspected I had only myself to talk to, but I pounded heftily on the door knocker, a cast-iron affair in the shape of a tree. Nobody answered.

I tried the door. It was locked.

I walked around the house. I couldn't tell how much of the surrounding land belonged to the Pynnes, because the trees gradually thickened into a wood without benefit of fences. But there was a conspicuous air of rural pursuits, with much cultivation and a sizable chicken run. I saw no chickens, however.

Nowhere from the building could I see either another house or even a cultivated field.

I had a look through the windows. The curtains were drawn and revealed an interior with sparse furnishing. What there was looked comfortable enough.

There didn't seem a lot more I could do. I got into my van and drove back to the roadside. I turned west and around the next bend I found another mailbox, with painted initials S.A.D. There was no road by it, but on the other side a gravel track led down a slight hill and I could just make out a small frame structure through a grove of trees.

I pulled across the highway into the track, assuming that S.A.D.'s S and D stood for Sharon Doans.

5

The gray board building was peaked like a chapel and looked old, far more a product of age than the log building I had just come from. A yellow VW Beetle stood on the gravel loop driveway and I parked behind it.

I walked toward the front door.

As I did so, it suddenly opened and inside the screen door a short woman appeared, hands on hips, framed in the doorway.

She was a startling figure, with red hair that fell in a divided waterfall across both her shoulders to below her waist. She wore a faded denim jacket and skirt, orange fishnet tights and navy-blue sneakers. On her belt there was a large hunting knife slotted into a holster.

Whatever I had expected, this wasn't it.

"You want me?" she asked.

"Are you Sharon Doans?"

"I am."

I took a step closer. "I was told you know Priscilla Pynne." She didn't deny it. "I would like to ask you a few questions about her. I've come down specially from Indianapolis. If it is at all possible, I'd appreciate it."

She wrinkled her nose and dropped her arms. "Oh hell. Come on in."

The inside was one large open room. Near the window next to the front door were a couple of wicker chairs and a table. She pointed me to one of the chairs, then suddenly stood in front of me again in the posture she'd appeared in the door with.

"Does this look active yet attractive?" she asked.

"Oh yes," I said. Or frightening. Depends on how you take it.

"O.K. Good."

She took off her hair.

"Excuse the rig-out," she said, waving the red wig. "I do lots of bits and pieces to make a living and sometimes it's book covers for this series of romantic novels." She pointed to a drawing board standing in a distant corner next to a table, a floor-to-ceiling mirror and an assortment of artist's paraphernalia.

"I'm on a book cover now. The book's about an unconventional woman who finds true love in the arms of a butcher."

"Many women do," I said.

"You really think so? I just haven't known that many butchers." She made it sound as if she'd been slightly irresponsible. "But I kind of thought maybe a woman who liked knives . . ." She patted the handle of the weapon at her waist absently. Then scratched under the base of the brown bun which had been revealed when the wig came off. "Hang on a sec."

She walked across the room and put the red wig carefully on the back of a chair. When she came back, she said, "I do most of my own modeling. I model a little bit for other people, so I figure why not for myself too."

"Why not indeed."

"Phew!" she said, and she dropped heavily into the other wicker chair. "I like to dress up anyway. I've got a big basket of clothes back there, all kinds of stuff. I get a charge out of it. And any other stuff I need, I borrow from stores in town. They're really helpful that way with people doing art around town."

"Do you read the books?"

"Enough to get the feel of them. Covers have to relate to what's inside."

"Then there are some pretty lively insides around."

Seriously she said, "The world's a modern Babylon." She looked up at me. "You wanted to talk about Cilla, but who are you?"

"A friend of hers has hired me to look for her."

"Hired?"

"That's right."

"Then you're not a cop?"

"No."

"Good. I'm going to make it breaktime and have a smoke. You want one?"

"No, thanks, I don't smoke."

"I don't mean a cigarette. I mean a joint."

"I don't joint either," I said.

"Too old, or what?"

"Too old," I said.

On the table in front of us was a small pottery bowl and in it there were four fusiform home-rolls. The table also bore an ashtray and a brick with a hollow full of stick matches. She took one of the cigarettes, striking a match on the side of the brick, and made herself comfortable.

She waved the cigarette at me. "It's good for you, you know."

"Delta-1-THC and its metabolites have too long a biological half-life to suit me," I said.

"What?"

"The active ingredients stick around in the body for too long."

"I hadn't heard that one before," she said. She thought. "But it sounds good rather than bad to me. Hey, do you mind if I write it down?"

I didn't, and she got up and brought over a piece of paper and a pencil. I repeated the chemical name for her.

"Wow!" she said. She leaned back. "I'm a little-bit person," she said. "I draw a little bit, I model a little bit. I like to write, so I write a little bit. Only I haven't got any imagination, so I just write down the stuff that happens to me, and the stuff that interests me." She drew on her cigarette. "So what did you want to know about Silly, then?"

"Silly?"

"Cilla. Priscilla Pynne."

"I see. I understand that you were perhaps her best friend."

She considered that. "I don't know about best or not. Who said 'best'?"

"Sheriff Dunlap."

"You've been talking to Jeanna?"

"Yes."

"She's been filling you up with a lot of idle gossip about me, I suppose."

"We didn't talk much about you, Miss Doans. Apart from what I've said, she suggested that more recently there might have been some trouble between you and Mrs. Pynne and that I should ask you about it."

"Ooooh." She waved her cigarette irritatedly. "It's not worth . . ." But she settled to tell it. "A couple of months ago there was this big party."

"Was that Billy Boyd's party?"

"You know about that?"

"Yes."

"Jeanna again, I suppose. All right, so Billy was making this big gesture with this party, inviting everybody he knew, even people he didn't like who'd been maybe friends of his mother's, right? But Billy's a stirrer, right? Now, I love him like . . . like a brother. I do. But he enjoys causing trouble, and so at this party he had a whisper to Silly and she came out to the garage and found me and Frank—that's her husband—in the middle of a friendly little kiss."

She made a face and vibrated her hands to show mock horror.

"Well, would she stay and find out what it was about? No. She just walked away and left the party." Shrug.

"What was it about?"

"Frank took me out there to talk about *her*. He was real worried about her. He knew she spent a lot of time here watching me draw and talking to me. She even modeled for me sometimes. I think underneath that cold exterior she liked dressing up even more than me."

I thought about asking whether Priscilla Pynne smoked with her, but, pre-empting my question, Sharon Doans said, "No, Silly hated this stuff."

I smiled and nodded, conceding that I had been wondering.

She waved the butt at me. "Makes you perceptive," she said, but her selling was soft. "Silly had a bad time with drugs sometime before she came here. She dropped out of college and a year or two later she OD'd in New York. They got her back together, and sent her home for Christmas."

"Where's home?"

"Springfield, Massachusetts. And that train ride was when she met Frank. Isn't it romantic?"

I kind of preferred the butcher, but I'm funny that way.

"Anyway, the party. Frank was just sort of saying thanks for the help when Silly walked in, and for a change she acted out her name. When I figured out what happened and who it was, I went to try to find her, but she had already gone. Then I saw Billy watching me with that bushy little smirk of his. I said, 'You sent her out there, you evil little bastard.' Oh, sorry," she said, covering her mouth. "I'm a little bit foulmouthed too."

"Let me know when it shows so I can cover my ears."

"He said, 'I cannot tell a lie,' and then he said, 'but it's not exactly a cherry tree I cut down, is it?' "

She watched my reaction to this. I smiled, and nodded gently.

"Well, I thought that was pretty funny, right off the cuff, you know," she said. "I wrote that one down, even though it couldn't be farther from the truth."

I nodded yet again. I didn't know whether I was an oil donkey or a junkie.

"Anyway, then he said, 'And she didn't even say thank you. Oh well, maybe she'll find some other way to show her gratitude.' "

"And you think that their running off together might have been tied to her finding a way to show her gratitude."

"If I know Billy—and do I know Billy!—Silly is busy showing her gratitude at this very moment." She laughed at that. "But seriously," she said, "Silly shouldn't have left because of anything to do with what happened at the party. There wasn't anything in it."

"But you think she might have left because of it?"

"It might have helped her make up her mind."

"But it had been brewing?"

"Hell, I don't know. I don't really know anything about her. Not to understand her. I know she'd had a rough time here, especially the first year. She was depressed from being so isolated and with nobody around she knew. She got some pills from Andy Kubiak at first, but lately she's seemed better. I do a litttle bit of acting, amateur stuff at the theater, you know? And she came down there with me and helped backstage with makeup and costumes. But she wasn't really happy."

"How long have the Pynnes been here?"

"Two and a half, three years. Something like that."

"And Mr. Pynne?"

"What about him?"

"What's he like?"

"Strong sort of guy. Knows what he wants. Short-tempered and kind of restless, though. I think he's looking for mountains to climb."

"Or pyramids?"

"Hey, you know about that." She cocked her head. "Are you pretty sharp or are you stringing me along already knowing this stuff I'm telling you?"

"I'm pretty sharp," I said.

She snorted. "Anyhow, he's not the easygoingest guy I've ever known. Though he's loosening up a little lately." She waved the remains of her cigarette. "He's started smoking again. When he came here, he was as much against it as Silly, from his time in Nam, but nowadays—"

"He was in Vietnam?"

"Yeah. Came out, went to college, then graduate school and now here. He's one of the ones that used it, getting himself together like they used to say the Army did."

"Except he is restless."

"Just wanting to push on for new things. He wants to be rich and he wants to be a daddy. And he thinks Silly is a prize bitch for walking out on him."

"Do you think Mrs. Pynne will come back?"

She thought for only a moment. "No. I'd bet she never comes back. She's away. She'll stay."

"Do you think she's been planning it for a long time?"

"I don't know. She didn't love Frank and maybe the more she became her own person, the more important that was."

"She told you she didn't love him?"

"Oh, the marriage was sort of one of convenience from the beginning. He helped her get back together and she gave him the pretty, housified wife that was part of his idea of how things should be."

"But no children?"

"He wanted them. She was holding out. Maybe that pushed her too."

"But you don't think she and Boyd had planned to leave for a long time?"

"Naw," she said. "Billy wouldn't have planned."

"Not at all?"

She shook her head dismissively.

"But running away takes money. He'd have had to arrange that."

"Billy always carried cash. Hundreds, at least."

"Would that have been part of his appeal to Mrs. Pynne?"

She mused. "Could be. I hadn't thought about it, but Frank is tight as a tick. She wouldn't have had any money of her own."

"And the appeal from Boyd's side?"

"Oh, the chance to crack the Ice Queen. He'd have jumped at that."

"The Ice Queen?"

"That's his pet name for her. She didn't exactly walk around radiating warmth and friendliness. But he'll melt her good, believe me. And then he'll leave the screwed-out hulk and wander home."

"You assume Boyd will be coming back?"

"Hell, yes. In fact, I'm surprised he's been away this long. Guess there's a little more to Silly than I thought." She looked at me slightly wickedly. "I look forward to hearing about it."

"You're in his confidence, then?"

She suddenly went quiet, and her face lost its animation.

"Miss Doans? Are you all right?"

Eventually she said, in a throaty whisper, "I was thinking about Billy. I . . . I'm a little bit bad, you know. I don't care enough what . . . Well, when he tries, Billy makes me . . . makes me feel better. It's just I miss him. I'll be glad when he's back. He's a laugh, Billy."

I sat and watched her.

She looked back. "I bet you don't make a girl feel small either, do you, mister? Not even a little bit of a little-bit girl."

"Not intentionally," I said.

"I didn't think so. Look, with all my other little bits I'm a little bit of a whore. Are you maybe a tomcat, like my absent friend? Would you keep me company for a while?"

It was terribly quiet, there in the forests of Brown County.

I said, "I don't think I'd be able to provide what you're really missing."

"You might help me forget for a while."

I didn't say anything.

"But you have work to do," she said.

"Yes."

"And you're going to go do it?"

"Yes."

"O.K.," she said. "Sorry."

"There's nothing to apologize for."

"O.K. I guess I better get back to work too."

We both got out of our chairs. She went to get the red wig and then carried it back to the door. "Anything else I can tell you?" she asked.

I said, "I would like to talk to Frank Pynne. I've been to the house, but he isn't there. I saw a car pulling out of the driveway which might have been him. It turned toward Bloomington. Would you know how I might go about getting in touch with him?"

Her head jumped back, as if I had slapped her. "Look, mister, I don't know what goddamn Jeanna Dunlap has been saying to you. Frank Pynne may have been around here a few times for a smoke and a shoulder to cry on since he got deserted, but that doesn't mean I keep track of his movements every day or have his phone number tattooed over my heart."

"Sheriff Dunlap didn't say a thing about you and Mr. Pynne, except what I told you before."

"Yeah, yeah. Well, I could tell you a thing or two about her, you know? She used to turn on too, did she tell you that?"

"No."

"That was before she got herself elected sheriff, but she's been in this room high as a cloud. You better believe it."

"I only asked because as a friend of the family it seemed you might know how I could phone him or get a message to him. That's all."

She breathed heavily before me. "Oh shit," she said, and threw the red wig onto her head. "Yeah. I'm sorry. I feel a little bit in pieces, that's all," she said. "Ah, hell. I don't know." She adjusted the wig. "How do I look? Great, huh?"

"If I were a butcher," I said, "I'd be at your mercy."

6

When I pulled up to the edge of the highway, I turned left, toward Bloomington, and in about fifteen miles I came to the Indiana University campus. The place was huge, big enough to rate a bypass all of its own. But I followed signs into the heart of things and hoped for the best.

Best turned out to be the Indiana Memorial Union. Mrs. Pynne's car had been found in the parking lot there and it seemed as good a place as any to base an attempt to get directions to Frank Pynne.

For fifteen cents I bought an hour's parking. It was five past three when I walked into the Union entrance. But before I started trying to locate Pynne, I went to a telephone and called the Indianapolis Police Department.

I caught my friend there in.

"Lieutenant Miller," he said, conveying more fatigue with his tone than a Greek chorus chanting "I'm tired" would.

I identified myself and said, "Jerry, you sound awful."

"I know," he said. "I am awful."

I knew things were bad. He never just talks to me. He carries on, he complains about my abuses of his position. It made me feel bad. I was calling to ask him to abuse his position.

"What's wrong?" I asked. "Are you sick?"

"I wish it was that simple," he said colorlessly. "Look, Al, I'm up to my neck. You want something, right? What is it?"

"I'm trying to trace a woman who's wanted for theft in Brown County. She ran off two months ago with a guy with a few business interests in Nashville. I'd like you to get one of your people onto the banks in Nashville to see if you can find his account. I'd like to know what money has gone out since April thirteenth and where it's been sent. Guy's name is Boyd. Billy, presumably William."

Miller just said, "All right." He didn't fight it. He didn't ask questions. "Is that all?"

"That's all. I'll call you back. How late will you be there?"

"How long is it till midnight?" he asked. He hung up.

I felt guilty about benefiting from his misery. But one learns to live with guilt.

I went next to a desk offering University Information. A sweetness-and-light coed offered help and before she could say "We're number one!" I had her on the phone to the university employment office tracking down Frank Pynne.

It took several minutes. I.U. employs a lot of people, but not enough at the employment office. Pynne was finally fixed in a building called Administrative Services and the same telephone put me through to the secretary who coordinated his department.

"I'm sorry. Mr. Pynne isn't in the office," she told me.

"Is he expected back soon?"

"No, I'm afraid he isn't. He's been in Indianapolis all day. He had a meeting this morning and this afternoon he is due to see several firms there about an absorbent-paper tender. He's not expected back in the office until Monday."

"Oh dear," I said.

"Can I take a message?"

"No. But you can tell me something, if you will. Is Mr. Pynne's car a red Ford Fiesta?"

Uncertain at first, but she said, "Why, I believe it is."

"Troubles?" my coed asked after I hung up.

"The story of my life, darling," I said. "The guy I've come from Indianapolis to see is away for the day in Indianapolis."

"Gee whiz," she said. "That's a real shame."

"Yup," I said. Wondering how Frank Pynne managed to be in both Indianapolis and his own driveway at the same time.

"Anything else we can do for you?"

"Not unless you were around this place during the dark hours of the morning on April thirteenth."

"No, sir. The building is closed up after midnight. Even the snack service."

"What sort of security patrols are there?"

"I'm afraid I don't know. But the director is around the building today. You could ask him."

The director's office was, conveniently, just across the lounge from the information desk.

The director was, inconveniently, not in his office.

I returned to my coed. "He's never gone for long," she said.

So I killed some time. I strolled through the Memorial Union to evaluate the quality of the backup services which modern educational establishments provide for our current college young people. Cafeteria, delicatessen, Sweet Shoppe ("for bulk candies and popcorn"), billiards, craft shop, bowling. There was even a bookstore.

I also passed a Ride Board, with "Need Ride" and "Want Ride" cards neatly organized among ten zones in Indiana and seventeen zones through the rest of the country. There seemed to be a lot of action among kids wanting to leave the campus. I would have been happy to come and take somebody's place for a few weeks. Or years. I would even be willing to learn something, if I had to.

After a few minutes I came back to earth. Also back to the director's office. The door was now open. Someone was inside. Always trust a coed.

He was a bulky little man. Too many stops at the Sweet Shoppe. He had a sweeping shiny forehead and eyes that glowed bloodshot. I had a momentary feeling that he no more belonged there than I did, but I knocked on the door. "Excuse me," I said.

"Yes?"

"I was hoping for a few words with the director."

He studied me. "You're not a student, are you?"

"No."

"A civilian. I've always got time for a civilian. Come in."

I went in.

"What's your problem?"

"I was steered to you in hopes of getting some information about a car that was left here in the early morning of April thirteenth."

"Here? You mean in the parking lot?"

"That's right."

"We have them towed away. We notify the campus police and then after forty-eight hours, pffft, they're gone. So you better ask them if the car's missing."

"It's not that. I'm looking for the woman who left the car in the first place. I'm wondering if there is any chance of finding anybody who saw her leave it."

"Hell," he said. "No one's going to pay attention to anybody parking a car in a parking lot."

"Not even at two or three or four a.m.? I was thinking, maybe, a security patrol."

"This is a college, mister. It's chock full of college kids and everybody knows that college kids are crazy. We could have the whole goddamn parking lot full up at three in the morning. They're loonies, kids, every single one."

I went back to the parking lot and stood by my van. I had a look at the loonies, the traffic, the buildings. I noticed a bus stop, a bicycle path. I felt uneasy about it all. I decided not to spend a few years here after all. Besides, at fifteen cents an hour, it was outside my reach.

And I couldn't think why Priscilla Pynne should take the trouble to leave her car here.

On the way back to Nashville, I stopped at the Pynnes' house again, but there was still nobody home. I felt I ought to talk to Frank Pynne, but it seemed that I would have to wait until he got back. From wherever.

I had a couple of other visits I could make, but after I parked in town, I went to the sheriff's office first.

An elderly man was reporting a grass fire to a muscular young deputy as I walked in. He had passed it as he was driving into town and he had seen a couple of children nearby.

"You reckon them kids are in danger?" the deputy asked.

"Naw," the man said. "Them kids was laughin' it up."

"So maybe they started it, huh?"

The deputy decided to have a look and he told my soft-voiced girl at the communications console that he was going out to Clay Lick Road.

"O.K., Peg?" the deputy said.

"I got it," she said.

As the deputy left, I stepped up to the counter. The girl remembered me. "Howdy, stranger," she said.

"Hello."

"You looking for Jeanna again?"

"Yes and no," I said. "I want to talk to her before I go back to Indianapolis, but there are some other people I want to see too. I stopped in to get an idea of her comings and goings so I wouldn't be interrupting her meals again."

"She's out now, but she's bound to be back here about five."

I looked at my watch. It was a little after four. "O.K., I'll try then."

"But I wouldn't worry none about her eating time. Jeanna's got a real strong stomach. She don't hardly never get indigestion."

Neither did I, lately. It takes food to get indigestion.

"Meanwhile, could you give me directions to a couple of people?"

"I'll try."

"An Andy Kubiak. Is he a doctor?"

"Sure is."

"And the person in charge of your theater here."

"George?"

"I don't know the name."

"George Keneally. He'll likely be down there."

"O.K., directions to down there."

I transcribed them and went on my way.

I walked out to the doctor's first. His house was on Greasy Creek Road, a few blocks east of the town center. From his shingle—well, a sign on the front—I learned that he was the county coroner as well as being a general practitioner. It also said that Friday office hours didn't start till six, but I rang the bell anyway, and the door was answered by a stocky white-haired woman carrying some needlework.

"I would appreciate a few words with Doctor Kubiak," I told her.

"It says plain as day on the sign that he don't see people until six o'clock. Can't you read, boy?"

"Yes, ma'am," I assured her. "But I'm not here as a patient. I'm trying to find a missing woman who was one of his patients and it's possible that he could help me."

"Now, you look kind of sensible," she said charitably. "You ought to know that a doctor can't just up and tell someone knocking on the door things about his patients."

"I wouldn't ask him to breach confidentiality, but he still might be able to help, if he would."

"Well, he won't."

"Could you ask him?"

"Nope," she said, " 'cause he ain't here."

"Oh. When will he be back?"

She had an obvious answer available for this, but instead she squinted at me. "This a local woman that's missing?"

"That's right."

"Priscilla Pynne, I'll wager."

"You'll win."

She shook her head. "I just never could fathom that girl. I didn't have no time for her. Got herself a good man there, one that pulled himself up by his bootstraps and made something of himself. Got themselves a nice little place too—damn sight nicer than most young people can afford—and so what if it's a little bit lonely. This whole town is isolated, it's no big city and there just ain't no point folks moving here and then bellyaching because it ain't Chicago. She should have just settled herself in and made the best of it. Had some kids. She came to Andy for the 'depression' when she first arrived in town and he gave her some pills, but I reckon she just wasn't making the effort. A woman's got to pull her weight and that's all there is to it. If she don't knuckle to it, what's the point in getting married in the first place? And it looks like she's asked herself the same question. Upped and run off with a banty cock like Billy Boyd. Well, it's her husband I feel sorry for, and that's the truth. You get someone like her comes to my Andy complaining how hard life is, nine times out of ten, ninety-nine out of a hundred, it's not them that needs the pitying, but the people that depend on them. Well, that's my opinion, and you can do with it what you like."

What I did was thank her for it.

The Brown County Theater was on the south side of town and from the front I couldn't see any obvious signs of life. On the off chance, I pushed at one of the front doors. It was open.

I wandered in.

The theater foyer itself was empty, animated only by a barrage of good-time posters. This was not Hamlet country. There were sounds of music coming from the auditorium. I followed them into the darkness.

I found myself faced by a stageful of singing children, being led by an enormous woman peering up at them from the orchestra pit.

As my eyes became accustomed to the dark, I was able to make out some people scattered through the seats. I picked the closest one and just as I drew her attention, the singers' leader stopped proceedings.

"No! No! No!" she shouted at them. "We do not pick the nose and sing at the same time. You, boy. When you've finished your business, we will begin again."

"And they say show biz is glamorous," I said to my shadowed neighbor. She looked at me as if I'd just been flicked down beside her by the offending finger.

"Can you tell me if George Keneally is around?"

Unsmiling she pointed to another shadow, at the back.

"Many thanks," I said, and made my way through the empty rows to the designated figure. I asked him for a few words.

"With pleasure," he said.

I believed him.

We went to the foyer. He was about fifty-five and wore a comfortable brown jacket with fourragère, an olive-green shirt and blue jeans. Also a captain's hat.

"Press?" he asked.

"Are you hoping I am," I asked, "or hoping I'm not?"

I gave him my name and occupation and explained that I wanted to get a little background information on Priscilla Pynne.

He had trouble placing the name.

"I think she helped backstage with some amateur productions," I said.

He cocked his head. "Is this the one who ran away with Billy Boyd?"

"That's her."

"Someone told me she'd been around here," he said, "but I couldn't for the life of me place her. They said she came with Sharon. Is that right?"

"Sharon Doans. Yes."

"And Sharon went off with the husband at that party too. You know the party?"

"Boyd's birthday, yes."

"And what a whale of a festivity that was. With all the undercurrents about his giving it so soon after his mother's death and then picking a fight with that Trust fellow."

"A fight? You mean fists?"

"Oh no. Talk, all talk, about some land or other."

"Which Trust fellow? Not Frank Pynne?"

"No, that lawyer. Hogue."

"David Hogue"

"That's the one."

"Life seems pretty complicated around this town," I said.

"I can tell you what makes a small town tick," Keneally said. "Gossip. If it's not who's been seen with who, then it's who said what about who. It takes some getting used to if you come into it from the outside, as I did. But I've always liked a touch of drama. And there's no shortage around here, believe me."

On the town square I stopped at a public telephone and called Lieutenant Miller at the Police Department in Indianapolis again. He sounded as if he had just been released too early from the hospital.

"Christ," I said, "you need a vacation, Jerry."

"I need more than a vacation," he said. "Oh. You want that stuff. Hang on."

I hung. He was away for nearly all my change.

"O.K. We found your bank. The Southern State. At first the guy there said he wouldn't go very far without a court order. But then he had a look at the records, and there wasn't much to say anyway."

"How's that?"

"Basically, the account has had no action the last couple of months."

"None?"

"There's a regular monthly payment, but nothing else at all since April thirteenth. Though there was a six hundred withdrawal on the eleventh. You interested in that?"

"I suppose so. Who is the monthly payment to?"

"He wouldn't say who. But it's for a thou, has been drawn on the account only since the first of April, and it's not to a business concern."

"That it?"

"That's it. You got enough to go back with a court order?"

"I don't know," I said. "I'll stop in a day or two with a CARE package for you and maybe we'll talk about it."

"I think I'm past CARE," he said.

It was almost on the stroke of five that I returned to the sheriff's office. I arrived just in time to see the unmistakable form of Jeanna Dunlap disappearing through the front door, and as I entered I heard her being told that I would be stopping by to see her again soon.

"There's my stranger now," Peg, the switchboard girl, said.

"Hail, Indianapolisite," Sheriff Dunlap said. "How have you been faring?"

"Well enough to have another question or two for you."

"Come into my parlor, then," she said, and she led me to a door with an opaque-glass upper half which had her name painted on it in big gold letters. She opened it for me, and I went in and sat on a wooden chair in front of her desk.

She unhitched her gun belt, and put it in a desk drawer as she sat down. "You found Cilla Pynne yet?"

"Nope."

"My my." She looked at her watch. "You been here hours and hours too."

"Sheriff, you're teasing me."

"I sure am."

"Do I understand correctly that you don't take Mrs. Pynne's and Mr. Boyd's absence very seriously?"

"Not terribly seriously, no," she said. "Do you?"

"I find myself feeling uneasy about it," I said.

"You'll accept my apologies if that, by itself, doesn't spur me to great agitation," she said.

"I will," I said.

"So what are your questions?"

"What has happened to Boyd's business since he left?"

"Seems all right."

'It's still open, this art gallery? It still runs?"

"It sure does."

"So he has a manager of some sort?"

"He always has. Cecil Tolley's girl, Mary. Worked there since Billy opened it." Sheriff Dunlap looked at me steadily. "What you are inching your way toward is asking me whether Billy's been in contact with Mary Tolley since he left."

"That's it."

"Well, he hasn't."

"Did he leave instructions before he left?"

"No."

"Isn't that surprising?"

"It doesn't worry me."

"Why not?"

"Because, Mr. Samson, it doesn't worry Mary. I know her pretty good, and that suffices for me."

I had to concede that she was likely to have a better feel for what should be worrisome in Nashville than me. I told her so.

"It sure does make me feel all warm inside to know I have your confidence," she said.

"The other thing that puzzles me is about cars," I said.

"I sure can hardly contain myself in the waiting."

"The assumption is that they left in Boyd's car, is that right?"

"They're gone and it's gone."

"What kind of car is it?"

"One of those Nip imports. A Datsun, a white sports car, but I forget the exact model name."

"Have you tried to find it?"

"I put it on the state list for a week."

"But no sightings?"

"No."

"Why not longer?"

"Car's not stolen. And I wouldn't have said that either Billy or Cilla Pynne was exactly a threat to society."

"O.K.," I said. "What about Mrs. Pynne's car?"

"Ah, now, I managed to find that one," the sheriff said mischievously.

"My question is why Mrs. Pynne would drive her car all the way to I.U. to meet Boyd if what they did there was just leave it behind."

The sheriff shrugged. "I'm not sure quite what there is you want answering."

"They could have met anywhere. Even in the center of town. If somebody saw them, so what? They probably weren't hiding the fact they were leaving together. And it wasn't a matter of gaining time, because Frank Pynne called you first thing the next morning. As long as she actually got out of the house without waking him up, she was away. Might actually have been a little safer if she walked to the road and he picked her up there. No risk from the noise of starting the car that way."

"Next time maybe they should come to you for help with their plans."

"It doesn't answer the question. Why did she drive to I.U.?"

"I don't know."

"All I could think of was that Boyd was away during the day somewhere that way. Do you know where Boyd was on Saturday, the twelfth?"

"No. Never occurred to me to find out."

"But it doesn't bother you?"

"Not a lot."

I shook my head with some frustration. "I don't understand why people are so uninterested in these two people leaving town."

"Oh, I wouldn't say we're uninterested. I'd say we're mostly dying to know all about it, and when Billy comes back folks will be plaguing him to tell them all the details."

"So you assume Boyd will come back?"

"Oh sure. Bound to. Billy's a hometown boy. He'll always come back."

"But not Mrs. Pynne?"

"Different sort of case," Sheriff Dunlap said. "From what I know, I wouldn't have said there would be a lot here for Cilla Pynne, not after all this hoo-hah."

"There's just a whiff of provincialism in that, Sheriff. Priscilla Pynne is an outsider here, so maybe you aren't as concerned about her as you would be if she was local born and bred."

Sheriff Dunlap said solemnly, "I don't think you have any facts to support that suggestion. If we know people, we have a better chance of understanding what is serious and what isn't. But we know how to provide protection and our other services to comparative strangers, and we do so to the best of our abilities. If two folks want to run away together, there's no way we're going to put that at the top of our priority list. We've got plenty of other things that are a damn sight more important to the peaceful and secure pursuit of life in this community."

I sighed. I was unhappy not to be able to get to grips with what was unsettling me. But I said, "No more questions, then, Sheriff. Sorry to take up so much of your time without seeming to be constructive to you."

"Don't you fret yourself, Mr. Samson. And if there's anything else we can do for you, why you just come on back and ask, hear?"

7

After I left the sheriff's office, I crossed the street. I intended to ask someone for directions to Billy Boyd's art gallery, but then I realized I didn't know what it was called.

I was a bit at loose ends.

I went back to the telephone box I'd used before. I called Frank Pynne's home number. There was no answer. I leafed through the Yellow Pages to see whether one art gallery seemed more likely than another on the basis of their ads.

The one called Boyd's seemed less than a long shot.

It was all of a block west of the courthouse, on a corner of Village Green Community Park. I went straight there, pleased to have someplace relevant to go.

It was closed.

What little time I spent looking through the windows made me think that it looked a lot like an art gallery.

When I turned around, I noticed a red Ford Fiesta parked near the opposite corner on Thomas Street. I stopped and looked at it for a minute. It seemed a little too chancy to be what I thought it might be. But I walked over to it. I had not recorded the license plate of the previous Fiesta in my life, so I couldn't tell for sure. This one had no cardboard boxes in the back, but it did sport a window decal of the Brown County Trust.

It was also parked in front of a restored frame building which bore a plaque identifying it as the place of business of David Hogue, Attorney-at-Law.

All praise to the smallness of small towns.

A second plaque traced the building's history since erection in 1887. And a mimeographed sheet in the window gave a list of the

B.C.T.'s activities in June. There was a committee meeting scheduled for seven that night.

I tried the door. It was open. I cheered up a lot.

I went in cautiously and turned left into a waiting room.

A secretary sat at a desk beside the front window. She looked as fresh as an Indiana tomato.

"Hello," she said. And smiled.

A plate on her desk told me her name. "Betty Weddle," I said, "you've just about made my day with that cheery greeting."

"That's kind of you to say so. Can I help you?"

"Am I right that Mr. Frank Pynne is here?"

"Yes. He's with Mr. Hogue."

"I've been trying to get a few words with him all afternoon. Do you know how long he's going to be?"

"I don't really know. They're talking about a meeting that's being held here tonight, but if I've got anything to say about it Mr. Hogue will be getting something to eat before then."

I gave her my name. "I'm a private detective from Indianapolis," I said, "and I've been hired to try to trace Mr. Pynne's wife. If it's at all possible, I'd like to arrange a time to speak to him before I have to go back tonight."

Betty Weddle looked thoughtful. Then she rose and said, "I think I'll just pop up and let them know the situation."

I couldn't have asked for better.

I spent the time admiring the room, which was particularly comfortable as lawyers' waiting rooms go. Us private detectives spend a lot of time in such places, when we are in regular work.

This room was anchored with a rich deep brown carpet and had solid maple furniture. Several large watercolors framed the full fire and brimstone of Brown County in autumn.

I sat down and bounced on the chair a little. It was the second place that day I would have been happy to live in for a few years. I had places to live on the mind.

Betty Weddle was back within five minutes. She was a robust woman in her thirties with an impressively tiny waist which her clothes showed off. She said, "They would like you to come up," and she seemed a bit surprised to have that message to convey.

Not nearly so surprised as I was.

I thought she would give me directions, but she led me springily up the stairs and through the doorway at the top.

Two men waited there. One was a casually dressed but carefully presented man of perhaps fifty. The other was about thirty, and wore a dark suit and tie.

"Mr. Samson," Betty Weddle announced as I entered the room. Then she left.

The older man came forward with his right hand extended. He was wiry but about six feet tall. "Dave Hogue," he said. "Glad to meet you. This is Frank Pynne."

Pynne, though about the same height as Hogue, was much fuller framed, apparently also without fat. He was dark, while Hogue was mostly gray, and Pynne had a tidy mustache which turned down at the ends.

Pynne shook hands with me, but without speaking.

"I'm pleased to meet you," I said. "I've tried to get a chance of a word with you at your house and at your office, but I was unlucky."

"What's your business with my wife?" he asked abruptly.

"I've been hired to find out what happened to her."

"She ran away with goddamn Billy Boyd, that's what happened to her. And that's nothing to what will happen to her when she comes crawling back."

"Frank," Hogue said, "we don't have a lot of time. I don't want to interfere. After all, the man wants to talk to you rather than to me. But if we're—"

"Sorry, Dave," Frank Pynne said. "And sorry to you too. I don't know what you are or what your business is, but I shouldn't sound off even if I do get mad every time I think about my so-called wife."

"I've been hired by a woman your wife knew at college, a woman named Elizabeth Staedtler. She may be moving to Indianapolis and wants to get in touch."

"Expensive way of getting in touch," Pynne said. He frowned over the name, but failed to place it.

"I came down from Indianapolis around midday and I've heard the superficial details of what happened. I gather nobody knows where Mrs. Pynne is, just at the moment."

"I wish I did," Frank Pynne said darkly. He saw Hogue make a face at his implied repetition of threat. He seemed, again, to control himself.

I said, "People also led me to believe that she may well not come back, but I certainly wanted to ask Mr. Pynne what he thought about that."

"What do I think? I think she'll be back all right. She'll be back because she hasn't got the stuffings to deal with life by herself. Billy will dump her and she won't have anyone to make all her decisions for her and then she'll be back. And I'll make a few decisions for her."

I was dealing with delicate areas, and not as a representative of one of the sides in the particular battle Pynne was tooling up for. It made questions more difficult to ask, since they had to be restricted in scope. "So I can take it, can I, that you haven't heard from her since she left?"

"That's right."

"I should say on Frank's behalf," Hogue said, "that his wife's de-camping suddenly with a man like Boyd was probably as upsetting and destructive a way for her to leave as she could possibly have chosen."

"So there was no real warning that she might leave?"

Pynne sighed. "None."

"May I ask why it was particularly bad of her to run off with Boyd?"

The two men looked at each other. Hogue said, "It's a rather com-plicated business, Mr. Samson. I don't know whether anyone has mentioned the Brown County Trust?"

"It's come up two or three times. I gather that it is a large and suc-cessful local conservation group."

Hogue nodded. "Yes, basically," he said. "And since he arrived in Brown County, Frank here has been one of our most active newer members. We are all impressed with his deep love of our county, his quick appreciation of the wonderful variety of terrain and natural phe-nomena, and of the rich balance of ecological systems here. It's really a special place, a unique area. And Frank has come to understand that and has shown great willingness to work not to petrify it or preserve the countryside just exactly as it is but to make sure that new use of old country is harmonious."

It was a pretty well worn sort of speech. It impressed me not with Pynne's described devotion, but Hogue's. He felt what he said.

"The particular sensitivity to Mr. Boyd in this context," he continued, "involves a tract of land which he inherited from"—he paused—"from his most regrettably recently deceased mother. Ida Boyd was, herself, an active member of B.C.T. and had wishes for the land which, unfortunately, she did not have time to make certain would be carried out. Billy's plans, as he's expressed them, are specifically contrary to his mother's, and there has been an enormous amount of controversy surrounding him, quite without recent events."

"Does that mean Boyd was actively working on plans for this land?"

"Actively enough to be able to talk in detail about several ways of ruining it," Hogue said acidly.

I thought for a moment.

"You look as if you have something on your mind, Mr. Samson," Hogue said.

"Without meaning to be offensive," I said, "it's Boyd's departure rather than Mrs. Pynne's that seems not quite right."

"How do you mean?" Hogue asked gravely.

"Boyd came into money and property recently, I gather."

"And threw a party to celebrate it," Pynne said.

"It's just that he seems to have had a lot going for him around here. It feels as if there is something missing to explain why he should suddenly leave the area altogether."

"He left once before," Hogue said quietly.

"Yes."

"Though he was young."

"Oh, cut the cackle, Dave," Frank Pynne said. "Billy was dying for an excuse to get away for a while, and if he could do it and knock off my wife at the same time, nothing could have pleased the little snake more."

"Why did he want to get away?" I asked.

"Because everyone in town thinks he killed his mother, that's why."

"Tell me about it," I said.

8

I left Hogue and Pynne about twenty past six. It was in comfortable time for me to get back to Indianapolis by eight o'clock, which was when I could call my client.

Risking starchy temptation, I stopped to eat between Morgantown and Samaria. It was at a diner-*cum*-general store, tacked onto a gas station, and it seemed full of beer coolers. But I managed to get a couple of hamburgers without buns and some space to bring my notebook up to minute.

The rest of the drive was a chance to ruminate on my afternoon's encounters, and I did some useful work on my mental cud. I was home ten minutes before the hour.

In the basket behind the mail slot in my outside door there was a hand-delivered message. It said that for my own advantage I should call Albert Connah, and the sooner the better. Connah was the man whose son's girl friend I had backgrounded. The note gave his home telephone number. The envelope also contained a check.

I called him.

"I liked your work, Samson. Clear, concise and cheap."

"Thanks," I said. "No problems, then?"

"Not for me. Just for you."

"Oh?"

"You're in a building that is being torn down, aren't you?"

"Yes," I said. I hadn't told him.

"So you're being kicked out of your place there?"

"I'm fighting it. I intend to have them relocate me."

"Don't jazz me. I made a phone call this afternoon and you've already lost."

"They might change their minds before Monday." Though Christian charity is often pretty hard to find in the Bible Belt.

"I want to see you tomorrow. I have an offer to put to you."

"I'm not sure that I'll be available tomorrow. I've got a client who may want me to do some work for her."

"Cut the bull. You're broke and we both know it."

"I'm calling my client in two minutes. I'll be making a verbal report to her, either tonight or tomorrow. After that I will know what I'm doing. Or not doing. I'll call you then."

"Yeah, yeah. Just be in my office tomorrow at . . . at twelve."

"I will if I'm free."

"Don't get me wrong. I'm not hiring you for another job."

"Great."

"But this offer you aren't going to refuse."

All of a sudden I led an exciting life.

Before I called my client, I called my mother, in case there was a message to change our arrangements.

"No business calls, Albert," she said. "But Lucy called to say her mother wants to know whether you'll be coming over tonight."

"O.K. Thanks, Mom."

"Son?"

"Yeah?"

"I was talking to Mrs. Portingale, you remember her?"

"No."

"She was in for lunch. And she's got this room, with a spare bed in it. Her son is going off to the Marines in ten days and if you don't mind sharing it till then you can have it. She won't charge anything. She'll be glad of the company."

"I'll think about it, Mom. But I've got to make a phone call now."

"You know I don't have a lot of room here, Albert."

"I know. Down to the last square centimeter."

"She's a nice woman. You could probably arrange meals too. Just as a stopgap."

"I will give it my earnest consideration and let you know in a day or two."

"All right, son."

I was glad I had something else to do rather than give it my earnest consideration immediately.

I dialed the number Elizabeth Staedtler had given me.

She answered it at the end of the first ring. "Is that Mr. Samson?"

I confessed.

"I was afraid you wouldn't call," she said.

"I make it a point of professional pride to do what I say I'll do," I said. For as long as the profession lasts.

"So," she said, "have you found out anything?"

"One way and another," I said, "quite a bit. Shall I come to wherever you are and tell you about it, or do you want to wait for a report until tomorrow?"

"I'm not busy," she said. "But I'll come to your office. Are you at your office?"

"Yes."

"I'll be there in about fifteen minutes."

I made my private-life phone call and spent the rest of the time dusting my desk and emptying the office wastebasket.

Elizabeth Staedtler was two minutes early. She wore the same subdued clothing as before.

"Come in. Sit down," I said.

She sat in my client's chair. She seemed extremely tense.

"Would you like some coffee?"

"No, thank you. Have you located Priscilla?"

I took my place behind the desk and opened my notebook. "No," I said, "I haven't located her."

She sighed. "I see. Well, what then?"

"I've confirmed that she has left her husband. She left Nashville early morning on April thirteenth. As far as I was able to find out, nobody knows where she is. I didn't find anybody who had heard from her, or who even had an educated guess to make."

"Is her husband looking for her?"

"Not actively. He keeps in contact with the sheriff to see whether there have been any developments, but the sheriff isn't making any effort either."

She seemed to think hard before saying, "What does it have to do with the sheriff?"

"There's an arrest warrant out on your friend."

She was shocked. "Arrest? What for? Leaving her husband?"

"No, no. But she took some money when she went and her husband is pressing charges."

She inhaled heavily and took this in.

"The charge seems to be a bit artificial. The husband is angry, and thought it would make the law work harder. Only it hasn't."

She considered this too. Then asked, "So what are the prospects of Priscilla being found?"

"I think people down there generally expect to have some information about her before too long."

"Really? How?" she asked quickly.

"They all seem to think that sooner or later the man she ran off with will come back, and that then they'll get the whole story."

Her eyes opened wide. "Man? What man?"

"The facts of the case seem to be that Mrs. Pynne left town in the middle of the night with a local businessman and stud-about-town, named Boyd."

She was speechless. She raised a hand to the side of her head and seemed to be steadying herself.

"Do you know the name, Doctor Staedtler?"

"What?"

"Boyd? Billy Boyd? I thought, perhaps, she might have mentioned him in a letter. But I guess not."

"No."

"He does not seem to be the world's most sensitive human being. His mother died in March just before she was about to tie up some land she owned in such a way that he would never be able to exploit it commercially. Her death, from a bathroom accident, could hardly have happened at a better time for Boyd's financial prospects and there is widespread suspicion that the timing was more than just macabre luck. There doesn't seem to be any proof. The coroner could only say that Mrs. Boyd's skull was unusually brittle. But the general level of suspicion wasn't reduced when Boyd went ahead with plans for a big party a few weeks after his mother died. They say his only acknowledgment of her was to invite some people who had been her friends rather than his. Even then, he apparently baited one of them about his plans for this land."

"I don't quite understand what it's all about," she said.

"There is some suggestion that he wanted to get away from town for a while to let suspicion die down. A chance to run away with Mrs. Pynne materialized and he jumped at it. I don't know how they got together, or any of the details. She seems to have been unhappy at home for some time. And at this same party Boyd steered her into finding her husband in a compromising situation. On Boyd's side, your friend was pretty and aloof, and her husband is active in a conservation group battling with him. It's possible there was an element of convenience in their departure."

She shook her head, but as if to clear it rather than to dispute anything. "I'm sorry," she said. "I just find this hard to take in."

I gave her a moment, then said, "I have to say, I find it a little hard to accept myself."

She frowned. "What do you mean?"

"I'm uneasy about what is supposed to have happened."

Her eyes narrowed. "In what way?"

"I worked out what I distrust most as I was driving back to Indianapolis," I said. "It's the fact that neither of them seems to have made contact with anyone in Nashville for two months."

"What's wrong with that?"

"Not so much for your friend, who appears to have had little in the way of ties there. But Boyd has not drawn money from his bank account, and he's not been in touch with the manager of his business. He's had a lot of women but he's not run off with one for years, and he seems to be the type for whom reporting that he had scored with the Ice Queen would be half the pleasure, or more."

"The Ice Queen?"

"I'm sorry. That's what somebody called your friend."

"How bitchy," she said.

"Yes, I guess so," I said.

"Sorry. Go on."

"O.K. Now, maybe Boyd and your friend are off somewhere having a hell of a time. If so, fine. She's away from her husband; he's away from accusing fingers and at least they have each other. But I wonder how it all reads if what seems to be the story isn't."

She was interested. "What would that mean?"

"We come back to what facts we know, and whether we can interpret them differently. First, they left town the same night."

"That could be coincidence, couldn't it?" she asked.

"Anything can be coincidence, but not very many things are. I have to think their departures are related."

She said nothing.

"Now the thing I'm trying to explain is why he should leave and not communicate with people in Nashville."

"And how do you explain that?"

"If he's not been in contact," I said, "I assume that he has a good reason for not being in contact. In effect, he is telling us that contact of any kind—even having his bank forward money—might hurt him."

She said nothing.

"If that's so, then he must have something to hide, something serious enough maybe to threaten the kind of life he's able to lead in Nashville."

I felt I was losing her attention slightly.

"I know it sounds a little extraordinary, but suppose we add a missing link. Suppose your friend Mrs. Pynne knew something positive to connect Boyd with his mother's death."

I paused. Eventually she said, "Yes?"

"It's just possible that he's done her some harm and he isn't coming back to Nashville because he would not be able to explain what happened to her satisfactorily."

"Harm?" she asked. "What are you saying, that she might be dead?"

That sounded bald. "Yes," I said.

She squinted and rubbed her eyes.

"I shouldn't speculate wildly," I said. "I'm sorry about that. I'm really saying that the situation doesn't feel fully explained to me. But the fundamental question for you is where you want to go from here."

"Go?" she asked. I had the feeling she was about to rise from her chair.

"I mean, whether you want to continue trying to find Mrs. Pynne."

"Oh yes," she said. She suddenly seemed terribly tired. I remembered that she had been interviewed and evaluated all day.

I had little more to say. "If you want to continue, I can get in touch with Mrs. Pynne's family and other friends, if you can help me locate them. Or I can do a little more to try to trace this man Boyd in the hopes of being able to get some news about her that way."

"I don't know," she said. "I just don't know." She put her hands over her eyes.

I suddenly realized that it had all been too much for her. I got up from my chair and sat on the front edge of my desk before her. I wanted to apologize for heaping information on her. I wanted to make some sort of impression on a human level. I nearly took her hands. Touching is part of my vocabulary, but I didn't know whether it was in hers.

I chickened out. I said, "Let me get you coffee or a drink or something, will you?"

She didn't say anything.

I felt stupid, unable to find sensible words. I said, "You must have had a hard day. Did you get your job?"

After a moment, she looked up at me. "Job?"

"At I.U.P.U.I.?"

"What? Oh yes. No."

"You got it, but you've decided not to take it?"

"I haven't decided what to do." It sounded pitiful.

"May I make a decision for you?"

"What's that?"

"Go to wherever you are staying. Get a little boozed, and then go to bed."

"With you, I suppose," she said.

I was shocked. "Certainly not. I'll happily walk you to your car, but that's as far as my professional services go."

"I . . . I'm sorry," she said.

"Go on, off with you," I said, trying to be avuncular. "Call me in the morning."

She got up, and she walked to the door. I followed her. We were both on the stairs when she turned and said, "What are you doing?"

"I'm walking you to your car."

"There's no need."

"It's quite all right."

"No. Please."

I shrugged. "O.K. Hear from you tomorrow."

"Yes." She continued down the stairs.

I stayed where I was until I saw my street door close. Then I went on down.

It was not late at night, but my neighborhood, my soon to be ex-neighborhood, is typically rough. It did not seem prudent to let my only current client walk to her car alone.

So I tagged along, at a distance.

The only problem with the plan was that she didn't walk to a car. She didn't even hail a cab. She just walked.

She kept a straight line, walking west on Maryland. We went past the Convention Center complex and straight to White River.

There's no bridge over White River on Maryland.

I didn't know whether she was going to look up in time to notice.

She stopped, however, when the roadway stopped. And she stood for several minutes. She seemed to look north, past the Washington Street Bridge. That's where I.U.P.U.I. is. Then she looked south for a moment, to a railroad bridge, and turned. I saw that she saw I was there. That is, that someone was there. I turned and walked around the corner of Blackford. I waited in the first deep doorway.

She crossed Blackford without a sideward glance. I fell in behind her again. She took a right, and then a left, and she went into a gray hotel, the Penrod, near the corner of Georgia and West. It's the Union Station area. There are still quite a few hotels around there, gray from the marginal existence which comes with being railroad hotels in what is now a car town.

Once home, I turned on my neon sign. A present from my daughter, it symbolizes the energy of youth for me. It was ready to blaze my wares all night long. I was only ready for bed.

It was hardly past nine-thirty, but I am an impulsive creature.

When I feel tired, I sleep.

I had boring dreams.

Then I had no dreams at all, because the telephone rang and woke me up.

"What?" I said as I answered it.

"Mr. Samson, this is Elizabeth Staedtler." Her voice was strong and firm and much much much too loud.

I opted for cliché. "Do you know what time it is?"

"Yes. Quarter past midnight," she said, as if it were a non sequitur and she was pausing in her purpose to help me set my clock.

"Jesus," I said.

"I don't want you to tie up your morning on my account. I've decided that I'm on my way back East, early. I want to formalize that my period of employing you is at an end."

"Oh."

"Frankly, some of your suggestions were incredible. I can't help thinking you produced them because they were the only way you could spin the job out. I've decided I've got better ways to flush away my money."

"All right," I said.

"That's that, then," she said. "Good. Goodbye."

She hung up.

"O.K.," I said to the dead receiver.

9

Saturday morning I lay in bed for a long time after I woke up. The Brown County hiatus from my life-problems was over. Thinking about it made me low. I much preferred going back to find out more about Boyd to packing my belongings.

But so it goes.

When the telephone rang at ten past ten, I had just resolved to roll out and make the best of life. Honest.

I rolled out and answered it.

"Mr. Samson?"

"At your service," I said.

"This is Dave Hogue. From Nashville. You came to my office yesterday."

"That's right. Hello, Mr. Hogue. How's things in Nashville today?"

"Fine, thanks."

"What can I do for you?" I asked, trying not to pant too hopefully.

"I was just calling out of curiosity," he said.

"About what?"

"You said you would be talking to this woman who hired you to find Priscilla Pynne. I wondered how that went."

"It went all right," I said. "What exactly were you interested in?"

"Well, I talked a little to Frank about you after you left us last night."

"Oh yes?"

"And it seemed that if you were continuing to look for Mrs. Pynne there might be a way for you to look on Frank's behalf as well as for your original client."

"I think I would be in considerable danger of his interests conflicting with my client's."

"I told him that, but it depended on what your client's interests were. If it were simply a matter of her wanting Mrs. Pynne's address, it seemed possible that she might not object to Frank's having the address as well."

"For what it's worth," I said, "I have the feeling that my client's interests were a little more active than that. She mentioned the conceivability of sharing an apartment with Mrs. Pynne, if she'd left home for good. She had a photograph of Mrs. Pynne and also seemed to find it very surprising to hear that Mrs. Pynne had run off with a man." Not that cliental proclivities are my concern.

"Did she?" Hogue asked sharply.

"On the other hand," I said, "I regret to say she is no longer a client. She decided last night that further expenditure was unlikely to be cost-effective."

"Mmm."

"So, unless Mr. Pynne would be interested in picking the file up . . ."

"Oh," Hogue said, "I don't think that's very likely."

"In which case, that's that," I said.

"Yes," he said thoughtfully. "Oh well. Bad luck, Mr. Samson."

"Since you've called," I said, "I wondered if I could ask you a small favor."

"Yes? What?"

"If you do find out any more about Mrs. Pynne or Billy Boyd, I'd be grateful to hear about it."

There was hesitation before he said measuredly, "Why is that?"

"I like to know about things," I said. "I like to know how they come out. That's all."

He hesitated again, but said, "All right. If there's some development, I'll give you a call."

"Great," I said. "Thanks."

That's the problem with being a private detective. The client defines you. Without client, you have no reason for asking your questions, for being curious. You have no justifiable identity.

I had suffered a lot of that kind of identity loss lately. I felt gray and marginal, like a railroad hotel.

And I didn't feel like facing the realities of preparing to move.

So I didn't. I made a gesture of independence and went to police headquarters in the time before I was due to see whether I could refuse an offer from Albert Connah. For half an hour I was my own client. It was one of the low points in my life.

Miller, in his office, looked tired, fed up, overworked. Much as usual. But, as on the telephone the previous day, he didn't posture with complaint and aggravation when I collared his attention. That was not as usual.

Instead, he looked up and said, "I'm going to quit. That's it. I've got enough years for some pension. I'm finished."

With some people that kind of thing pours forth with Old Faithful regularity. I'd never heard it from Miller before. He was a career cop, dedicated in the old-fashioned way. Some of the pieces in my puzzle are old-fashioned too. I can appreciate old-fashioned.

"You just tell your Uncle Albert all about it," I said.

"I'm getting out," he said, as if to convince me. "I'm tired of being passed over and ignored. My opinions don't count for anything. If I get in a difficult spot, my so-called superiors don't back me up the way they should. All I get is crap for all the work I put in. Nobody works harder than me. Nobody gets less for it. I'm getting out."

"It sounds serious," I said. Because it did.

"It is. I am. I'll stick it through my vacation in the fall. Then I'll find something else."

He waggled his head, as if agreeing with himself.

A man came into the office and dropped two folders on the desk. Miller said, "I'm up to my eyeballs, Al. What do you want?"

"I'd like you to put a car on the list, see if anybody notices it."

"What's its number?" he asked.

"I don't know. It is a white Datsun sports car and belongs to a William Boyd of Nashville."

"Same guy as yesterday, huh?"

"Yeah."

"O.K.," he said.

I knew things were bad. He always wants to know what's happening, in case of an easy arrest.

He just wrote the details down, picked up the phone and put the information people to work on finding the license number.

Then he stared at me. "William Boyd?" he asked. "William Boyd? Are you having me chase after fucking Hopalong Cassidy?"

"It's a car you're after. Not a horse."

He looked at me. Then managed to laugh. "You're a nut case," he said.

"I would find it hard to defend myself against that charge."

"Jesus, that's the first laugh I've had in weeks. A pitiful little laugh at that. Heard any jokes lately?"

"Only the one about the guy marooned on a desert island with his dog. The guy ate everything in sight and then ate the dog and, as he was chewing the last scrap of meat off it, thought to himself, Boy, Rover would really love these bones."

He listened quietly.

I said, "So what's the problem, Jerry?"

"Hell, if you think those guys out there are trying hard to be President, you should see the politics going on in here."

"Anybody got time left to catch crooks?"

"If they put all their energy into it, this would be the cleanest town in the country."

"O.K. You get my vote."

The phone rang. It was Boyd's license number. Miller took it, then asked, "What do you want to know about it?"

"Just where it is."

He shrugged. "Tell me, would I like being a private eye?"

"You'd love it. No internal politics at all."

"Want a partner?"

"Certainly. Especially one with premises."

"Sounds great, when do I start?"

"Soon as you pass your nut-case test."

10

Albert Connah greeted me warmly. A thickset black man with bright eyes, he was about my age: forty-two.

"Mr. Samson, Mr. Samson," he said heartily. "Kind of you to make time to see me."

"A pleasure, Mr. Connah, a pleasure."

"The deal is this," he said, not being a man to waste valuable time, "you're about to be out of a home, right?"

"So my client tells me."

"I've got a place for you. You can have it rent free, in exchange for some night-watchful eye-type duties and your private-eye service up to ten days a year for expenses only. I'll guarantee it to you on this basis for five years, but I'm really thinking in terms of ten or fifteen. Interested?"

Are kids interested in birthday presents?

We drove out to the property in question. It was a run-down former wholesale timber business on the west side, near Washington High School.

"It was folding up anyway," Connah told me. "Family business with debts, but then the guy killed himself. I got it cheap."

The land area involved was large, with a big storage structure around a central open loading yard. The building I was to occupy included an unprepossessing trade counter on the street with three small rooms behind it. One of these opened onto the yard.

"I'll take the counter out," he said, "and have a shower put in beside the toilet. What you do about a kitchen is your problem, but you got one room for that, one room to sleep in and one for a little Ping-Pong table if you want it. The front can double as living room and office, or you can divide it. That's up to you. In any case, the whole thing is twice as much space as you've got now."

I made it closer to four times as much. "What are you going to use the place for?" I asked him.

"I'm a crank," he said, with a grin. "I buy things and sell things and I make a goddamn fortune at it. I bought this place so I can make a lot of money while everybody else suffers. I'm going two ways here. This is a crappy part of town now, but in ten or fifteen years it's going to be important again and this land is going to be worth a mint. Now isn't the right time to develop it, so in the meantime I'm going to fill it up with glass."

"With what?"

"Yeah, you laugh, whitey, but see who comes out on top."

"I'm not laughing." Smiling, that's all.

"Everybody complains about goddamn inflation and goddamn energy prices. I'm gambling they ain't seen nothing yet. Next ten years the energy pressure from the Third World is going to drive the thing out of sight. People don't see the writing on the goddamn wall. So I'm going to cash in."

"With glass?"

"That's it. Anything it takes energy to make is going to be worth its weight. So I buy now and let it sit and it gets more valuable. I pick glass because glass keeps and doesn't need upkeep. I don't have to heat it, or humidify it. It won't explode, and the only thing that can replace it is plastic and that's made out of oil in the first place: I'm going to fill the place up with quality glass. It's going to get worth more, enough to cover the interest on my investment in the land here. Then I sell it, I sell the land, I get even richer than I am now. So what do you think of that?"

"I think you're a crank, Mr. Connah."

He gave me another big grin.

"One thing," I said.

"Yeah?"

"I'm kind of fussy about the way things are where I live," I said. "I was thinking maybe it would be a good idea if I was living on the premises while you had the alterations done. That way I'd be close at hand to consult with the builders in case of difficulties."

"And the architects, huh?" he said.

"That's it," I said.

"So you want to move in on Monday, right?"

We understood each other. "Where do I sign?" I said.

Not that it was quite so simple, but Glass Albert checked out as what he said he was and our respective men of law needed little time to produce the agreement on paper.

I actually moved in the first week of July, after two weeks of transition accommodation.

One of the first things I did when the phone was connected was call Miller, and in the course of conversation I asked whether Boyd's car had been sighted.

"What's your problem?" he asked. "Paper doesn't get dusty on my desk. If anybody'd seen Hoppy's car, you'd have been the first to know."

I decided he was feeling better.

And I forgot all about my last case on Maryland Street.

I was feeling better too. It felt like a chance for a new beginning. Dying embers of enthusiasm glowed hot again. I polished my furniture. I painted the outside of the new office and hung my neon sign. I went off my diet and lost weight anyway. I mounted my old office door, with its invitation "Walk right in," in a place of honor on a side wall, like a first dollar. I used the fact that I had changed addresses as an excuse to circularize all the law offices in town, and I borrowed money to advertise for a month in the newspaper. I turned the neon sign on for the first time on Bastille Day and as an office-warming present my woman got my telephone-answering machine out of hock.

Through the course of the summer, as the timber bays filled with glass, I even got some work.

I was not bound by the tenancy agreement to be on the premises for any set number of hours each day or week. My irregular pattern of work and usual attendance on the premises at night provided my contribution to the protection of Glass Albert's appreciating assets. He chipped in a chain fence topped with barbed wire and I became the best-protected private detective in town.

I began to dream sometimes about children throwing stones and about sopranos with piercing voices.

With reasonable notice, Glass Albert had claim to ten of my working days a year. His idea was that I might do the same background work on other prospective offspring-in-law that I had already done on his eldest son's friend.

"I've got seven children," he said, "and they are all goddamn stubborn. I'm not fussy about who they marry, but I want to make sure their lives aren't centered around sucking up to me for money."

There was also the prospect, in time, that I would come in for some of his regular investigation work, above and beyond the ten days. "Getting information is the hard part of what I do," he said. "If you know things, understand things, you get rich."

I took his word for it.

In September, I also agreed to make an addition to our arrangement.

"I've been thinking," he said, "about all that space in the loading yard."

"Don't tell me you're going to roof it and fill it up with marbles."

He looked up and gave it a moment's thought before he said, "Nah. I want to put a basket up out there. That all right with you?"

"A basket? Like basketball?"

"Yeah."

"Oh, my man!"

The basket projected from the back of my living quarters and was erected the next day by a pair of carpenters. Glass Albert came along in the afternoon with a ball.

"Sometimes I feel like shooting a few hoops," he said, "but these days I get embarrassed going to the parks among all those kids."

I sympathized.

"I always wanted a basket, someplace to shoot in private. My family's gone so goddamn soft and fancy, they try to make me feel bad about liking this game. My wife calls it a nigger game and wants me to strut around a goddamn golf course. To hell with that. And even my young kids won't watch the goddamn Pacers with me."

I told him what a hard life he led, and offered, as a special favor, to let him store his ball with me. I even undertook to look at it occasionally and check that it had enough air.

By the standards of my adult life, it was an idyllic summer.

12

I read about the discovery of Billy Boyd's body on the first Tuesday in November. I'd set the day aside to catch up on paperwork, so I was reading the *Star* with a thoroughness I don't always apply to it. Especially in a time of elections.

It was a brief notice. It said that a body discovered in Brown County by campers on Sunday had been identified as that of a local businessman, William Boyd.

When I read the story the first time, my reaction was interest. That it was something from my past, far removed because of all the things which had happened to me in the intervening four and a half months.

I began to read on in the paper. But I stopped. I went back to the story and read it again.

Spectator detachment started to give way to something sharper, more immediate. My heartbeat increased.

It suddenly seemed conceivable that I was involved.

I couldn't decide at first. It seemed superficially so unlikely that there would be any real need to change my comfortable plans for the day.

But Boyd dead . . . If he'd been dead all the time . . .

I put the *Star* aside and went to my files. I found the notes on the work I'd done for Elizabeth Staedtler, and I read them through.

The question remained open. The newspaper report was too short, hadn't said how long Boyd had been dead, whether he'd been killed, died naturally or committed suicide. But it was possible that they were looking for Priscilla Pynne. If they were, they might want to find Elizabeth Staedtler. And in the whole world I was probably their best link to her, weak as I was.

I had to go to Nashville.

I did that part of my paperwork which was essential.

I turned on the answering machine and got out the van.

In the old days I had a human answering service, a woman I never met called Dorrie. But she went out of business. When she called me to say she was folding up, she cried. "I'm an anachronism," she said.

I thought a lot about things like that as I drove south. I found I didn't enjoy the late-season foliage or the unseasonably warm weather at all.

My first stop was the sheriff's office.

I had expected it to be buzzing with activity, but it was empty, except for my soft-spoken switchboard operator. My notes said her name was Peg.

When I walked in, she was on the telephone. She looked tired and strained. She could not be the only communications operator employed by the department, but if Boyd's body had been found two days before, I could understand that there was enough tension to go around.

"Yes, sir?" she asked. "Help you?"

"I want to speak to Sheriff Dunlap about the Boyd case."

"Doesn't everybody?" she asked rhetorically. Then she looked at me again. "Do I know you?"

"I was in here in June, trying to trace Priscilla Pynne."

"Haven't you lost some weight?"

Woman after my own heart. "I have," I said.

She nodded. "Jeanna's gone out to see how the search party's getting on. I don't know when she's going to be back."

"What search party is that?"

"Billy, he was found in the woods." She paused. "You know about this or not?"

"I know what was in the *Star* this morning."

"Well, he was found in the woods and they're out looking for Mrs. Pynne's body."

It sounded stark, and rocked me slightly. "Oh."

"You knew they went away together?"

"Yes," I said.

"Well, it's like my mama used to say, Where one is, the other is. When I was trying to find my shoes or my gloves or something."

"How long have they been looking?"

"Since yesterday afternoon."

"So they knew it was Boyd then?"

"Jeanna took one look on Sunday night when the body came in and she knew it was Billy. With him missing, there wasn't much chance remains that size was going to be anybody else."

The switchboard sounded. She turned from me and answered a phone call. She explained that they were sorry Deputy Cohee had missed an appointment to give the caller advice on home security, but an unavoidable emergency had come up and he was required to stay in the office.

When she turned back to me, I asked, "Where is Deputy Cohee, then?"

"Eating lunch," she said sourly. "You want me to call Jeanna?"

"I'll go out to her, if you tell me where to go."

"You follow State 46 out of town, toward Columbus."

"East?"

"Yes, sir. And you'll likely see the cars and that on the road. It's after 135 branches off, a mile or so this side of Gnaw Bone. The land doesn't have a name, but it's the north side of the road."

"This isn't the land that Boyd inherited from his mother, is it?"

"That's right. You know where it is?"

"No, but I was told about it. It's a large area, isn't it?"

"Couple of square miles, I think."

"And it's all woods and hills?"

"Sure is."

"And they're searching it all?"

"They sure are."

I found the cluster of cars easily. There were perhaps a dozen, though the only people among them were a picnicking family, two adults and three near-teenage children. The adults were resting on folding aluminum chairs, drinking from a giant thermos bottle. One child was eating cake amidst the debris of a meal while the other two grappled in the grass.

I was going to interrupt them, but as I approached, the woman saw me and nudged her husband. He got up immediately and trotted to me with a hand extended. "Maurie Mappes," he said. "Glad to meet you."

"I was coming over to ask if you know where everybody is."

"Up in the woods," he said.

His wife joined us. "They're looking for a body to go with the one they found day before yesterday."

"I know," I said.

He nodded. "You press? State police? Federal? Or what?"

"What," I said. "Do you know which way in the woods? And how far?"

"Well," the wife said, "we can't hear them anymore, can we, Maurie?"

"No. They been out of earshot now for more than an hour." He checked his watch. "Yup. They're going through the whole place, you know."

"The whole forest," Mrs. Mappes said.

"But they'll find her, all right. And then they'll have him dead to rights, they will."

"Dead to rights," Mrs. Mappes echoed.

"Who?" I asked.

"Why, the husband!" he said.

"The husband of the woman they're finding," she said.

"They've arrested him. It's a bit of a surprise to me he doesn't just tell them where he put her and save them all this trouble," he said.

"Though it's possible he doesn't remember, Maurie. That's possible."

"Anything's possible," he agreed. "But you'd think he would remember where he buried his wife, wouldn't you? I mean, that's only reasonable."

13

I made my way into the woods. There was no clear footpath, but it was the gnarled roots of the established trees rather than the light undergrowth that made me pick my steps with care.

I walked up a short rise from the roadside and then dropped into deepening forest. Half the trees were bare now, patchily dressing the forest floor with a fresh and florid cloak.

I soon felt very much alone and once woke out of woody distractions to find myself poking a clump of heart-shaped leaves to look for second-flowering violets.

I had to force my mind back onto work, against the magnet of bosky musings on man's insignificances and the effect of a dry fall.

As the terrain rolled and rocked, I tried to keep a straight line in from the road.

It was several minutes before I heard voices and found the searchers.

Jeanna Dunlap stood watching them dourly, hands on her hips. A line of thirty men and boys moved slowly forward, prodding the earth with poles. Half were in civilian dress, four were sheriff's deputies and the rest were Boy Scouts.

The line produced nonstop chatter, but Sheriff Dunlap said nothing as she watched me approach. When I stopped in front of her, she said, "Remind me."

I gave her my name. "I'm the private detective who was here in June looking for Priscilla Pynne."

She swayed in affirmation. "I knew I recollected you. Wait here."

She walked to one of the deputies and he stepped out of the line to take her supervisory position. The sheriff then led me several yards away.

"Now, Mr. Samson," she said, "what brings you back to our fair county?" She spoke heavily, and looked as if she hadn't slept for days.

"I read about Boyd in the *Star* this morning."

"I think I'd worked that much out for myself," she said.

"How was he found?"

She eyed me before answering, but said, "A couple of folks from Seymour way were camping. The woman was looking for some firewood and disturbed a snake. She hit at it and chased it. There were some rocks and the snake went under them. She turned a couple over, and she found the toe of his shoe. She dug away a little and it didn't come loose. Called her husband. He called us."

"A snake?" I asked.

"There's quite a few in these parts. Even some rattlers. We get a few bites each year. Usually kids looking for arrowheads." She shrugged. "Probably some little old rock snake, this one. But he found Billy for us."

"You expected Boyd to return," I said.

"Sure as hell didn't expect it to be like this," she said.

I asked, "Is this land open for camping?"

"No."

"Why were they on it?"

"Experienced campers. Wanting to get away from people."

"Bit late in the season, isn't it?"

"They say they wanted to camp out through the elections. Idea was to come in on the Saturday, leave the week on Sunday. They picked this part of the area because there are no facilities."

"Where are they now?"

"What's that to you, Mr. Samson?"

Quite a good question. "That's a good question. I just feel involved."

"That's obvious from you being here so quick," she said. It was not a casual, passing comment.

I volunteered my explanation. "I was hired to find Mrs. Pynne. I couldn't do it, but by now the woman who hired me might have found her herself. Or Mrs. Pynne might have got in touch with her. If that's so, then it has to be followed up."

"Except she didn't find Mrs. Pynne and Mrs. Pynne didn't find her," Sheriff Dunlap said.

"Why's that?"

"Because Mrs. Pynne is in here," she said. She waved her hand around. "Pushing up grass and rattlesnakes, waiting for us to find her. I know that like I know my own name."

She did not encourage questions on the subject. I said, "Has Boyd's body been here the full time since he went missing?"

"Near as we can tell."

"Has Boyd's car been found?"

"No, it hasn't. But it might even be one of the things we find somewhere in here."

"The car?"

"Billy's grave was prepared carefully. Way back from the road, in a nice little hollow, piled with rocks and with a goddamn poison ivy in the middle. Guy did that might take the trouble to do something fancy getting rid of the car."

She seemed defensive and convinced, however unlikely getting rid of a car in a wood seemed to me.

"We could find a lot of things in here," she said. "We're looking at everything. Not just for Cilla Pynne."

I went back to the idea of the preparation of the grave. "You haven't said it, but I assume Boyd was murdered."

"Yup."

"Do you know how he was killed?"

"Andy's called in somebody from Indianapolis to look at it today. No broken bones, no bullet. Nothing simple like that. Andy reckons he was strangled, but we should have it for sure"—she looked at her watch—"pretty soon."

"Do you know who did it?"

"We've got us a working hypothesis," she said steadily.

"I hear that you have Frank Pynne in custody."

She said quietly, "Now, that wasn't in no newspaper, Mr. Samson."

"No. Some bloodthirsty sightseers on the road told me."

She didn't believe me.

"There's a family picnicking down there. They're waiting for you to bring Mrs. Pynne's corpse down so they can look and see if it has all its fingers and whether she died smiling. You know the type."

"I know the type. I just don't know how they know we've got Frank locked up."

"It's true, then?"

"It's true," she said. She scratched the back of her neck. "I bet it's goddamn Milt. I saw him talking to some people. I thought he was telling them to go away."

"One of your deputies?"

"Yes."

"Why Frank Pynne?" I asked.

She looked at me as if I had gone too stupid for belief. "Up in the big city you folks may go in a lot for changing your partners, but down here a man runs off with your wife, we take it serious."

"Jeanna!" The call came from the search line.

Sheriff Dunlap looked from me to the caller. "Don't suppose you want to join in the search?" she asked.

"No," I said.

She left me to mull over what she had been saying. It didn't take me long. I didn't credit it. Indeed, the social piousness even sounded out of character. I followed her back toward the line and saw that the deputy she'd left in charge was holding up a soiled sneaker. It looked like a man's, and a large one at that. Sheriff Dunlap didn't seem very interested.

Neither was I.

I turned back toward where I thought the road was and walked for a while. Then I lost certainty of my direction. On the way in I had stopped paying attention to my route when I'd heard voices ahead of me. Now the more I looked around, the less idea I had of which way the road lay. Trees look pretty much the same to a timber-yard dweller.

I was about to go back to the sheriff when I saw a burly little Boy Scout sauntering in a direction which would pass near me. He was going at about right angles to what I would have guessed was the right way. He carried a hatchet and now and then he took a swipe at a tree.

"Excuse me," I called to him.

"Huh?" He stopped.

"You going back to the road?"

"Yes, sir."

"I'm a little bit disoriented. I'll follow along with you, if that's all right."

"It's all right," he said.

He resumed his jaunt as if I hadn't ever appeared. A troll on a stroll. I had to make an effort to keep up with him. "You guys been out here all day?" I asked.

"Uh-huh."

"Is it a school holiday of some sort?"

"Naw. They let us out special. Mr. Jacobs, the scoutmaster, he gets us out."

It struck me as a gruesome project, but I didn't know quite how to put it. "Wouldn't it be kind of creepy if you find what you're looking for?"

"Naw," he said. "Mr. Jacobs, he gets us helping on a lot of stuff. Accidents and people lost in the woods."

"I see."

"Besides, you gotta face death sometime," he said. He took a hatchet-swipe at a tree. "Like over there," he said.

I looked where he pointed with his blade and saw a rocky hollow in which much of the earth had been disturbed. "That's where they found him?"

"Yes, sir. We spent yesterday digging the whole place up. Then filling it in again."

He stood looking at it for a moment, and without further ceremony started for the road again.

He chopped a hunk off a tree about every twenty steps. He seemed to enjoy it. I wondered how the trees felt on the subject.

When we emerged on the roadside, the Mappes family was playing Wiffle Ball. Maurie Mappes sacrificed a pop fly when he saw me.

"Hey, hello!" he called. He waved and trotted over. "How you doing?"

"I'm doing fine." I could see Ma Mappes accosting the scout.

"They found anything yet?"

"Yes, some dead . . ." I let it hang.

Mappes nearly had a hemorrhage.

"Some dead leaves. In fact quite a lot of dead leaves."

He didn't understand.

I tried to explain. "You gotta face death sometime," I said.

I felt him growing angry, but I was saved possible violence by his wife calling, "A rusty knife, Maurie! They found a rusty knife."

The scout's audience doubled. I was left alone and I made use of the opportunity to find my panel truck.

As I got in, I heard an urgent voice. "Jeanna? You there, Jeanna? Please answer."

It was the sheriff's car radio. I started to get out again. But then I didn't. It wasn't my business to send scouts to get sheriffs to respond to their unattended radios.

I drove back toward Nashville.

Not that much around here was my business.

14

In Nashville, I went back to the sheriff's office. There I found Dave Hogue badgering my soft-voiced switchboard lady.

"I'm trying to raise her! I'm trying!" Peg pleaded. She sounded exasperated. "I don't know what else you expect me to do."

"I expect you to get the sheriff here right away," he said with ominous passion in his voice. "You are her communications officer. This is a legal order." He waved a document, and I doubted whether it was the first time he'd swung it around. "If it is ignored, everybody in this office is vulnerable."

The receptionist saw me. "Mister," she said, "I've been trying to get Jeanna on the two-way, but she doesn't answer. Do you know where she is? Did you find her?"

Hogue turned to me with fire in his eyes. The blaze obscured any recognition process.

I said, "She's with the people combing the woods and she's out of earshot of her car's radio."

"That's crass irresponsibility," Hogue said.

"What's the problem?" I asked. Like everything else, it was none of my business. But Hogue hardly needed encouragement to repeat his complaint.

"I've got a judicial order that my client be either charged or released. Jeanna Dunlap leaves a deputy in charge who takes two hours for lunch and wouldn't be able to make a decision for himself anyway. She clears out to play needle-in-the-haystack and that leaves my client locked up back there when he should be out on the streets." He waved his document in the direction of a heavy door, which seemed, in the context, to locate the sheriff's jail for me.

Peg had regained her composure. "There's only so much I can do,

Dave, and there's no point in carrying on to me about it."

"Looks like Deputy Cohee should be found and sent out for the sheriff," I said.

"The sheriff should be within radio contact," Hogue said pigheadedly.

"But she isn't. So next best is to go send someone out to her."

"I *can* find her myself. Looks like I'm going to have to."

"They're not close to the road," I said. "It might be just as well to get Cohee to do it."

"What's that supposed to mean?" Hogue asked me icily.

"I had trouble finding my way around in the woods there," I said. "That's all."

"I won't have any trouble finding my way around," he said.

And he left.

I said, "I suppose it is obvious, but I take it Mr. Hogue's client is Frank Pynne."

"It sure is."

"Could I go through and talk to him?"

She stared at me, as if surprised I should ask. "No, sir, you can't. And you know I couldn't authorize it neither."

"I'm sorry," I said.

She didn't take the apology. She'd been having some hard days.

"I am sorry," I said. "I didn't think. It's just I need to find out more about what's happened so I can decide whether I'm needed."

"What would you be needed for?"

"It is just conceivable that I might be a witness."

"A witness? Against Frank?"

"Not necessarily against him, but in the case."

She registered this.

"I also take it Pynne hasn't confessed."

"No, sir. He says the whole thing is a load of . . ."

"Falsehoods?"

"That's it."

I grew silent.

"Look, mister," she said. "What is it you want? Waiting for Jeanna again, or what?"

"I have a few questions, but I can only ask them of the sheriff or of ?ynne's lawyer. So I've just got to kill some time."

She began to say something but the telephone rang. At the same :ime, a short, round man in his sixties, with thin white hair both on his 1ead and on his upper lip, came into the room. He seemed comfortable there, and my switchboard lady seemed to know him. He stood quietly, fingering a manila folder, while she dealt with the call. I sat down off to the side.

When she finished, he said, "Peg, I have the preliminary findings for Jeanna. I'll go home and write them up tonight, but she wanted the results as soon as possible. She here?"

"No, Andy. But she'll likely be back any time now."

"O.K. Hey, I was right. He was strangled."

"Oh my."

"But I was also wrong. There was a little fracture, in his back, just below the neck."

Andy seemed more enthusiastic about these details than Peg was.

"The pathologist who came down says it's likely Billy was strangled from behind, either lying down or thrown face down, by someone who put a knee between his shoulder blades while he was pulling on the rope or the wire around the neck. Christ, the guy is good. I sure did miss that crack in the back."

"Well, I'll tell Jeanna. Soon as she comes in."

"See, it all comes together, doesn't it?"

"What?"

"That kind of killing. That's the sort of thing they teach in the Army, isn't it?"

"What do you mean?"

"Well, Frank was in the Army, wasn't he? He was in Vietnam."

"Lots of folks been in the Army, Andy." From my place on the side I applauded this observation. Too many things are found the way they are because people look for them to be that way.

"I know, I know," the doctor said. "It wasn't me that made the point about the services. It was the pathologist. He's seen a lot of it. He served with them. It's not me setting Frank up. Frank's all right. I think he had a dud for a wife. I'm sorry if he's responsible for all this but if he is, then she gave him cause and I, for one, can't fault him all that much for it."

"Well, I'll tell Jeanna. The formal report will be with her—when, tomorrow morning?"

"Yeah. That's fine," he said. "There's some other lab work to do on organs and blood, but they'll come to her direct from Indianapolis."

"O.K."

"I'm on home, then; you take care of yourself, Peg."

"And you too, Andy."

As he was about to leave, I caught his attention. "You're Doctor Kubiak, aren't you?"

"That's right."

"Did you happen to notice, in the remains of Mr. Boyd's clothing, whether his wallet was still there and whether there was any money in it?"

He looked at me hard. "Who are you?" He turned to Peg. "Who is he?"

She shrugged.

"I'm a private detective."

"Debt collection?" he said. "Sheriff Dunlap will let you know any aspects of my report which she thinks you are entitled to know. Excuse me." He walked out.

As Kubiak left, a tall young man in deputy's uniform came in. I began to feel as if I should have paid admission. People at work, while I watched.

"Walter, where the deuce you been? What you doing not coming back? People here been screaming for your neck, no joke."

"There was an accident, Peg. Right as I was a-walking by. I cain't ignore something like that."

At that moment the voice of Jeanna Dunlap crackled over her two-way radio. "Peggy? Peggy? This is Jeanna. Over."

"I read you, Jeanna."

"I'm coming in in a couple minutes. Andy bring a report in yet? Over."

"Yes. Just now. Hey, Jeanna, Dave Hogue caught up with you yet?"

"No. He looking for me? Over."

"Sure is. Jumping around like a jackrabbit in a frying pan. He wants you to charge Frank Pynne or let him out."

"Hell, we've only had him a little more than a day. We'll have him for a whole lot longer than that, too. Over."

"Well, Dave's on his way out to you now."

"I'll wait here till he comes, then. Anything else? Over."

"Nope."

"Ten four, then."

"Bye-bye."

"Wow, Peg," Deputy Cohee said, "if'n Dave Hogue's that hopped up, sure am glad I'm here and not out there."

I asked, "What are the chances of Hogue getting Frank Pynne out?"

Cohee turned to me smiling, but as he realized he didn't know me, his good humor faded. "Who are you, mister? Who is he, Peg?"

"I think he's waiting to see Jeanna. He says he may be a witness."

"A witness?" Cohee lit up again, but not with a smile. "You saw Frank at it on the night?"

I felt packaged. No more comfortable because it was a box of my own making. "No, nothing like that."

"What is it like? You try me, mister."

"No, it's nothing simple."

"It don't have to be simple for me to comprehend it," Cohee said. "I got my diploma. I'm no dummy."

"That's not what I meant. It is only that if Frank Pynne committed these murders, then nothing of what I think is relevant. But if he didn't, then I might be able to help."

"Murders," Cohee repeated. "Murders? Who said anything about there being more than one? They found another body yet, Peg? They got more than one yet?"

"No," she said, "but—"

"There you are, fella," Cohee said. "Why you talking about more than one? And why you talking about someone other than Frank killing people? What do you know about it all? You tell me that, what do you know about it all?"

I addressed Peg. "I'm going across the road to get something to eat. Could you try to explain things to the gentleman in words of two syllables or less, and then tell Sheriff Dunlap I'll stop back later this afternoon?"

I didn't give her a chance to answer, and turned to leave.

I made it to the door.

But I couldn't open it. Not after Cohee pushed me up against it, kicked at my legs and whispered sweet nothings in my ear like "You ain't going nowhere, clown. You take the position so I can see if you're carrying, or I'll blow your fool head off."

15

Cohee's attitude was neither flexible nor constructive. He threatened that if I didn't answer his questions, he'd lock me up.

I told him I wouldn't talk to him anymore until he apologized nicely.

That kind of made him mad.

He took me to the cells, shoved me into the first empty one and secured the door. It showed me he was as good as his word.

I was as good as my word too. I didn't say a thing. I didn't even ask what the charges were or what he thought would happen when Jeanna found out he'd done all this without benefit of the formalities.

It wasn't that I minded irritating him with such trivial little questions. It was kind of a matter of principle.

I hadn't been locked in a jail for years. I was pleasantly surprised by its cleanliness and comfort. It was a design-conscious two-cell-by-two-cell layout, with toilet and beds provided. If I hadn't already found accommodation and premises, I would have considered making an offer.

Cohee seemed to think that locking me away for a while would make me think and become more willing to talk.

He was partly right. I hadn't expected him to make a gesture to distract Jeanna Dunlap from roasting him about his stupid two-hour lunch. But as it was happening, it occurred to me that it might not be such a bad way of passing the time. And I was willing to talk, I was.

To Frank Pynne.

Pynne was in the cell next to mine. He sat on the lower bunk staring at the jail door. He had a couple of books, but wasn't reading. As Cohee left, Pynne looked momentarily through the bars at me.

"We'll have to stop meeting like this," I said.

He looked away.

"I've met you before, Mr. Pynne," I said.

He turned back. "You know me?"

"About four months ago I was hired to look for your wife. I spent half a day at it, and talked to you and lawyer Hogue in his office in the late afternoon."

He nodded. "I remember now. You didn't find her."

"No."

"Damn bitch," he said.

We both contemplated that for a moment.

He said, "Goddamn Boyd." He lay down on the bed and stared at the bottom of the upper bunk.

I asked, "Have you been charged yet?"

He didn't look at me. "No."

"Held for questioning?"

"Yeah."

"I think Hogue's going to have you out soon."

He sat up. He faced me. "What the hell do you know about it?"

"I was in the office out there. He's got some sort of order, to make them either charge you or let you out."

I paused. He didn't speak.

"So unless they have some evidence, they'll probably spring you."

It was a delicate fishing expedition.

"Fuck evidence," he said.

I wasn't sure if I'd caught nothing or not. I cast again. "What are they going on so far? Motive and opportunity?"

"What the hell business is it of yours?" he asked.

I shrugged.

He lay down again.

And I found myself locked in a jail in southern Indiana.

The question of what business of mine it was kept coming up. If it wasn't me asking, it was someone else. I was tired of it as an issue. I decided to make it my business. A client? I would be my own client.

Might not do much for me financially, but it did wonders philosophically. Who says incarceration isn't rehabilitative?

I said, "Mr. Pynne, I'm still trying to find your wife."

"You should be out in the woods with a shovel," he said. "If you believe Jeanna Dunlap."

"Should I believe Jeanna Dunlap?"

"Half the town does, why not you?" he said.

He seemed disinclined to latch on to the straightforward opportunity I was giving him to deny his guilt.

I asked, "Why only half the town?"

I saw a flicker of a smile at the springs of the upper bunk. "Why only half?" he repeated. "Good question."

I waited him out for a good answer.

"I figure half," he said, finally, "because this town is divided into pro–Billy Boyd and anti–Billy Boyd. I figure the pro-Billys all want to lynch me and the anti-Billys all want to buy me a drink."

"Why is Boyd such an issue?"

"'Cause he makes it that way. Made it. He liked to shake things up for the rattle they made. Always talking you down, always arguing. I've seen him take on both church people and atheists. I've seen him push Dave Hogue as if he wanted to cement over the whole county. Yet if B.C.T. was all women, Billy'd have been in the middle of it and all for tearing the town down to grow the forest back."

"A stirrer," I said.

Pynne rubbed his eyes with both hands. "Ah, fuck," he said. "How did I end up here? What the fuck am I doing here?"

And I was suddenly back where I started. I didn't know whether he was regretting what he had done, or regretting that he hadn't done anything.

I didn't have time to unravel it. The door at the end of the corridor opened and suddenly the quiet jail was filled with people and noise. Jeanna Dunlap, Dave Hogue, Walter Cohee, and all talking at once.

They walked past my cell to Pynne's and unlocked his door.

I felt a moment of panic, stood up and pressed myself against the bars. You hear things about strangers in country towns languishing in country jails.

But Sheriff Dunlap came and let me out too. Behind her, I heard Hogue explaining to Pynne that he wasn't allowed to leave the county. Pynne asked about his job being in Bloomington.

But then I lost what he was told. Jeanna Dunlap occupied my attention. "Had a nice little rap session?" she asked.

"Quite nice," I said. "Find your other body?"

"Not yet," she said.

16

Before leaving the cluster of people at the sheriff's office, I told Dave Hogue that I wanted to see him as soon as was convenient. He asked that I give him three-quarters of an hour to clear up matters with Pynne. I used it to eat.

It was quarter to three when I presented myself before the desk of Betty Weddle.

She asked if I had an appointment. I told her what Hogue had said to me and she gave a terrible moan. "But he promised," she said.

"Did I come in in the middle of something?"

"He hasn't had a bite to eat since this morning. He's got Mr. Pynne up there now, and he promised me that when Mr. Pynne left, he would go out and have a proper meal, a no-work meal, where he just sat and relaxed."

"I'm sorry," I said.

"Honestly, that man will be the death of me," she said.

"Mmm," I said.

"If he isn't the death of himself first. He's got a bad heart, you know."

"I didn't know."

"A very bad heart. He could be gone in a moment, pffft, just like that."

I didn't know what to say. I said, "Has he had heart trouble long?"

"Since he was thirty-two," she said, almost proudly. "He doesn't like people to know about it. He's lucky to be alive. But I tell him, just because he's been lucky so far is no reason for him to abuse his body."

"And does he listen?"

"Not today," she said. Angrily, yet equally crediting herself with successes at other times. She shook her head. "But it's always like this when he's worked up about something. He gets too involved, he forgets to think about himself. I tell him and tell him, he's got to remember himself, it's for the good of all of us, but he just goes ahead as if I hadn't said a word. Well, I can't sit by without speaking up. That's what he says about things, like B.C.T. Well, I say the same about him."

"Men are foolish creatures," I offered.

She looked at me as if I were crazy. "I don't know about that," she said. "But he should eat."

Footsteps on the stairs outside spared me further opportunities to prove my sexist generalization. Betty Weddle went to the hallway door and we both heard Dave Hogue saying, "You try and get your mind off it. Relax if you can."

"That's easy to say," Pynne said harshly.

"Just trust me, Frank."

"All right. But sure as shit I'm not going to sit around and get railroaded. You better realize that."

"There's no way that you are going to be railroaded for this," Hogue said.

Frank Pynne said, "O.K., Dave," and left.

Weddle waited till the outside door was closed, then said, "David, you promised me you would eat, but now there's a Mr. Samson who says you asked him to come here. Won't you please tell him to come back later?"

Hogue didn't answer until they were both in the waiting room with me. "I'm not really hungry, Betty," he said. "This way, Mr. Samson."

When we were alone in the large room I'd been in before, I said, "I can come back, if that would be more convenient."

"Betty mothers me a bit," he said. "Maybe I encourage her sometimes. But other times . . ." He raised his eyebrows and shook his head slightly.

"Has she been with you long?"

"Oh yes. The year after I opened, which would make it since . . ." He thought. "Since 1965. Then I helped her through a little trouble a few years later, and—well, here we are."

I nodded.

"Damn good legal secretary," he said. "Most of the time she could do as good a job in this practice as I do. I expected her to get married again, or I would have encouraged her to take law classes."

"That's not a very modern attitude," I said.

"I guess not," he said.

"She's not too old now."

"Thirty-five?" He thought. "Maybe I'll talk to her about it." He wrote something on a note pad. "And now," he said, "what did you want to see me about? Surely you didn't come down just to chide me about not calling you when they found Boyd's body?"

"No. I came down to find some more facts, because I might be of use."

He raised his eyebrows, then asked, "What facts?"

"Has Mrs. Pynne been heard from since she left?"

"No."

"What evidence is there against her husband that supports Sheriff Dunlap's notion of a double murder?"

"Nothing concrete," he said.

"Come on, Mr. Hogue," I said. "It hasn't been pulled out of a hat."

"It's primarily a matter of motive, so far," Hogue said. "The idea is revenge because Boyd ran away with Mrs. Pynne."

"Ran away? They didn't seem to get very far if Jeanna Dunlap is right."

Hogue shrugged. "There are only three other points that I know of. First, that Frank is a part of B.C.T., which was having trouble with Boyd. Second, that Frank and his wife had an argument in public on the night she left."

"Where was that?"

"We—the B.C.T.—had a square dance. It was just clear that they were not getting along that evening. They left early."

"I see. And third?"

"That Frank has been seeing a lot of another woman since his wife left."

"Who? Not the woman she caught him with at Boyd's party?"

"Yes. Sharon Doans."

"Which is thought to be an extra motive?"

"I assume so."

"And that's it?"

"Unless they find Mrs. Pynne's body, yes."

"Well," I said, "I don't like it."

"Why not?"

"Because I don't think Mrs. Pynne's body is out there."

Solemnly he asked, "Why do you think that?"

"Boyd was buried with care. Far from the road, in a hollow. Sheriff Dunlap says there was even some poison ivy on the grave. If Priscilla Pynne was killed at the same time by the same person, she would have been buried in the same place."

He thought about that.

I said, "It seems clear that Boyd was not meant to be discovered. It was only accident that the body was found. If there were two graves, there would be twice as much chance that one would be come across. So what would be the point? No advantage to preparing two sites. So if there were two bodies, I figure they would both be there. Which means, alive or dead, Priscilla Pynne is elsewhere."

Finally Hogue nodded. "I think you're right," he said.

"If that is so, then the simple story that they got together and then got killed together doesn't work. And it looks to me as if Sheriff Dunlap is on the wrong tack altogether."

He nodded again, looking very serious.

"The reason I came down here," I said, "was to see whether Priscilla Pynne still needed to be looked for. Based on what we know, it seems to me that she does."

Hogue said, "That would appear to be inescapable."

"It is partly a matter of helping your client's case. But it may be more serious than that. If a couple of people are supposed to have run off together, but one of them turns up dead, there is pretty good reason to want to ask the other one some questions."

17

For the time being, Hogue hired me to work on behalf of Frank Pynne. He decided it was not in his client's interests to wait until Sheriff Dunlap gave up woodland rambles.

I didn't object.

We talked about what I would do. I explained about Elizabeth Staedtler and the chance that in the intervening time she had been in contact with Priscilla Pynne. We agreed that I would follow that up. We also agreed that I would have another try at talking to Frank Pynne. He was our best source of information about other leads in Priscilla Pynne's background.

I also wished to try to reconstruct as much as possible of what had happened the night of the double disappearance.

Taking the hypothesis that Mrs. Pynne was alive raised certain questions. Boyd's car was missing. If she took it, why was her own car left at I.U.?

I also asked Hogue if he could find out who Boyd's thousand a month had been paid to.

"What thousand a month?" he asked.

"When I was here before, I found that the only activity in his bank account was a regular payment to someone for that amount. But I couldn't find who the money went to."

"I'm surprised he had that much money," Hogue said.

"Certainly, since his mother died . . ."

"Of course," he said. "I was forgetting that."

If he had been solemn while we talked about Frank Pynne's plight, he became positively gloomy at the memory of Ida Boyd.

"A fine woman," he said. "Not an easy woman, but a fine one."

"You were among the people who felt Billy was involved in her death, weren't you?"

"It was too convenient for him," Hogue said.

"That was because his mother was about to make a will, wasn't it?"

"Yes."

"Did she not have a will before? Or was she just about to change an existing will?"

"She had no other will," Hogue said. "It would have been her first."

"She was in her fifties, wasn't she?"

"Fifty-seven."

"And—"

"And yes, she should have had a will drawn up long before."

"But she didn't."

"Ida was a superstitious woman," he began. "She had a number of"—he searched for words—"a number of foibles. She believed in ghosts, for instance, and 'atmospheres' and almost anything in the area of the E.S.P.-parapsychology-occult hocus-pocus."

"Yes," I said.

"I'm not taking anything away from her sensitivity and love of the countryside. We were close friends. We had even just about decided to marry."

"I didn't realize that."

"It was not a public matter," he said gravely. "We started to give it serious thought toward the end of last year. And we did spend considerable time talking about matters of concern to her."

"Like her will?"

"Ida's husband, Billy's father, died suddenly of heart trouble in 1960. It was in January, and was only a few days after he had signed his own will. Ida suffered terribly during that time."

"And associated wills with that suffering?"

"Wills," Hogue said, "and New Year's resolutions and sudden warm spells and eating shrimp and half a dozen other things."

"I see."

"And it was also then that Billy ran away."

"You said before that he was very young."

"Yes. Fifteen. He ran away with a woman who was in her thirties and a sculptor. I don't know anything else about her. She was not one of Ida's approved subjects for discussion."

"How long was he gone?"

"He came back in 1967. I'd been here for three years. Billy just reappeared, took over a property his father had owned, and was back."

"Had he been in touch with his mother in the seven years before he returned?"

"Not until the months immediately beforehand. He wrote to her saying that he was willing to come back as long as she made various financial undertakings. She was deliriously happy to hear from him again and she did everything he asked."

"Do you know what he asked?"

"No. At that time I was not her lawyer. I've never seen the papers."

"And the woman?"

"She never figured in his life again, as far as one knows. I was told her name, but I don't recall it. I can't remember how long it's been since anybody talked about this. Years and years."

"I see."

Slightly ironically, Hogue commented, "In a small town, one never suffers from lack of tittle-tattle."

"Suffers from too much of it, perhaps?"

"I admit I've never managed breathlessness while waiting for the latest nuance of who's with who. But I'm reasonably well adjusted to life here. And very very fond of the surrounding area. I don't know what I'd do without it now."

"What I was getting at when I asked about wills," I said, "was this. If Billy was involved in his mother's death, he must have known about the will his mother was going to make. How would he have known about it?"

Hogue said, "I don't know for sure. But one is never surprised when people know things around here."

"Would his mother have told him what she was planning?"

"It's certainly possible," he said. "Billy never seemed cut out for the role of dutiful child, but they conversed. And he had been after her about the land. She was resisting the kind of plans he had for it. That's what the will was about, and she had come to feel strongly enough about it to overcome the great fears she had. I respected her a lot for that. However little I respected the fears, they were real for her."

"Did Billy and his mother live in the same house?"

"Yes. Part of their arrangement, although it was more than large enough for him to"—hesitation—"maintain his privacy. The house is just across the street, in fact."

He pointed to a very substantial brick building across Thomas Street, a little bit farther from the corner than the building I was in. In the pre-car age, people actually lived in towns and wanted to be near their work.

"So Billy could have been there when Mrs. Boyd died?"

"Oh yes. Except he seems to have been elsewhere."

"I assume that if there had been any leads in Mrs. Boyd's death, you would have followed them up at the time."

He didn't answer.

"Mr. Hogue?"

"I . . . I was . . . If Ida resented his running away when she needed him, she also felt maternal guilt about him. She would say, 'He *is* my only child.' I . . . I could hear her voice just now, saying that." He hung his head.

One of the real kinds of ghost.

Then Betty Weddle walked in. She carried a tray with two cups on it and a large white paper bag. "I'm sorry to disturb you, Mr. Samson, but David must eat, and if he has to work while he's doing it, then he has to."

"Betty, this is not—"

"I've been out for a few things, and I have a Danish and coffee for Mr. Samson. Just let me lay it out and I'll leave. I will not be swayed."

Swiftly and deftly, food was unpacked and distributed. Hogue was given soup, a sandwich, a large salad, tea and an apple.

Good as her word, Weddle left as soon as things were set out.

"This is embarrassing," Hogue said.

"I'm impressed," I said, from the perspective of someone who'd taken care of himself unaided for years. "And she said that you'd had some heart trouble, so it's only right that—"

"Did she tell you that?" he asked sharply.

"Yes, before I came up."

He sighed heavily. "That's too much, it really is."

"It was only in the context of the necessity of your taking care of yourself."

"She's in a . . . a mood, or something. Somehow my authority is being eroded. She's taking over in areas in which she has no business. This has been going on for weeks now, but it's getting critical. I've really got to do something about it."

It didn't involve me.

"What makes it the more incomprehensible is that she was on the point of leaving just after Christmas."

"Leaving? Why?"

"Too long in one place, she said. I don't really know." He shook his head. He drank from his soup. "However, it is not your problem."

"No," I said.

But while I had my sweet roll and coffee, I mulled over whether Hogue could be as unaware of his secretary's attachment for him as he seemed to be.

18

I drove west out of Nashville. After finding no one at home at Frank Pynne's cabin I drove on to Sharon Doans' house. I was not surprised, as I turned left at the S.A.D. mailbox, to see a red Fiesta next to Doans' yellow Beetle. The two colors seemed highlights in the late-autumn landscape in which the chapel-like house was set.

A few moments after I knocked, Sharon Doans opened the door, took one look at me and said, "Well, speak of the devil."

She stood with a hand behind her back and seemed, for a moment, ready to let the conversational development rest where it started.

I said, "I'd like a few words, if it isn't too inconvenient, Miss Doans."

"Sure. Come on in."

I went in. Frank Pynne sat on one of the wicker chairs near the front windows. He, too, held a hand conspicuously out of sight.

Doans walked ahead of me. She showed me a cigarette, raised her eyebrows and then drew deeply on it. She was completely without the dramatic dress-up trappings of my first visit. She wore faded jeans and a brown flannel shirt. I looked across the room and saw that the easel was bare. She must have been between covers.

I said to Pynne, "I've just come from your lawyer."

"Bully for you."

"In case you're interested, he's retained me to work on your behalf."

I'd expected a reaction, but he only took a puff on his home-roll. It was Sharon Doans who asked, "What can you do for Frank?"

"Try to find his wife."

"That's what you were trying to do when you came here before, wasn't it?"

"You have a good memory," I said.

"No, I don't. I have a lousy memory," she said. "I'm rotten like that. I didn't remember any of it till Frank said. So I looked you up."

"Oh?"

"I write the things that happen to me sometimes. You dropped in out of the blue and told me how much longer pot lasts than booze. So I wrote you down for that day. It was June thirteenth."

I noticed a red book on the table.

"So I've been reading you to Frank, all the stuff I told you about Silly."

"Fucking busybody," Pynne said.

"In which case," I said, "you won't be surprised to hear that I'm here wanting more information about Mrs. Pynne."

"There ain't no more," Frank Pynne said, now laconic.

I said, "Your lawyer believes you are innocent of the murder or murders that other people seem to think you committed. I'd have thought you could muster at least an iota of attention for the efforts being made on your behalf."

"I didn't kill anybody," he said. "I may when she comes back, but not so far."

"Great," I said. "But suppose the police turn someone up who saw your car near Boyd's place on the night. Or saw you walking in the woods where he was found. Or suppose they find your wife's body. How easy do you think it is going to be then for Dave Hogue to spring you from the sheriff's jail so you can light up with your friend? Can you prove where you were on the night of April twelfth? Are you ready for the grilling you're going to get when the law gets around to you again after its walk in the woods? If you think you're going to get a smooth ride through this, then you're off your skateboard."

"All right, all right," he said. He turned dark and inward, like a man reminded of a past he thought he'd escaped. Only, Pynne's past was happening now.

"When did you last see your wife?" I asked.

"When I went back to my side of the bed about one in the morning the night she left," he said.

"Oh, poor Frankie," Sharon Doans said.

"So she left after you went to sleep that night?"

"Looks like," he said.

"Are you a heavy sleeper?"

"I didn't hear her go. I didn't wake up and wave goodbye."

"Let me put it this way. Did she take clothes with her? A suitcase?"

"Yeah. A lot of her stuff was gone."

"When did she pack?"

"How the hell do I know when she packed? She didn't ask me to help her."

"You were out together that night, at a square dance," I said.

"Yeah," he said, looking at me as if I had no right to know such a thing.

"And you left it together?"

"Yeah."

"And came home?"

"And parked the car and walked in the door and—"

"I'm trying to find out whether she had time to pack her things that night without your knowing about it. Did you leave her alone for any length of time after the dance?"

He thought. "No."

"So," I said, with a sigh, "either she packed after you were asleep or she packed sometime before. Could she have packed without waking you up?"

"I sleep when I sleep," he said. "But . . . I wouldn't have thought so."

"Which suggests she had made plans," I said patiently.

"The bitch," he said. "The goddamn bitch." He stubbed his cigarette butt out between his fingers and stood up. "I don't know what the hell is going on." He walked around the room, uncomfortable in the cage of anger against his wife which he'd lived in over half a year.

Sharon Doans and I watched him pace the room. He dominated attention. He got a glass and ran some water into it. He drank it fiercely.

He sat down again, dropping himself in the chair, making it seem frail. "Hell," he said. He shook his head. "We didn't get along that well. Never. I led. She followed, only she didn't like following so much lately. Like, I wanted a baby. If two, three years ago I'd said baby, boom, those pills would be in the john. Now she tells me she wants to wait and I know that means she doesn't want one."

I didn't know what to say.

I said, "I'd like names and addresses of your wife's friends and family."

"Huh," he said bitterly. "That won't take long. She didn't have any friends and I don't know where her parents are. And they were the only relatives I ever met."

"Elizabeth Staedtler, the friend of your wife's who originally hired me, told me that she and your wife wrote once or twice a year over the last five years or so."

"First I've heard of it," he said. In a way that made it clear he'd heard a lot of things for the first time recently.

"And her parents?"

"Springfield, Mass., six years ago. Her mother turned out for the wedding. Her father was too drunk."

"Did the parents live together?"

"Yeah."

"And you don't know where they might have gone if they're not still in Springfield?"

"No."

"What street did they live on then?"

"It was something like Cawly or . . ."

"And your wife was never in touch with them since you were married?"

"No," he said. But ironically, because he now meant, "Not as far as I know."

"What was her maiden name?"

"Pitman."

"And can't you remember anything that might fill the picture a little?"

"Sharon already told you more than I remember," Pynne said. "I could tell you more about Nam."

"Did you kill Boyd?"

He glared ferociously. I took that for an answer in the negative.

"O.K., what do you think happened to him?"

The question stopped him. I said, "Hadn't you asked yourself that?"

"Nope," he said. "What happened?" rhetorically. "Huh. I suppose the bastard didn't kill himself after a blinding moment of lucidity?"

"He was strangled and the top of his back was broken."

Pynne thought about it.

Sharon Doans fainted.

I'd never been in the presence of someone who had actually passed out without being slugged or something. I didn't know what to do. We laid her out on the floor and checked her breathing. While I was considering further examination, she came around.

"Oh God," she said. "What happened?"

We told her.

"It was what you said about Billy. I pictured it. I'm a little bit squeamish."

She sat up. It was her turn for a drink of water.

"I'm all right. I'm O.K." She moved to a chair.

Pynne brought us back. "I wouldn't have thought Cilla could have killed him that way." But he said it in such a way that it was clear he was giving it careful consideration.

I was interested that I hadn't been the one to raise the possibility that she had killed Boyd.

"How strong was she? Is she?"

"Hell, I don't know. Pretty strong."

"Even small dead men are pretty heavy when you carry them through the woods."

"She'd be as strong as she had to be," he decided.

"And suppose they are both dead?" I said. "If you didn't do it, who did?"

He shook his head and shrugged.

"Miss Doans?"

"Someone to kill them both? God, I don't know."

"Or suppose she's alive and didn't do it. Who benefits from Boyd dying?"

"Everybody," Pynne said.

"A really useful answer," I said. "They'll love it in court."

"I don't know. I don't know. Shit."

Sharon Doans was recovered enough to be solicitous of Pynne's deteriorating emotional state. She told me to leave him alone.

"Do you know who gets the property?" I asked her before I left. "I gather there's quite a lot here and there."

"Especially here," she said. "He owned this house."

"Who will it go to?"

"I don't know."

"What about relatives?"

"There aren't any. None that I know about."

19

I left Pynne and Doans consoling each other in a cloud of velvet smoke. I carried my own kind of cloud with me. It was thin, hazy mental stuff, an unease. But unease seemed a perpetual characteristic of my ramblings in southern Indiana.

I parked in Nashville and walked to Boyd's art gallery.

I managed to get there in business hours this time, shortly before five. But nobody was visible inside.

I went in. Within a minute I was joined from a back room by a substantial woman of about forty. She wore an autumn-red suit, pink coral jewelry and a big smile.

I had an immediate sense that I wouldn't want to play poker with her. There was a basic brightness about her manner and smile which made me suspicious in the way that fit the old story about a Hoosier boy coming across a poker game on a train. He has a roll of bills visible in one of his shirt pockets and after watching for a minute asks, "Gee, watcha playin', fellers?" The kid gets off the train at the next stop with rolls of bills in both shirt pockets.

"Howdy," the woman said. "I'm Mary Tolley, the manager here. If you see something you want to know more about, you let me know, hear?"

I introduced myself.

"Oh, I remember you," she said.

Which surprised me, since we'd never met.

"You talked to Jeanna about me a few months back. Asking whether I'd heard from Bill Boyd in the time he was gone. You made Jeanna feel a little bad, so she come over to check it again with me."

"And," I asked, nodding, "do you remember what you told her?"

"Sure do. I hadn't heard from Bill. And I reckon now we know why." She referred to it factually, solemn but without grief.

"Mrs. Tolley," I said impulsively, "I want very much to understand what happened to Mr. Boyd, because I want to find out who killed him. I'd appreciate it if you'd let me ask you a few questions."

"Well, sir," she said brightly, "I'll do my best, but I've only got a few minutes. I've got to get off and pick my daddy up for a doctor's appointment."

"A few minutes would do fine, Mrs. Tolley."

"Could I ask one favor of you?"

"What's that?"

"It's not 'Mrs.' Tolley. I have never married, and I kind of prefer to be called 'Ms.,' if that's all right with you. Makes me feel like I'm keeping up with the times. And you know, it's also pretty much the way folks always said the other round these parts anyhow."

"O.K. Ms. 'tis."

"Only problem," she said, "odds are I don't know the half of what you're going to ask me."

"We can try."

"That we can."

"Do you know who benefits from Boyd dying?"

"In a money way, you mean?"

"Yes."

"No, sir, I don't. There is likely going to be a will come out, 'cause he mentioned having one, but I don't know anything of what's in it."

"And you don't know who the gallery will go to?"

"No, sir. But it don't worry me."

"Why not?"

She chuckled. "Mostways 'cause I'm not a worrying sort, I guess. But Bill trusted me and I trust him." She shrugged.

"I gather he let you run this business with a pretty free hand."

"After the first few years, that's right, he did. This point, I reckon I know the buying and selling of art round these parts pretty much better than he did. We more than pay our way, which was all Bill asked. Apart from being here to let him show a little special attention to one artist or another who caught his eye."

"That would be mostly lady artists, would it?"

Smile. "Sure would."

"Before he went missing, was there anyone whose talent was catching his eye?"

"His eye found some talent in a lot of places," she said.

I said, "I've been told what Mrs. Pynne was doing the evening before she left, but nobody has said anything about Mr. Boyd's activities that night. From what I hear about him, it doesn't seem likely that he was sitting home. Would you have an educated guess as to who he might have spent a little time with that evening?"

"I do recollect that he was speaking of buying a few pieces of work from Celene Deckard about that time. Celene is a specialist in the ceramical line, and she has her some ceramical landscape work that is unique. She's also a fine-looking young woman."

"Where should I go to express some interest in ceramical landscape?"

"She has a house up Lake Lemon way," Ms. Tolley said, and she gave me directions. "Although," she continued, "on any particular night Bill could have been any of half a dozen places where they was always glad to see him."

"These all artistical ladies?"

"I suppose they are. You know, I was that tiny way surprised when folks told me Bill had run off with that Mrs. Pynne."

"Why was that?"

"Just because she was too kind of thought out, you know? And while Bill would have him a casual shot at most anything in a skirt, I never saw him try, you know, make much of an effort with a female who wasn't sort of kooky, the way a lot of them are."

"I see."

"Not that I've got anything against artists. Once you get to know them, they're just like folks."

"You know Boyd a long time?"

"Oh yes. My daddy, he run this place as a drugstore for Bill's daddy, long before Bill made it what it is now."

"I see."

"When he was a young un, Bill used to hang out here. He and my daddy got along. My daddy always treated him like a man, Bill, from the time he started coming round when he was maybe eleven. Bill was always tiny little, but Daddy treated him big. Bill always liked my daddy for that, and when he come back and changed this place over he helped set my daddy up in something different and he took me on here."

"Was Boyd always interested in art?"

"No no. Only after he come back. You knowed he run away?"

"Yes."

"That woman—Tee-Dee Askew was her name, with the Tee-Dee from her initials—she was a sculptor and I'm sure that the art side was her influence."

"Am I to assume that he went away with her in the first place because she treated him like a man too?"

"I think you're getting the understanding of Bill just fine. On the surface of it, lots of folks just couldn't understand that, her running off with Bill, and Bill running off with her and her little girl."

"Little girl?"

"Tee-Dee had her a girl of about nine or ten. Lovely little thing she was." Mary Tolley looked at her watch. "I have to go in a minute now. But you know, you sure should have a little look around the gallery while you're here. We got some fine things, some fine fine things. Look good and keep their value good too."

"The nails you hang your pictures from are outside my price range," I said.

"Uh-huh," she said. "Well, we do credit terms."

It seemed a good time for me to be running along.

Celene Deckard's studio was ten miles from Nashville, on the North Shore Road around Lake Lemon. Near where it intersects with Possum Trot Road, my instructions said. And there I found a small frame house, accompanied by what looked like a large garage.

I also found Celene Deckard. Nor was she alone. She had a friend there, and they wore matching muslin dresses. Deckard was a dark-haired woman and her cheeks were pink. Her friend was lanky and nearly six feet tall, bald with a bushy brown beard.

"Sorry to bother you," I said as I came in, following an invitation at the door.

"No bother," Deckard said.

"If you were in the middle of something—?"

"Nope. In the middle of nothing."

"A whole lot of nothing," the friend said.

"I mean," I said, "sewing, turning up hems or whatever."

Deckard nodded. "I think he's talking about your dress, Eddie. Though I don't know if he thinks something that would fit around your waist would be likely to fit around mine."

"It's my dress," Eddie said.

"Of course," I said. "Whose else would it be?"

"Women wear pants," he said. His voice was guttural, and not quite clear. "Why shouldn't I wear a dress?"

"No reason at all," I said. I tried to sound earnest. It wasn't what I had come to talk about.

"You got guys with earrings these days and girls with crew cuts. Dresses have some advantages sometimes, so why should that be taboo and none of that other stuff?"

"I'm convinced," I said. "I was caught by surprise, that's all. Trend-setters have to be prepared for stereotyped reactions from people who walk into their homes on other business."

"Trend-setters," Eddie said slowly. "I think he's making fun of me now. Is he making fun of me, Celene?"

How could I be making fun of him just because he was wearing a dress that matched his girl friend's? What kind of narrow-minded oaf did he take me for?

The kind I am, I suppose.

"Even if he is, don't worry about it, Eddie," Deckard said. "He's here on business, he says."

"I'm feeling aggressive, Celene," Eddie said.

I was getting tired. I came close to telling him that the dress didn't go with his eyes, but it seemed a childish tack.

Deckard said, "Go on to the bedroom. I'll be along in a couple minutes."

Eddie scowled, but he left.

"It's not buying of ceramic work. I'm a private detective."

She looked at me. Then she laughed.

It went on too long. I began to feel aggressive. "What's the problem? Jokes coming across a TelePrompTer behind me, or what?"

"I don't know which of you is farther into daydreamsville."

"Me or your bit of rough? You'll only have half a chance to decide. I've got a couple of questions which I'd like to ask you. You don't have to answer me, and even if you do it probably won't keep other people from asking the same things soon."

"What kind of questions?"

"Primarily about the night of April twelfth."

"Oh," she said. "Billy."

"That's right. The first question is whether you saw him that evening. That was the Saturday which seems to be the last day he was seen."

"Yeah, I know which day it was. Because I was supposed to see him on the Sunday night and he never showed."

"Did you see him the Saturday?"

"For a while, yeah. We were out here in the late afternoon, but Eddie came back when he'd said he wouldn't."

"Eddie? This Eddie?"

"Of course this Eddie. What other Eddie?"

"How long could you have had him around?"

"He's my inspiration," she said. "I've known him for a long time."

"But you were friendly with Boyd?"

"I was balling him because he was going to buy some of my stuff, if that's what you were asking. He was supposed to pick some things out that Saturday. Only, Eddie got in some trouble in Bloomington and got scared. He came home early and that scared the pants off Billy."

"Eddie scared the pants off Billy?" There seemed a shortage of pants altogether.

"So Billy left early. About nine. I never saw him again. When he didn't show up or call on Sunday, I went around to his place but nobody answered the door. I didn't hear till later that he'd probably left town."

"When he left you on the Saturday, do you know where he intended to go?"

"Nope. Didn't seem right to ask. And I was tending to Eddie. He got into a fight, and was cut pretty badly."

"Eddie? In a fight?"

"Look, fella," she said, waving a finger at me. "You don't know Eddie. You got no reason to crap on him. I've known him a long time. I've known him from before he went funny. If I spend time with him, it's my business, not yours."

"You are absolutely right," I said, chastened. "I'm sorry. I had no reason to make rude remarks just because he rubbed me the wrong way."

She didn't know whether I was being sarcastic or straight.

I said, "I've had a long day in a business I don't understand. It's made me less open to the variability of humanity than I am accustomed to being. And more prickly. I've not meant to be offensive."

She decided she knew I was being sarcastic now. "Go on. Get out," she said.

I couldn't think of any way to retrieve the situation.

I got out.

I felt genuine regret as I drove back to Nashville. I wasn't very nice to Deckard and friend. Usually I am interested in people who are different. I positively like bearded men who wear dresses.

But not that day.

Maybe I was getting old-fashioned in more profound ways than I admitted to myself. Maybe I was heavily into daydreamsville, as the lady said.

Only I couldn't find Daydreamsville on the map. Needmore, Fruitdale and Bean Blossom, I found. Also Trevlac, which they say was named by spelling Calvert backward. I passed through Helmsburg and by six railroad cabooses which had been converted once to be motel rooms.

Maybe I fit into the real world after all.

I drove to Dave Hogue's office. I parked in front of it and tried the door. It was locked. I didn't know whether he lived on the premises or elsewhere. It looked a large place. He might live there. I rang the bell and waited and rang again.

No one answered. Out of curiosity I walked to the side of the house where there was a driveway and I followed it around back. There was a yard with a few trees, and a double garage.

I looked through a small window in a door on the side of the garage and saw an empty space in one bay and a great pile of odds and ends filling the other. No one answered a knock on the back door either.

All things being considered, I decided to leave the man in peace. I would report what I'd been up to by phone from Indianapolis in the morning.

I also decided to eat. I went to the Nashville House half expecting to see Sheriff Dunlap tucking into today's special. But she wasn't there.

I had myself a big meal, including their fried biscuits.

I took a long time over the food, and by the end I felt a lot better. I was, after all, employed. To be irritable just because I didn't understand some things was to be a sore winner in a race like mine.

After dessert I walked across the street to the sheriff's office. I soon had a clue why she'd not been eating. There were three state police cars in the reserved space in front of her office. That wasn't the clue. The clue was the raised voices that came through the door as I approached it. I even thought I saw somebody inside waving his arms.

I decided it wasn't the time for me to wander in. They scared my pants off. I walked back to my van.

The state police were with Jeanna Dunlap. Maybe giving her a hell's hard time for not bringing them into the Boyd case earlier. That would mean she had not found her second body and had begun to suspect she wasn't going to find it. It meant her particular theory was now out. Some new theory was in. The thing was up for grabs.

I mused about language for a moment, the susceptibility of common phrases to double meaning. Up for grabs. Rubbed me the wrong way.

I decided I shouldn't use so many common phrases. Then I decided that was stupid. I was common. I am common. He is, she is, I are common.

I got in the van and drove back to Indianapolis. Once there, I did no more work except to sort out the telephone number Elizabeth Staedtler had given me. I tried it twice. The first time it was busy; the second, nobody answered.

I called it a day. I went to visit my woman. There I went to sleep. It's common knowledge that a rest is as good as a change.

20

After breakfast I called Dave Hogue's number. But he wasn't at his office. "He's over trying to get Frank Pynne out again," Betty Weddle told me. "The state police took Frank in for questioning last night. In fact the town is swarming with state police now."

"And there's no way you can tell when Mr. Hogue will be back, then?"

"Not really, no."

"All right. Could you tell him that I'll be in Indianapolis this morning trying to track down Elizabeth Staedtler? I'll try to call him later on."

"I'll tell him, Mr. Samson."

"And could you ask him to do one other thing for me?"

"What's that?"

"I would like to know who inherits from Billy Boyd."

She hesitated. "Why is that?" she asked.

"There is no point in being completely bemused by all the gossip and small-town politics," I said. "When people are murdered, it's for reasons, and so it may be helpful to know who benefited materially from Boyd's death."

"Mr. Samson," she said, "isn't your interest exceeding what you've been hired to do?"

"What do you mean?"

"You are not in this case as a law enforcement officer; you have no responsibility to assign likely guilt. You are involved in the legal defense of a client against possible charges or conviction."

"I don't need to tell you that if we find who did do it, that's the best defense available."

"And I shouldn't need to tell you that Frank Pynne may well not care to pay for anything beyond the minimum necessary to get himself off. That is our object. Nothing more."

I thought that I had clear enough in my mind what was in bounds and what wasn't, but I said, "Well, when I come down I'll have a word with Mr. Hogue just to make sure we all understand what I'm supposed to be doing."

Perceptively she said, "I'm not meaning to undermine any understanding you have with David. But once Frank is cleared, that's going to be that."

"And at the moment, helping the forces of law and order to find a hypothesis which doesn't involve Frank Pynne is as good a step toward that goal as any."

"I see. Yes. When will you be back in Nashville?"

"I would think this afternoon."

"All right. I'll tell David."

. . .

I went through my notes on Elizabeth Staedtler, and returned to the phone. I tried the telephone number she had given me again, but it was busy.

So I tried I.U.P.U.I. From their own information number I got the number for the sociology offices. There I got a harassed secretary.

I explained that I was trying to locate a woman who had been interviewed for a job in her department in June.

"Trying to locate?" she repeated back to me as if in utter disbelief. "What's that supposed to mean?"

"Madam," I said, "I am working on a murder case and this person may know how to get in touch with a vital witness."

"Murder," she repeated. "I can't believe it. First the darn car won't start and now someone's calling about murder cases. What are you? A cop?"

"I'm a private detective working for the lawyer who is defending a man being accused of murder."

"And what is it you want?"

"I want the home address and telephone number of Doctor Elizabeth Staedtler. She was interviewed for some kind of job on June twelfth this year."

There was a silence at the other end of the line. In an optimistic moment I thought she'd gone to get the file.

"I don't know," the secretary said, at last. "Just over the phone, somebody's address and telephone number? I don't think I can do that. I mean I'm sure you are who you say you are, but how do I know you're not someone else? Not necessarily criminal or something, but like a finance company? I don't see how I can do that. Not over the phone. Not unofficial. Maybe if you came over and talked to our head of department, the head could authorize it, but otherwise I have to treat job applications as confidential. No, I can't do it. Sorry."

I had to accept it. So I did.

I tried the number which Staedtler had given me again. This time nobody answered after twenty rings.

It was going to be one of those days.

Come to think of it, mine was one of those lives.

I called information for Bridgeport, Connecticut. I could have told the operator what she told me. "I have no listing for an Elizabeth Staedtler. In fact I have no listing for any Staedtlers of that spelling at all in Bridgeport."

"Thank you," I said. But I didn't mean it.

All my client had told me was that she had come to Indianapolis from Bridgeport. She never said she lived there. And when she called to sign me off she said she was going back to the East.

The East is a big place.

I had several ways to go. I decided to cast a net at the Police Department. Miller had been so helpful before, I knew he was just dying to pursue a few little things for me so I would be free to amble down south again.

Miller wasn't there.

"Well, where is he?" I asked Sergeant Mable, the reception officer at Homicides and Robberies with Violence. "On a case or downstairs being reprimanded or what?"

"In Nebraska," Sergeant Mable said.

Shocked, I asked, "Has he retired?"

"Naw. He's on vacation."

"Vacation? In Nebraska?" Nobody goes on vacation in Nebraska. Except maybe Miller.

"How long's he away?"

"Another two weeks."

"Oh terrific."

"What did you want to see him about?" Mable asked.

"I'm trying to find somebody," I said, unguardedly.

Mable shrugged. "Try Missing Persons?"

It would never have occurred to me, but there were worse notions. "Where do I go?"

Missing Persons was down the hall from Communications and a stairwell away from the friendly computers of I. & I.—Identification and Information. The office was a clearinghouse for search activities elsewhere, not big in itself.

And there was no danger warning on the door.

The first person I saw as I walked in was a stocky man of about fifty with thinning gray hair, swept back so it looked as if his head had jumped forward leaving the hair behind. I knew him. Lieutenant Leroy Powder.

He saw me immediately. He must have been looking at the inside of his door.

"Oh God!" I said.

"But my friends call me Roy," he said. Then to the others in the room, a non-uniform clerical assistant and a junior officer, he said, "Hey, guys, look! This here is an old-style specimen like you don't hardly see out of a zoo nowadays. Have a good look before he becomes extinct."

"I didn't know you were up here," I said. "I thought you were one of those guys that disintegrated when he was hit by sunlight."

"I've been here more than three years. Just about getting things into shape," he said with some pride. When we'd met before, he was the long-entrenched supremo of the department's night cover system, a legend in his own nighttime.

I hadn't enjoyed dealing with the legend.

"So what you want?" he asked, challenging me.

It was a jump ball as to whether I walked out, but I said, "Nothing you can help me with. Just a missing person."

"I didn't think even you thought this place was the goddamn toilets," he said. "Of course you got a missing person. Now, who the hell is it?"

"A former client," I said.

He wrung his hands. "A client. A client! My galloping God, the sleuth wants us to go out and find his client for him."

"Only if you're up to it," I said.

"Bit careless to misplace a client, isn't it, gumshoe? Wouldn't have thought you had so many as one could get lost in the shuffle of tiny feet in and out of your office."

"When the performance is finished, and these two captives do their audience number and stand and cheer and holler 'bravo' and stamp their feet, maybe we can do the necessary so I can get out of here."

"Oh, my humblest pardons, gumshoe," he said. "Gumshoe is a busy gumshoe and doesn't have time to put up with the idiosyncrasies of silly old lieutenant policeman person."

"Right first time," I said.

"Well," he said, "I'm in a hurry, so if you got anything to say come through to my desk and make it snappy."

I was as concise as I knew how to be.

"So," Powder said, "your problem is that when you had your client sitting across the desk from you, you didn't get her home address."

"I plead guilty," I said.

"And you came in here to get your friend Miller to help you make amends for this carelessness. What things did you want Miller to do for you?" He picked up a pencil and held it ready above a sheet of paper.

I was encouraged. I said, "I wanted him to call I.U.P.U.I. to lubricate the wheels for me there. I wanted him to call the University of Bridgeport to get the student records of Elizabeth Staedtler and Priscilla Pynne including home details. And I also wanted him to get onto the Pentagon."

"The Pentagon," he repeated. "Naturally. And why was that?"

"I would like to know where Billy Boyd went when he ran away in 1960. He became eighteen when he was away, so he would have registered for the draft. They would know where he was living at the time."

Powder wrote it down. "I see," he said. "And would your friend Miller get all this stuff for you?"

"Probably, yes."

"Then he ought to be drummed out of the goddamn force," Powder said.

"That's a narrow and stupid—"

"Narrow! Stupid! To beef because a cop spends public time getting stuff for a lawyer defending a guy who hasn't even been charged yet? With no chance of clearing up a crime?"

"You got a murder down there. Or two. Or even three."

"But they're not our murders, are they?"

"Narrow and—"

"Button it!" he said, his voice ringing. "Let's put you in my leather-soled shoes, hypothetical though that may be since you ain't even half big enough to fill one of them. Suppose you're me and you walk in spouting all this guff. What would you do in my place?"

"I'd call I.U.P.U.I. I'd call the University of Bridgeport. I'd—"

"On your horse," he said. "Go on. I'm busy. Your time is up. You got a missing-person case sometime, come and see me."

I left quietly. It had been one of those things that seemed like a good idea at the time.

21

On my way to the halls of academe, I stopped at the Hotel Penrod, where I'd seen Elizabeth Staedtler enter.

Five bucks and a quick flash of my investigator's card got me a look at the hotel register for June, nearly as quickly as the five bucks alone would have. I found Elizabeth Staedtler's entry easily. She'd checked in on the day before she'd come to me and she'd checked out the day after. All as she had said. The only address given was Connecticut.

I pointed this out to the clerk, an elderly man who moved slowly enough to make me suspect he was really dead. "Shouldn't you get more home address than this?"

"What for?"

"In case they leave something behind that you want to send on to them to keep their good impression of the hotel so they'll come back when they're next in town."

"Anything gets left we keep for a couple of days and then divide up. You get some funny stuff sometimes. Had a bottle of booze with a worm in it last month once. A worm!"

"Do you remember this woman?" I asked.

"No."

"How do you know? I haven't even described her yet."

"I don't remember her."

"Would some more cash help your memory?"

"Not a lot. I only started working here in July."

I.U.P.U.I. is an enormous exercise in cooperation between the two oldest rival Indiana state universities, Indiana and Purdue. Neither of them originated in Indianapolis; now they both have a major base there in a complex but seemingly unplanned campus built in brick and concrete around a series of parking lots.

I found my sociology secretary, though with some difficulty. She was a lively little woman who remembered talking to me. "You're the guy said you were a private eye on a murder, right?"

"Not only said but am."

"Christ, what a day!"

"I know the feeling," I said.

"It didn't stop there, you know."

"What? Where?"

"After you called, I had three lectures to cancel. Three! What a day!"

I nodded. "About Elizabeth Staedtler?"

"I talked to the head of department about that after you called, because I thought from your voice, you know, I thought that you'd probably be coming by." She smiled. "And here you are."

"And here I are. What did he say?"

"She. Our head's a she. Anyway, I talked to her, and we talked about it and then a little while ago I got this other funny phone call. Now I hardly never get funny calls, but today! And he said he was a policeman. Well, first I thought it was you again, even though the voice was kind of different, I thought it was you and after all you were what you said you weren't and from a finance company or even an old boyfriend, you know? Only he said to call him back at the Police Department. He gave the number and I did and it was the Police Department and so he was, you know?"

"I know," I said.

"Well, he said that I shouldn't give you any information. And, or course, in a way, that made me happy I hadn't done it in the first place, 'cause I was suspicious, or—well, if not exactly suspicious, then at least cautious, because a secretary in a big department has access to some pretty important things sometimes, you know. But then I told him, see."

"Told him what?" I asked in edgewise.

"Well, what happened after I talked to the head. She asked me to get the file, so we could see what we were dealing with, because she didn't remember it. And I'm not surprised she couldn't remember it, because it wasn't there."

"The file?"

"That's right. Stetler, Staedtler, it didn't matter how you spelled it, because it wasn't there."

"You mean it's been stolen?"

"I mean it never was there."

"Hang on. I don't understand."

"Well, we've never heard of her."

"What do you mean, you've never heard of her?"

"I mean we weren't hiring anybody in June. We didn't interview anybody in June and we've never heard of anybody called Doctor Elizabeth Staedtler."

"Oh," I said.

"Well, at least you're not laughing," she said. "The policeman, he laughed his head off."

"Is there any chance of a mistake about this?"

"No. I mean we can't keep track of everybody who makes an application for a job, you know. We get so many because jobs are so scarce in this day and age. But we certainly know who we interview. And we know when we interview, and . . . all that. We saw some prospective students that week, some late applications and a man who wanted to transfer from Duquesne. But no hiring. And then when I told him that, the policeman, he said that it was all right to tell you when you came in after all. The kind of day it was, that seemed to mean that you probably wouldn't come in, you know. But here you are."

22

By the time I'd driven back to my office, I had figured out that Elizabeth Staedtler had been in Indianapolis for some reason other than applying for a job at the sociology department of I.U.P.U.I.

I'm quick that way.

But I couldn't be sure of anything else. Sure, she'd checked in and out of the hotel when she'd said. But who knows where she spent the rest of her life?

I tried the number she'd given me. It was busy again.

I called the University of Bridgeport.

I was in no mood to mess around. "I'm calling from the Indianapolis Police Department," I said. "I would like the addresses and telephone numbers you have for two former students. Would you put me through to someone with alumni records, please?"

They put me through. After doing my explanation bit, I demanded the records of Elizabeth Staedtler and of Priscilla Pitman.

"You want to hang on? Or shall I call you back?"

"I'll hang on," I said.

They were quick and they were efficient.

"O.K., Officer," the records man said. "I have them. You ready?"

"I'm ready."

"Elizabeth Sanderson Staedtler entered in the fall semester of 1971 and graduated in June, 1975. Four point oh oh grade point average. Whew, that's top grades. You want that kind of thing?"

"Why not?" I said.

"Majored in history, double minor in education and psychology."

"Yes?"

"You don't want me to read the transcript, do you?"

"No. How about addresses?"

"I've got a home address. It's 15 Bayview Drive, Stonington, Connecticut 06378."

"Good. And a phone?"

He gave me a phone number.

"That's the address she applied to college from?"

"Yes, sir."

"Any others on there?"

"No, sir."

"O.K. What about Priscilla Pitman?"

"Yes," he said, slowly. Finding his page. Or whatever. "Priscilla Howell Donohue Pitman. Also entered in fall, 1971. But she didn't complete the year. She left before finals. Her transcript is all F's and I's. I is for incomplete."

"And addresses?"

"I've got 781 Croxley Boulevard, Apartment 4A, Springfield, Massachusetts 01107. But no phone number. Information is pretty thin on this file."

"Thanks. You've been a great help."

"Just doing my job," he said.

I tried the Indianapolis number I'd been trying. It rang and rang. I didn't understand.

But . . .

I called Stonington, Connecticut. It went to the eight count before it was answered by a woman.

"May I speak to Elizabeth Staedtler, please?"

"Liz? Good heavens, she hasn't lived at home for years!"

"I've just had this number from the University of Bridgeport. Do you know another number where I might be able to get her?"

"You can get her here tomorrow," the woman said. "Herb and she are coming for an extra-long weekend. Do you know Herb?"

"No, I don't."

"Of course you don't. Liz is not a Staedtler anymore. She's a Weaver."

"I'd like to speak to her today, if it's possible."

The woman gave me another Connecticut number, in Hartford.

I called the Indianapolis number again. It was not a busy-signal try; it was a no-answer try.

Until the thirteenth ring.

"Hello."

"Hello," I said. "Who is this, please?"

"I, um, my name is Carl Kovaleski."

"I'm trying to get some information on a woman called Elizabeth Staedtler," I said. "Does that name mean anything to you?"

"Uh, no."

"I called her at this number in the middle of June. Does that help?"

"No sir, mister, it doesn't."

"Well, is there anybody else there who might remember or who might know something?"

"I dunno, mister. This here is a public telephone in the bus station. I'm from Saint Louis, so you better tell me exactly who you want me to ask."

It was the hard way to learn how a phone could be either busy or unanswered with nothing in between. And it left me with an image of Elizabeth Staedtler, in her gray coat, camping in the phone booth waiting for my call.

I was getting upset. My last client on Maryland Street was turning out more complicated every step I took. I felt absurd now just to have accepted her at face value at the time.

I called Hartford, Connecticut.

A woman answered. "Hello."

"Is that Mrs. Weaver?"

"It is."

"Formerly Miss Staedtler?"

"Yes, that's right. Who's calling, please?"

"My name is Albert Samson," I said.

"Yes?"

"Of Indianapolis."

"Yes? So?"

"I'm a private detective. You hired me in June."

"Like hell I did," she said.

I heard a voice in the background, asking a question.

Faintly, as the receiver hit the cradle, I heard her saying, "Some new kind of dirty phone call."

23

I was in the Hartford airport by a little after five.

I didn't have Herbert Weaver's home address, but I matched the telephone number to an address in the phone book.

The wrong side of town, in the rush hour. I arrived by taxi at their comfortable suburb doorstep almost at 6 p.m. exactly.

I rang the bell and was answered by a woman of about twenty-seven.

"Yes?"

"Mrs. Weaver?"

"Yes?"

"I was afraid of that."

It was another half an hour before two Weaver children were fed and occupied enough to leave me some clear time with their parents. Herbert Weaver was older than his wife, a man with a strikingly expressive face and restricted to a wheelchair. Elizabeth Weaver was on the tall side, and, though tired, she carried an immediately attractive vitality. Her movements were bright. She swung herself, even if it was just to drop into a comfortable armchair, pleading exhaustion.

She had definitely never hired me to do anything.

"You say someone's been using Elizabeth's name?" Herbert Weaver said.

"Your wife's maiden name. I was hired in June by a woman who called herself Doctor Elizabeth Staedtler."

"A doctor," Mrs. Weaver said. "Mmm. That would save a lot in medical bills."

"A Ph.D. doctor, in sociology," I said.

"And what was this person trying to accomplish, Mr. Samson?"

"She hired me to look for a woman who I believe you once knew, Mrs. Weaver."

"Who?"

"A woman who entered the University of Bridgeport the same time you did. Priscilla Pitman."

She appeared not to place the name.

"The story was that you and Miss Pitman—who has married and is now Mrs. Pynne—corresponded once or twice a year and considered yourselves friends."

"I don't quite . . ."

"Miss Pitman left U.B. before the end of the first year."

"Oh!" she said suddenly. "Her!"

"What was it, dear?" her husband asked.

"There was this girl in the dorm who I bet it was. She came to my room once and asked me to be her friend. It was terribly unnerving. She sat on the bed and just kept talking, about how much trouble she was having concentrating on her work even though she knew it was easy, and how she needed someone she could feel she was working for, who would help make her bear down. It was frightening, because she had this intensity. Talking very calmly, but as if she were going to explode. God, I haven't thought about it for years."

"You always did attract the lame ducks," her husband said.

I took the picture which my Elizabeth Staedtler had given me and showed it to the world's Elizabeth Staedtler. "Is this the girl?"

She looked at it a long time. "It's the same brooding frown," she said. "That's her." She passed it to her husband.

"Well, well," he said. "Not backward about coming forward." He passed the picture back to me.

I said, "I take it that you did not go on to be her mentor-friend."

"No," Elizabeth Weaver said. "I felt sorry for the girl, but she scared me."

"What happened to her?" I asked.

"There were some incidents," she said. "And then she was found naked in the cafeteria one morning in the spring. She was gone that afternoon, poor child. She was one of those, you know, who go away from home for the first time and can't handle it."

"And I take it," I said, "that there was no other student at the time who was a friend of you both?"

"I don't feel that Priscilla had any friends," Elizabeth Weaver said.

The Weavers drove me back to town and I asked to be dropped at the bus station. From a pay phone I called Dave Hogue collect.

"Hartford, Connecticut?" he asked. "I thought you were coming down here this afternoon."

"As you gather, I didn't make it. Has anything happened?"

"The state police have been making a repetitive meal out of questioning Frank Pynne. They've been at it all day, though they're not getting anyplace."

"Anything else?"

"I've had a look at Billy Boyd's will."

"And who benefits?"

"A lot of people," he said measuredly. "And quite a stir there's going to be too."

"Why?"

"Because he's left a list of forty-nine women, each one to get a bequest between a hundred and a thousand dollars."

"That's going to make some fur fly."

"It certainly is. Especially since it specifies that the money is 'for services rendered,' and that a list of the people he left money to should be carved on his tombstone."

I thought about it for a moment. "That's a wicked will."

"You are very right," he said somberly. "Anybody whose name is on that list stands damned, with no effective defense."

"What a charming fellow this Boyd was," I said. "Who is on the list?"

"I don't have a copy," Hogue said.

"But you read through it?"

"Yes."

"So you know whether there are any interesting names or not."

"They are mostly people that I think you don't know."

"But some that I do know. Who, for instance?"

He took a breath. "Betty, for one," he said.

"Betty? Your secretary?"

"Yes. For a thousand dollars."

"A case in point about condemning without a defense?"

"I haven't asked her about it. I . . . I don't think I really have the right, if it is a matter of her private life."

I said, "A list of that size must cover quite a period of time. Perhaps her appearance relates to something from long ago."

He was silent.

"You don't buy that?"

"No."

"Why not?"

"Because the format of the will has been established for more than twelve years, and he has just added names and amounts from time to time."

"And they would have to be dated, I suppose."

"They would."

"And the date for Betty?"

"The end of February. This year."

I let it go. "What other names were on this infamous list?"

"Forty-eight people with secrets."

"All local?"

"Yes. While I daresay some services were rendered to our Mr. Boyd elsewhere, he chose to limit his posthumous generosity to residents of Brown County."

"Jeanna Dunlap?"

"Yes, but her relationship with Billy was not something she ever hid."

"I can go through the list of names I know, but why don't you tell me whether there is anything interesting."

"Priscilla Pynne is not on the list."

"What about Celene Deckard?"

"Who?"

"An artist who lives near Lake Lemon. She saw Boyd about nine o'clock the night he went missing."

"Did she?" He seemed interested. "I hadn't heard that."

"I'm sure that the state police will have gotten to her by now."

"I can check. I don't remember the name from the will, but I wouldn't swear it's not there."

"You said that the select forty-nine received individual bequests."

"Yes."

"What about the bulk of the estate?"

"The gallery to Mary Tolley," he said.

"And the rest?"

"To be sold off, with the proceeds going to Miss Sharon A. Doans, 'who will know what I wish done with it.' "

"Sharon Doans?" I asked. "What was she to Boyd?"

"I don't know," he said, "nor do I know what Boyd wished to be done with the money. Nor do I know what will become of the tract of land."

"You sound pretty fed up, Mr. Hogue."

"It's been a very trying day."

"I've been trying to track down Elizabeth Staedtler," I said.

"In Hartford?"

"She lives here."

"Oh."

"And I think I have turned up a witness who saw Priscilla Pynne alive two months after she disappeared."

"You have?"

"Yes."

"Who is it?"

"Me."

24

I explained to Hogue how my conversation with the real Elizabeth Staedtler seemed to undermine completely the story the person who had hired me had given.

"Unless there is someone else altogether involved, who sent me to ask questions about one while using the name of the other, I have to assume that my client was actually Priscilla Pynne."

"But didn't you recognize her?" he asked tiredly.

"I never knew her. She gave me a picture of Mrs. Pynne but the woman I saw looked very different. She was the right height, as far as I can remember. Weight and hair color can be tinkered with. Eyes can be disguised with contact lenses. And clothes are clothes."

"But why should she hire you to look for herself?"

"At the moment, it is my most ardent wish in life to ask her that question."

About seven-thirty there was a bus to Springfield, Massachusetts. Near the Springfield bus station I found a hotel which reminded me only too strongly of the Penrod near Union Station. After checking in, I went out to buy a toothbrush and paste, a map of Springfield and a newspaper . When I got back, I watched television in the lounge for a while. But I found it hard to concentrate on the disjointed antics of whatever it was that was on the screen.

I went to bed.

In the morning I had a light breakfast and went by taxi to 781 Croxley Boulevard.

Like my hotel and me, it had seen better days. A five-story brick apartment building on a corner, with a dirt alleyway running behind it off the boulevard. Garbage cans stood in a battered row along the side wall, lids ajar in various angles of ragged salute.

The main entrance was recessed a few yards from the street. There were two cement benches either side of the entry walk. One was smashed in the middle, like a balsa board stepped on by a giant foot. The other looked as if it would last forever.

There was no name on the mailbox for 4A. I climbed to the fourth floor. One apartment door had a plastic "A" screwed tightly at eye level. I knocked. And again.

The door behind me, marked "D," opened a few inches and a woman with long strands of white hair among a majority of black stared blandly at me.

"He's in there," she said. "He's in there, but he ain't gonna answer."

"No?"

"He had a bucketful last night. He'll sleep till five, he will."

"I see," I said. "But I'm not even sure I have the right place. I'm looking for some people named Pitman."

The head nodded, like a jerky puppet's. "It's the right place."

"Well, ma'am," I said, trying to be ingratiating, "I'm a private detective and I'm looking for the Pitmans' daughter Priscilla. A few months back she left her husband and he wants to find her. So I came by here to see if maybe she'd been in touch."

The woman looked at me. "Priscilla? That married the soldier?"

"I believe so, yes."

"She left him?"

"Yes."

The woman detonated a shriek of laughter. Her shaking knocked the door open, and she stood in a tattered nightdress, vibrating. Finally she stopped, and said, "That's the funniest thing I've ever heard."

While I had already suspected that, I asked, "Why is that, ma'am?"

"Because the mother has been swanking around on that marriage ever since it happened, that's why. Oh, how are the mighty fallen!"

"I take it Mrs. Pitman isn't at home now?"

"No. She works. Always out before eight."

"Do you know where?"

"Supermarket. She's on the checkout at A. and P. It's down the main road about a mile."

"Did you know the girl?"

"Missy Prissy? Sure I knew her. Too good for the likes of me, and the rest of us living round here. Not smart enough for her, ordinary people. Only, I saw her when they sent her back from New York. We all saw her then, and it was a little harder to tell who was the ups in life and who was the downs. Till she hooked that poor soldier boy. I saw his picture in the paper. They never brought him around here. But we all saw her when they sent her back."

"Has Priscilla been around here lately?"

"No."

"Do you know if she's written or been in touch otherwise?"

"I don't know. *She* wouldn't tell the likes of us that the precious picture girl left her old man. Someone too good to lend a neighbor a couple of bucks wouldn't tell anything ugly and ordinary like that."

The apartment building was on Croxley Boulevard's intersection with Arbor Avenue, and Arbor was the major road. I walked toward town, and found the A. & P.

I went to the manager's office, elevated and enclosed with glass, in a position to survey the premises. I asked for a few words with Mrs. Pitman without explaining what sort of words they would be.

The manager, a bald man whose stomach was inadequately restrained by a tight belt, didn't ask any questions. I suspected men in well-worn jackets had asked for words with Mrs. Pitman before, that the men had come and gone but Mrs. Pitman remained a fixture to be relied on.

He took me to the checkouts where a gray-haired woman was ringing up a dozen items for a child-mother.

"Man to see you, Marjory," he said.

Mrs. Pitman looked over her shoulder at me, then slid without hesitation off her seat. The manager picked up the checkout rhythm where she had left it.

I led her out of casual earshot.

"What's he done now?" she asked. A careful layer of makeup covered a wrinkled face. She was about fifty, and was the source of the fine structure, bone and otherwise, which showed in the picture I had of her daughter.

"I'm not a policeman," I said. "And it is not about your husband."

The statements did not bring her relief. She could tell I was bringing her trouble.

"What, then?"

I explained my business in the same way that I had explained it to her neighbor.

"Left him?" she repeated. "Why?"

"I don't know. She took off one night and he hasn't heard from her since. I thought that maybe she had been in touch with you."

"Fat chance," she said. "I had two letters from Chicago. Last one on February seventeenth, 1977, saying that Francis got him a job somewhere in goddamn Indiana."

"That's right. Bloomington."

"Well, you know more than I do."

"You've had no word of her in the last six months, then?"

"I just said so."

She had. And I believed her.

"Six months?" she said then. "Ran away six months ago?"

"A little more than that."

She eyed me with an impersonal suspicion. "Where are you from, mister?"

"Indianapolis."

"You come out here all the way from Indianapolis?"

"Yes."

"Then you aren't telling me the half of it. You wouldn't come all the way from Indianapolis if all she did was run away from her husband six months ago. That ain't life."

"No," I admitted. "I suppose it isn't."

"Are you a cop?"

"No. I've told you no lies," I said.

"I didn't think so. But you haven't told me much truth, neither."

"I have been hired by her husband's lawyer. A man has been

killed. Her husband is suspected, and it is possible that your daughter knows some things that may help."

"Don't flannel me, country boy. You're trying to pin this killing on my girl. Now that's the right of it, isn't it?"

"No," I said.

She nodded, in confirmation. "Oh yes, it is."

"I'm not trying to pin anything on anybody. I'm trying to find her. When I find her, she'll speak for herself."

"I suppose she will," Mrs. Pitman said. "Except she always was an actions-speak-louder-than-words sort of child. So if she's run away, maybe that says a lot."

"It is knowing the meaning of what it says that is the problem."

"You'll work it out, too," she said. "I can see it in your eyes. There's a kind of spark I see there." She peered hard at me.

I just went on: "Is there anybody else your daughter might have kept in touch with over the years?"

"You mean somebody else she might have turned to round here instead of me?"

"Your daughter seems to have lived very much alone. Her husband doesn't understand much about her and I haven't found anyone she confides in where she lived. She hasn't kept close to you. If there's anybody she might have got in touch with, I would like to know about it."

"Mr. Catherman," she said.

Kenneth Catherman was a high-school English teacher. I got the school's number from the operator. But the secretary there said he was not at work.

I tried him at home. He answered with the nasal blur of a cold in full flower. I asked if I could come and see him. He asked what about and I said, "Priscilla Howell Donohue Pitman."

"Good God!" he said.

He gave me the address. By the time I acquired a taxi, it was eleven-thirty.

The house was the lower half of a stucco duplex, in a comfortable residential area. Catherman saw me walk in from the street and opened the door before I rang the bell.

He invited me in and offered coffee. I accepted, and while he prepared it I sat waiting in the living room.

"There we are," he said. He put a tray on the coffee table and sat down opposite me. He wore the trousers and waistcoat of a three-piece suit, a tall, solid man of about forty.

I said, "You knew Priscilla Pitman's name immediately."

"Certainly. She is etched on my memory."

"I'm trying to find her," I said.

"Is she lost?" he asked with a detached air.

"Her whereabouts are not known," I said, formally. "Her mother thought that you would be the person she would have stayed in touch with around here."

"I'm afraid not. I would have liked to correspond with her and keep track of how her life unfolded, but it didn't happen that way."

"You don't know where she is?"

"No. Sorry."

I scratched my head. "I see."

"A memorable girl," he said. "Teachers—teachers who care—get precious few memorable students passing through their tender mercies."

"When did you know her?"

"She graduated in 1971," he said. "A dedicated student. Very hard-working, yet intuitive enough. A rare combination, especially from her background. And put together with the kind of Greek beauty she had, dear oh dear, an unusual creature indeed."

"Your description sounds rather more than pedagogical," I said.

"They are people, you know, these kids. I try to see them as people."

"Did you have a relationship with her outside of school hours?"

"Certainly!" he said. But coyly, he added, "Mind you, I try to have relationships with all my better students outside of school hours."

I wondered whether I was being toyed with.

I upped the stakes. "You haven't asked me why I am trying to find her," I said. "She may be a witness in a murder case in Indianapolis and I am trying to locate her for the defense." I gave him my card.

"I see," he said.

"You don't seem surprised."

"How surprised is surprised? You state it as a fact; I accept your statement as such. I had no expectations to be contradicted."

"You say Priscilla Pitman was a hard-working student in high school. Yet she ran amok at college. Why should that be?"

"These things are always complex," he said, saying nothing. "I see her as . . . a phenomenon. In that sense, one just observes what happens without judging."

"Were you physically involved with her?"

"Certainly not. Not my type, I'm afraid, old boy."

"And did she know that?"

Serious for the first time, he said, "Not for a long time."

"You last spoke to her in June, 1971?"

"Spoke?" He thought carefully. "Spoke? Sometime in the summer of 1971."

I did not have good feelings about this conversation. But I was not sure that it wasn't just that the man's style wasn't sympathetic. And I couldn't think of how to push it farther, disappointing as what he'd had to say had been.

I asked, "Is there anyone else you know of who she might go to in an emergency?"

"I gather she married a soldier some time ago. You could try him."

"You speak as if you don't expect them still to be together," I said.

"I'm surprised they got together in the first place."

"Why is that?"

"Priscilla, with a soldier?"

"Why not?"

"As a stepping-stone, or a rehabilitative stop, perhaps. But not for life. Not that I've met the fellow." He laughed. "But I flatter myself that I understand something about Priscilla."

25

The quickest way home was a train to Boston and a plane from there back to Indianapolis. I was in my office by the middle of the evening, having used the travel time to seek perspectives on what I had and hadn't found out.

There were some messages on my answering machine. One of them was even from someone other than family or tantamount to family. It was cryptic and nasty. It said, "Impersonation of a police officer is grounds for revocation of a gumshoe license as well as being a criminal offense."

Made me quiver in my sneakers.

Before I set off for Nashville in the morning, I stopped at Missing Persons. "Decided to surrender yourself," Powder said with menace as I walked into the office. "Very sensible."

"What's your problem?"

His extensive forehead gleamed and a vein stood out, nearly vertically. "Your problem," he said. "Impersonation of police."

"I do imitations of policemen I have known and loved," I said, "but I don't impersonate them."

"You told the records people at the University of Bridgeport that you were a cop."

"No, I didn't."

"They said you did. They'll identify your voice."

"I told them I was phoning from the Indianapolis Police Department. That's different. That's a lie, but I never said I was a cop." Private eyes can be as good as philosophers at splitting hairs.

"Tell it to the judge," he said. He rubbed his face. "Enjoy your visit to I.U.P.U.I.?" he asked.

"I thought you were having nothing to do with this case."

"We found everybody missing in Indianapolis before ten yesterday. I made a couple of phone calls to avoid dying of boredom. They barely worked."

"That include one about draft records?"

"Venice," he said.

"Italy?"

"California. It's a suburb of Los Angeles."

"Address and phone number?"

"No longer effective for providing anyone who has heard of your man. So I'm happy to give them to you."

He had them written out on a piece of paper, which he passed across to me.

"So," he said, "found your client yet?"

"Not exactly."

"How surprised I am," he said, yawning. Subtle fellow.

"But I found out who she is."

"I thought you already knew that."

"I knew who she said she was."

"So who is she?"

"The woman she asked me to find."

I expected an eruption of abuse, but Powder leaned forward, rested his chin on his knuckles and thought about it. "And she hired you to find herself," he said.

"But since she already knew where she was," I said, in Dick and Jane logic, "she wanted some other information from me."

"Which was?"

"Whether she was being actively looked for."

"And you told her she wasn't."

"So she took me off the case."

"Only, now you are looking for her."

"Yes," I said.

"Have you got a sighting since your own?"

"Not yet," I said.

When I got to Dave Hogue's office, I found a state police car in front of it.

Inside in the waiting room a middle-aged trooper, whose head and long neck extended like a stem from his pear-shaped body, towered over Betty Weddle as she sat at her desk. She looked uncomfortable, even flustered, and she turned to me with obvious relief when I walked in.

"Mr. Samson. You want to see David?"

"That's right. Is he in?"

"Yes. Upstairs. I . . . " She seemed hesitant and rose from her chair.

"I'll find my own way," I said. "I don't want to interrupt."

"He'll be all right alone, Miss Weddle," the trooper said.

She turned to him with a pained expression, but sat down again. I went up to Hogue.

The door to his big second-floor room was open. He was staring out the window, but he stood up as he heard me enter. I closed the door behind me.

"Hello, Samson," he said.

He looked terribly tired. "You look awful," I said.

"Yes."

"You have an Indiana law enforcement officer interviewing your secretary down there."

"I know," he said. "It's about this business of Boyd's will. They seem to be going down the list."

"What for? Prurience value?"

"I suspect it's all they can think of to do, but it is certainly unimaginative and insensitive," Hogue said.

"Your secretary looked pretty uncomfortable."

"I can well believe that." He looked gloomy. "I feel responsible," he said, looking at me, then away.

"How?"

He didn't answer at first. Then he sighed and said, "Oh, maybe I should have kept up closer track of her social life."

That sounded vague to me. "Kept up? Does that mean you did know more about it once?"

"I got rather involved in her private life when she was being beaten by her second husband. But that was ten-odd years ago."

"Involved in other than a legal capacity?"

"She confided in me a good deal and there was a critical time when I gave her some shelter."

"He injured her seriously?"

"A number of times. But she is a loyal and resilient person."

"But in the end she came to you? After a beating?"

"In the middle of a beating sequence," he said. "But her fear was that she would lose control of herself, that she would shoot the man. Feeling she was nearing the limit of her own control, she finally sought help."

"Men like that are usually possessive too. Did he follow her?"

He sighed. "Yes, Mr. Samson, he did. There was a confrontation and I resisted him physically."

"Isn't that risky for someone with a bad heart?"

"Yes," he said. "But I get involved when I believe in things. And a gross, drunken man beating his wife and screaming obscene accusations is something I find it hard to step back from."

"Accusations? Involving you?"

"Among others, yes."

"I see."

"I doubt that you do, but that is really neither here nor there. I represented Betty in divorce proceedings and injunction procedures to keep the brute from her door. And, I'm pleased to say, he has moved away."

"I don't mean to intrude," I said, "but now to find that she had been involved with Billy Boyd—"

"Putatively involved," he interrupted.

"It must have been quite a shock for you."

"It was," he said. "It is."

"And you haven't talked to her about it?"

"No."

"Will you?"

"I don't know."

"Having butted in this far, may I ask another question?"

He shrugged tiredly.

"Did she know you were considering marrying Ida Boyd?"

"Certainly not," he snapped. "That was not public knowledge. It wasn't even settled between Ida and myself. We didn't talk to anyone else about it."

Then he seemed to recall something. But it didn't change his point of view. "Why do you ask that?" he asked.

"Only putting things you've said side by side. Betty Weddle is clearly very loyal to you. Yet at the end of last year, when you say you were thinking about marriage to Ida Boyd, you also say she suddenly talked about quitting her job here, and we also find that she, putatively, began to take up with someone you were having battles with."

"The B.C.T. was having battles with him. It was not personal," Hogue said.

"Nevertheless . . ."

"I never told Betty about my plans," he said, to close the subject. "What have you been up to?"

His personal life was not my business, so I accepted the shift to more comfortable ground readily. I got out my notebook and summarized my interviews.

After my report, he said, "But you're not actually closer to finding Priscilla Pynne?"

"You mean, do I have her address? No. But she's out there. I'm sure of it."

"I see."

He didn't say anything more. He seemed terribly weighted under by events. When I saw he wasn't going to comment, I said, "It has to be good for our client. It undercuts the simplicity of the jealous-revenge theory or the free-myself-for-another-woman theory."

He nodded. "Yes."

"Is Pynne still in custody?"

"No. The state police investigator released him yesterday. They are short of hard evidence, and he didn't crack under their intimidation. But the pressure is still on him. The local paper came out yesterday with his picture on the front page."

I asked, "How is Pynne taking it all?"

"He's trying to shrug it off. Keeping busy with various projects he has going."

"What sort of projects? Things to do with his job?"

"Only peripherally," Hogue said. "But I.U. has given him vacation time he had coming. They haven't suspended him or anything like that. They're not as much under pressure as they might be if he were in contact with students."

"Is Jeanna Dunlap still walking in the woods?"

"I don't know what Jeanna is up to. She seems to be out of the picture."

"What is the state investigator's name?"

"Darrow Junkersfield."

"I'm going to have to see him," I said.

"Why?"

"He should know that Priscilla Pynne was alive two months after she disappeared."

"Of course," Hogue said, and exhaled heavily.

"Look, Mr. Hogue," I said, "I'll go now and see some of these people and get back to you later."

"I think that would be just as well," he said. "I feel rather grim."

"But could you do one thing for me?"

"What's that?"

"Maybe you already know. Did Boyd's body have any money on it?"

He studied me again. "Money? Cash money?"

"That's right."

"I . . . I don't think it did. I don't remember mention of it."

"And other papers? Credit cards?"

"I don't really know, Samson. What—?"

"Mrs. Pynne, leaving home, needed money. If Boyd was buried with his cash, that would tend to rule her out. If the cash and credit cards were gone, that would argue against her too, because the credit cards probably wouldn't be any good to her. But if the cash was gone, and that's all, that puts her in again. And he was known to carry cash."

"You are thinking that Mrs. Pynne killed Boyd?" he asked.

"It's a hypothesis. One that doesn't involve Frank Pynne."

"True."

"And it fits something else that's been bothering me," I said.

"Which is?"

"Her car being left at I.U."

He frowned.

"If she killed Boyd," I said, "she wouldn't want to be seen driving his car, and she certainly wouldn't run away in it. So driving to I.U. in her own car, and using other means of transportation from there makes sense. From Bloomington she could connect to anywhere."

"And Boyd's car?" Hogue asked.

"Hidden? Disposed of? I don't know. But out of circulation somehow, which explains why there have been no police sightings of it."

He nodded slowly.

"One way or the other, it seems to be leading away from Frank Pynne," I said.

26

As I left Hogue's building, I saw the struthious state trooper sitting in his car making notes. I knocked on his passenger-side window and he rolled it down.

"I want to have a few words with Darrow Junkersfield," I told him. "Do you know where I can find him?"

The man had a rich and resonant voice which belied his odd shape. He said, "When I saw him last, he was going to an interview, somewhere to the north of town. But he is using the local sheriff's office as a base. You could wait for him there."

North of town could well mean Celene Deckard.

"Thank you," I said. "I'll try there in a few minutes."

First I took the short walk to Boyd's gallery.

Mary Tolley, dressed in pale blue and bright orange, was engaged with a Japanese couple. She spent several minutes with them while I waited, passing my time studying brushwork and texture.

Then she left the couple to come over to me. She said, "Sorry to keep you waiting, Mr. Samson."

"Quite all right. Business before business. How are you doing?"

"I reckon it's only a matter of how much of their baggage allowance they have left."

"If you reckon it, I'll bet you're right," I said.

"Do I sense that you have decided to purchase one of our fine works of art after all?"

"No, ma'am," I said. "Though if they are good investments, maybe my best idea is to get some paints and find out whether I'm an undiscovered primitive genius."

"Everybody has art in him. That's my belief."

"I'll give you first refusal once I get in production," I said.

Mary Tolley said, "If you didn't come for a picture, maybe you come in to talk about something else."

I nodded. "About Billy Boyd's will."

"There's quite a bit of talk about that round town."

"Did you know he intended leaving you the gallery?"

She stiffened slightly. "I believe I already told you that I didn't know who the gallery would go to, but that I wasn't worried."

"I didn't mean to be offensive, Ms. Tolley. And do I gather that some police questioning has been rather direct?"

She paused, then laughed quietly at herself. "Well, they ain't exactly brought in the bright lights to shine down on me, but they sure did want to know where I was on the night of whenever."

I didn't ask where she was. It showed her I was different. I said, "Perhaps it occurred to them, as it did to me, that you run this place so well and so completely that you might have known more of Boyd's intentions than anybody else."

"I don't think nothing occurred to them," she said. "I think they got themselves a list and they're going down it."

"And quite a list too."

"So I hear," she said, without smiling. "Though sounds to me like stirring up a whole lot of trouble for no good reason."

"I've been wondering about something else since I spoke to you last," I said.

"Uh-huh."

"About Tee-Dee Askew."

"Uh-huh."

"Boyd spent a long time with her, as far as one knows, and she seems to have been quite an influence, yet from what I understand she is not mentioned in his will."

"I haven't seen it," she said cautiously.

"Do you know whether she is dead?"

"No, sir, I don't."

"He remembered a lot of other people who seem to have meant a lot less to him."

"I can't explain the omission," she said.

"O.K. Can I ask another thing about the list?"

"You sure can ask."

"What are the chances that there is a fictitious element in it?"

"You mean that he made up some of the names?"

"Or put some women on the list just to cause them trouble."

She didn't like the sound of that. She frowned and scratched the back of her neck and said, "I wouldn't have thought so."

"Why not?"

"Bill didn't have no plans to die just now. Not for another forty years, and what kind of trouble could he cause then?"

Not a lot.

"O.K.," I said. "Something else. You said that Boyd occasionally used the gallery as a bargaining point in his relationship with some lady artists."

"I don't recall having said it exactly like that," she said, with a smile.

"What I wanted to know is whether he ever bought or exhibited Sharon Doans' work?"

"What work?" Mary Tolley asked.

"She's something of an artist, isn't she?"

"Not so's I've ever seen."

"She told me she does some book covers. I assumed that she did other artistic work too."

"I'd of said her inclinations would put her in a somewhat older profession," Mary Tolley said.

"I see," I said, not having expected a comment quite so sharp.

She was aware of a needle point having shown through. She said, "Bill seemed to like her. He spent him some time with her over the years, so maybe she has her some qualities underneath the glassy little surface."

The Japanese couple indicated all too scrutably that they wished to speak to Ms. Tolley, so she left me again, before I had quite finished asking what I wanted to know about Sharon Doans.

However, pictures were selected, and with the packing and paying to be done the odds were that it would be quite a while before Mary Tolley was available again. I decided to ask my questions of Sharon Doans herself.

But first I walked over to the sheriff's office.

Inevitably, it seemed, I found the soft-spoken receptionist Peggy on duty. "Don't you ever get time off?"

"When duty to my county calls," she said, "you'll know that I'll be here."

"I hope you get extra money for overtime," I said.

"No, sir," she said. "Round these parts the only way to get some extra money is to get your name put into Billy Boyd's will. You heard about that, I suppose."

"Yes," I said.

"If I could do it," she said, "I'd put my own name on it. Sure could use another hundred dollars just now. Don't think anybody would believe me for any more."

"You weren't well acquainted with Mr. Boyd, then?"

"No, sir, he never got around to me. No excitement in my life, no fun. All the men I know just want to get married and settle down. Plumb boring existence I lead, I do declare."

"So for thrills, you stay on duty here during lunchtime."

"Yes, sir, you got it first shot," she said.

"I'd like to see the state policeman, Junkersfield," I said. "Do you know where he is?"

"He's at lunch, across the way," she said.

"And I suppose Sheriff Dunlap is across the street at lunch too."

"Now, there you're wrong," she said. "Jeanna's holed up in her office." She indicated the door behind me with the sheriff's name written on its upper-half frosted glass. She lowered her voice. "Jeanna, she's not very happy."

"I see. Can I have a word with her?"

"You can try."

I went to the door and knocked on it.

"Go away!" an unambiguous voice said.

I opened the door and walked in.

Jeanna Dunlap was sitting looking out the window. The view was of some grass and the public toilets. I felt she was preoccupied with other things.

"I told you to go away," she said without turning to look at me.

"I know."

"Another goddamn interloper," she said. Though she still hadn't looked, she seemed to know who I was. That meant she could hear conversations that took place outside her office.

"At least I'm not an official interloper. Nothing I do can make you look bad."

I was trying to be understanding.

"Stuff it," she said.

"I'd like to know what you think about all this now," I said.

"I think in a hundred years we'll all be dead."

"Look, Sheriff," I said, "if you've stopped caring, get off your ass and resign. Until then, pull your weight. I've got a lot of things I'd be interested in talking with you about, but if you want it short and sour, do you still think Frank Pynne killed Billy Boyd?"

She swiveled in her chair slowly and looked me in the eye. Her depression and desperation were far deeper than I had expected.

"Yes, I think Frank killed Billy," she said. "He's the obvious suspect. I suspect him. Go away."

The instruction was so passionately felt and her gloom so pervasive that I just turned and left, closing the door behind me.

I walked back to Peggy, the receptionist. I leaned over her desk and said quietly, "She's terribly depressed."

"Yes, sir, I know."

"How long has she been like that?"

"Yesterday and today."

"What triggered it? The state police?"

"They sure are treating her like a piece of shit, if you'll excuse my language. But I believe she is bothered about Mr. Boyd's will too. Jeanna, she read that through and a little while later she was in there." Peggy seemed pleasantly willing to confide in me.

"What was it about the will?" I asked.

"It may just be that it brought home for her that he was really gone."

Behind me the door flew open with a crash. The glass in the upper half shattered and Jeanna Dunlap stood, a towering silhouette, outlined by the light from her office window.

"If you don't stop yammering to that man, Margaret, you'll be gone. And, you, I told you to go away."

It seemed a good time to take my leave. As I left, Jeanna Dunlap said, "Now, Peg, call the maintenance department about the glass in my goddamn door."

27

I went across the road to the Nashville Inn. Through the window I saw two men in state police uniform, and when I went in I walked to their table.

I said, "Excuse me, but is one of you Darrow Junkersfield?"

The taller of them, a youngish man with massive sideburns, looked up and said, "Me."

I introduced myself.

"You're working for the lawyer, aren't you?" he asked.

"That's right."

Junkersfield said to the other, "Paul saw him outside Hogue's office a little while ago."

"If it's all right," I said, "I'd like a few words with you."

"I'm busy," Junkersfield said peremptorily. "Try me again tomorrow."

"I wouldn't take much of your time."

"You won't take any of it today," he said. "Anything you want to say, say it through Hogue."

"But it's about Priscilla—"

He stood up. "No 'but's. I'm busy. We're both busy. Run along now."

He sat down again and they began to talk.

I felt frustrated, but there was little I could do but leave.

I walked to my car and drove west out of town.

There was no one at home down the gravel track across from the mailbox marked S.A.D. Despite no car being visible and no answer to my knockings, I stood in front of the house for quite a time. I was thinking about going into the place anyway. It was an impulse; just one of those pleasant little notions that pop into one's mind from time to time. Especially one in a nosy line of work who feels frustrated.

I tried the door.

It was locked.

I tried the big sliding window near the door.

It didn't slide.

I took a casual little stroll around the whole building.

Nothing budged.

Just preparing to give the lady some advice on guarding her home from intruders, Officer.

Only, she seemed to know all she needed already.

It meant I'd have to make an effort to get inside. I thought about what I would be looking for.

Nothing specific in mind.

Boyd's car?

Souvenirs of California?

The arms of a butcher?

The more I thought about it, the more my impulse seemed to be a form of retaliation against abusive officers of the local law.

Foolish me, wanting to break and enter.

I took hold of myself.

I abandoned my impulse and followed a hunch instead. I went to Frank Pynne's log cabin.

I was rewarded. I found both Pynne's Fiesta and Doans' Beetle.

I pounded with the wrought-iron-tree door knocker.

Pynne answered the door quickly.

"Oh," he said.

"May I come in?" I asked. I walked in.

Doans was not in evidence at first sight. But she soon appeared in the sparsely furnished living room, wearing an apron.

"Oh, it's Mr. Samson," she said. "Frank has to go out soon so I'm making him lunch. Do you want some?"

"I don't think he's staying," Frank Pynne said.

"You know," I said chattily, "I don't understand that."

"What?" Pynne asked.

"People I talk to seem to like you well enough, but with me you are always surly. Here I am, hired by your lawyer to work on your behalf, and yet I feel nothing but irritation from you."

He said, "I'm irritated with my whole fucking life."

"All right," I said. "I'll leave Dave Hogue to talk to you."

"Waste of money," Pynne said.

"Dave Hogue?"

"You."

"Tell him to take me off it. You're the client."

He made a sucking sound. "He wouldn't listen."

"Why not?"

"He won't talk to me about money. He says we'll work it out when things are finished."

I shrugged. "It's Hogue that retained me, so it's him that's responsible for me. I'm cheap, but I'm not free."

"Frankie's terribly depressed by this business," Doans said.

"I don't mean to make it worse," I said. "But if the world's thrown him a curve, he's got to swing his bat if he's going to knock the thing back where it came from." I looked from Doans to Pynne.

He shrugged and sat down.

I was disappointed. I thought it was quite a pretty speech.

But that's show biz. I changed audiences. I said, "I've come for a few words with you, Miss Doans. Shall we go to the kitchen?"

"I'm making a meat loaf," she said when we had walked through.

"It smells good."

"Thanks. And a salad there, too. See?"

She showed me a large mixed salad with things crinkle-cut and fancy.

"A cook too, among your other talents."

"Well, maybe a little bit," she said. "I don't cook much for myself. It's kind of nice to have an excuse. And poor Frankie is so down."

I was a little bit tired of poor Frankie. I said, "What I wanted to talk to you about was Billy Boyd's will."

She left her salad and her busyness to examine my face. She tried to sustain a chatty matter-of-factness. "That was amazing, wasn't it? Billy had a lawyer in Columbus who called me. I went over there and he explained about it. It was such a surprise."

I said, "Boyd didn't just pull your name out of a hat, Miss Doans. He says you know what he wants done with the proceeds."

"How do you know that?" she asked sharply. "That's supposed to be a private thing."

"What did Boyd want you to do with the money?"

"That's between Billy and myself," she said.

"What was your relationship with him?"

"Friends. Hey, you're sounding like that cop that talked to me, day before yesterday."

"Junkersfield?"

"Yeah. And I'm not on trial, you know."

"I'm just trying to tie up some loose ends. Get things straight in my own mind, so I can work better for Frank."

I had caught her by a handle. She said, "Well, you can ask. I won't promise to answer. And I'm saying nothing about what Billy wants me to do, because if he'd wanted people to know, he'd have written it out in the will, wouldn't he?"

"O.K.," I said. "When did you come to Nashville?"

"1968," she said.

"How old were you?"

"Older than I looked," she said peevishly. "Like now."

"You were nineteen? Twenty?"

"Nearly nineteen."

"And did you come to Nashville alone?"

"Yes."

"To do what?"

After a moment she said, "To paint and draw."

"Did you live where you live now?"

"I don't think I want to talk about this."

"There's no harm in my asking you where you lived when you moved here. I can check it elsewhere anyway."

"I lived where I live now," she said.

"A house which Boyd owned. Or was it still Mrs. Boyd's? How did you get it?"

She didn't say anything.

"How much rent did you pay for it?"

"That's not your business," she said.

"What's your middle name, Miss Doans?"

Her eyes opened wide. "What?"

"Your middle name. Is it Askew?"

"How did you know that?" she asked, wide-eyed, and threatened, as if somehow I had magic access to the secrets of her mind and was dangerous.

"I didn't. That's why I asked. But since your last two initials are A.D. and I think your mother's are D.A. I thought you might just have reversed your names for the sake of a little anonymity. That makes your middle name Askew and hers Doans."

"What do you know about my mother?"

"Before now, nothing. I'd guessed that she was Tee-Dee Askew. Just like I'm guessing that what you're to do with Boyd's money has to do with her."

Sharon Doans steadied herself on the edge of the kitchen work surface. "Nobody knows about this," she said. "Nobody knows about this. I haven't told anybody."

"Where is your mother, Miss Doans?"

"That's my business."

"It's not going to be hard for me to find out. Just harder than if you tell me."

"The harder the better."

"It's a matter of going to Venice and checking the records there and—"

"She's in a hospital!" It burst out. "She's in a hospital, and she's paralyzed and a vegetable, all right? Is that what you want to know? Is that what you wanted me to tell you? And yes, Billy wants me to see she's taken care of, without all the crap of the lawyer. Because he knows I'll do it. All right?"

Quietly, I asked, "What happened to her?"

"She tried to kill herself, only she wasn't very good at it, not being of a mechanical turn of mind," Doans said acidly.

"This has to have been a long time ago," I said.

"Yeah."

"Not long before you and Billy came here."

"Billy came first," she said. She was gulping at her air now.

"Was what happened why Billy came back?"

She looked at me poisonously. "You know damn well it was."

"I'm guessing," I said. "I'm guessing that an arrangement with his mother was the only way he had of getting the money to pay for the care for her."

"Close enough," she said, quietly now.

"And if that was so, then he felt responsible for what happened to her. And if you followed him here, maybe you were involved too."

"I'm saying nothing about that," she said sharply. "Nothing. Nothing."

Which in its own way said quite a lot.

As I stood silently in front of her, Sharon Doans began to sob. Frank Pynne materialized by her side and comforted her while looking at me.

She gripped him tightly. She bit at his shirt, held it tightly in her teeth, pulled at the fabric.

He said, "Go away."

28

I stopped to eat once again at the diner on the road from Morgantown to Samaria.

Between Dunlap, Junkersfield and Pynne, I'd been told to go away three times in barely an hour. That was pushing a record, even for me. And after thinking about it, I had decided to take them seriously. I was on my way back to Indianapolis.

There was little more I could do around Nashville until some dust settled, and I had thought of a favor I could ask Powder to do. A fourth "go away" would hardly faze me.

Not that I am insensitive to rejection. Such things scar my psychical core. But psychotraumatic scar tissue is an occupational hazard.

In the diner I ordered meat loaf. I enjoyed it. I had pie à la mode. I enjoyed that too.

And the waitress, a slight woman with long dark hair and half-closed eyes, actually said, "Come again, now, hear?"

I took it personally and fell in love with her.

Powder was talking to a woman when I entered the Missing Persons office. She was clearly distraught.

"No, she's never been out overnight before," the woman said. "I'm scared to death. I made the dinner at the usual time but she just never came back for it. And not all night, and now it's been the whole morning and she's still away. I'm just petrified. I don't know what to do. I didn't know how I could get help."

The woman cried freely and dropped tears on the counter.

Powder was soft and fatherly. "You know, these things happen, dear. And it's only been over one night."

"But I'm afraid for her! Genuinely afraid for her safety. Who knows what might happen. The way the world is . . . accidents, or even worse. Oh God!" The sobs continued.

Powder took the woman's hands. "Try to relax, if you can. You don't want to be a nervous wreck when she does walk in, do you?"

"You think she'll come back?"

"Yes," he said convincingly, "I feel sure of it."

"Really?"

"Really," he said.

"Really really?"

"Really really." He patted her on the shoulder. "You go on home. Get her box ready and a can of food out."

"I've got last night's in the icebox," she said, "with some of that plastic wrap on it."

"O. K., good. Then you watch some TV and keep busy, and before you know it there'll be a scratching at the door."

"I've got a cat flap," she said.

"All the better," he said soothingly.

I felt soothed.

"Bye, now," the woman said.

"Bye-bye. Take care."

The woman left.

I took her place at the counter in front of Powder. I was ready to make a crack, but then I didn't. I didn't want to.

Powder and I stared at each other for a moment.

I just nodded. I could appreciate a man who was strong enough to wait to worry about what would happen if everybody with a missing cat came in until everybody did come in.

In my hesitation he nearly killed me with a shock. "I'm glad you stopped in," he said.

We went to his desk. When we were settled, he asked, "Have a good time in Venice?"

I said, "I've managed to find out what I wanted to know about that."

"What?" he asked baldly.

I told him about my conversation with Sharon Askew Doans.

Powder asked, "So what did Boyd and the lady do to make the mother try to top herself?"

"I can guess," I said.

"Didn't you ask her?"

"No. She was pretty upset."

"You had her going, spouting her life history, and you didn't ask her?" He looked at me, disbelieving.

"No."

"You're too fucking soft," Powder said. "If you'd kept at her, she would probably have admitted killing Boyd."

"I don't think she did it," I said. "She was the main beneficiary of his will, and the statement about knowing what he wanted done with it meant she knew she was beneficiary, but I don't think she did it."

Powder shrugged. "You're lucky you're not a sergeant investigating this under me," he said.

"Luck has nothing to do with it," I said.

"The killing's not what I have to work on anyway," he said.

"It's not?"

"Not my business. You lost a client. You came to me at the Missing Clients office. So that's what I work on. And I want to ask you a hypothetical question."

"O.K."

"You're this lady you're looking for."

"O.K."

"Why do you hire you? What can a crummy P.I. do for you?"

"I don't know," I said to be cooperative. "What?"

"Shit," he said with disgust. "That's a goddamn gumshoe for you. Does a job and doesn't even know what he did for her. That apply to you and women too? Come on, come on. What did you do? Tell her whether they'd found the body?"

"No," I said. "She could have checked the newspapers for that. What I did was tell her that nobody was looking for her and that nobody seemed likely to want to look for her."

"But why did she want to know that?" Powder shouted. "Why does she care? Why does she need to know badly enough to hire a stranger to find out? But not badly enough to ask someone herself? Why? Why?"

I said, "Already today I've been told to go away by half the world, and I've fallen in love, and I've listened to two grown people talking about a missing cat. That kind of thing takes what little intelligence I have to offer out of me."

"What you did," he said portentously, "was to indicate to her that it was probably safe to go ahead with her plans." He sat back, leaned back. He rubbed his face.

I said, "What plans?"

"I don't know what plans," he said. "How the hell do I know what plans? But I can tell you this. She's not far away."

"You're going to have to spell it out for me, Powder."

He sat up and sighed. "She runs away from home. Two months later, having changed her appearance, she comes to Indianapolis and goes to you. She asks you to find out whether she is being actively sought and you tell her she isn't. Now, to me that means she wants to do something somewhere around here. If all she needed to know was whether the law was after her, she didn't have to dress up and give you a picture. The way I read it, she wants to pass casual inspection without being recognized, and she even used you to test how good her disguising was."

"And if I recognize her," I said, "all she does is walk out."

"Mind you," Powder said, "it's a goddamn joke. Hires you to find someone sitting on the chair across the desk from you. Goddamn P.I.s. I always said they wouldn't know the nose on their faces."

I ignored the editorial comments. "She's changed her appearance," I said, "and she's not being chased. She's worried about being recognized."

"Which means," Powder said, "that she's somewhere not a million miles from here."

"More like within, say, a hundred."

He smiled. "Which kind of brings it all into my line of country, doesn't it, gumshoe?"

"You know so much," I said. "What's she doing out there?"

"I haven't done that piece of thinking for you yet," he said. "But I'll tell you something else for free."

"What?"

"She ran away alone."

"Why?"

"Because if she'd just run away with somebody, she wouldn't care whether she was being looked for. People leave with the milkman all the time. No big deal."

"Unless she has something she has to hide."

"Like killing a guy?" he asked.

"Could be," I said.

And it could. I felt a cumulative sense of the growing insistence in Priscilla Pynne to control her own destiny. Possibly whatever the cost.

"O.K.," I said, "she's getting on with what she planned. She planned it on her own. It has to be done around here. What is it?"

"Fucking riddle," Powder said. "Answer comes out of why she left, what kind of woman she was. Just the kind of blurry, wishy-washy gruel that ought to be saved for private eyes to suck on."

"Suits me fine," I said. "And I've got some routine leather-pounding that seems just about right for you people."

"Oh yeah?"

"Mrs. Pynne drove her car to Bloomington in the middle of the night, but nobody knows where she went after that or how she went there. I'd say it was time to start checking taxis and buses. And in the building she parked outside, there's a Ride Board, with student notices wanting riders to go all over the country."

Seriously, he said, "How long ago was this again?"

"April twelfth, nearly seven months. But if you're lucky maybe she took a cab in the middle of the night, either to the bus station or somewhere else. Maybe they'll remember because of that and because she is a striking-looking woman." I took the picture of Priscilla Pynne and flipped it across the desk to him.

He picked it up and raised his eyebrows.

I said, "And we can see who finds her faster. Wishy-washy private eyes trying to guess where she is, or routine-bound leather-scrapers picking up the trail after more than half a year."

He put the picture down and rubbed his face again. "I might just be able to get some cooperation from Bloomington," he said.

· · ·

I left police headquarters to walk to the parking lot where I'd left my van. It was in the lot built on the site of the first office I'd been evicted from, on the corner of Ohio and Alabama.

I hadn't parked there from the sentimentality to do with times past. I'd parked from the sentimentality of it being cheaper and the Market Square lot being full.

While I was waiting for the light on Wabash to change, a woman next to me said, "You! Cut that out!"

"What?"

"Oh, all innocence when somebody has the nerve to speak up. Just cut the crap and stop looking at me like that."

The light changed.

She harangued me all the way to the other side. "People like you ought to be locked up," she said. "I ought to call the cops."

She turned left. I walked straight on.

I didn't feel indignant. I had been looking at her. From the time I left Powder, I'd been looking at all women more carefully than usual.

I'd been looking for Priscilla Pynne, who was out there, somewhere.

29

When I got home, Glass Albert's Caddy was parked outside my office. That meant he was in the back, shooting hoops. I walked around. When I got on court, his back was to me and he was about to shoot. I sneakered up and checked him from behind. Being able to move without being heard is why we wear gumshoes. You're also silent when the soles of your shoes are thin as skin.

"Son of a bitch," Glass Albert said as the ball trickled out of his hands and down his back.

"You take the ball over your head to shoot," I said. "Makes you vulnerable from behind. Keep it in front, where your hairline used to be."

"You didn't tell me you were a private eye just because you were between coaching jobs," he said.

"Best of twenty free throws for an empty glass bottle?"

"You mock, whitey," he said. "Just wait for the fortune I make out of this."

"I'm only trying to keep you around," I said. "The longer you're here, the longer your gas guzzler's parked out front. It raises my prestige among the neighbors."

"I'm glad somebody besides me likes it," he said. "My wife calls it a nigger car and drives around in a box of matches."

After I beat him on free throws, we went inside and shared the can of beer I found in my refrigerator. Being in work doesn't leave a lot of time for shopping.

We sat in the room I'd made my kitchen. "This is where the guy who owned it before me killed himself," Glass Albert said. "I told you that, didn't I?"

He hadn't. "Thanks a lot," I said.

"There was a woman came around just after I got here," Glass Albert said.

I sat up suddenly.

"What's the matter? Spring pop through the cushion?"

"Who?" I asked.

"Says you hadn't called her and she wanted to see if you had been swallowed by the earth."

I sat back. "I've been neglecting family and friends," I said.

"She family or friend?"

"Friend."

"Bit young for you, isn't she?"

"No, I'm too young for her. Inside."

"Take some advice from a rich man," Glass Albert said. "Never let your career get so important that it breaks into the time you spend with people close to you."

"Thanks a lot."

"Who did you think this lady was?" he asked.

"There is a woman out there," I said, waving a pointed finger rudely at the surrounding world. "And I've got to find her."

"And you thought she'd saved you the trouble by coming here?"

"I can hope."

"How do you set about finding 'a woman'?"

"I think she's within a hundred miles."

"Still lots to choose from. What do you do first?"

"I try to think where I would be if I were her."

"And when that doesn't work?"

"I think some more."

"Think like a woman? What she would do?" He shook his head. "Shit."

"What do you mean, 'think like a woman'? What kind of atavistic concept is that?"

"It's not *my* concept," I protested.

"It's just *tanto, tanto!*" Lucy, the daughter, said.

"Isn't it your bedtime?" I asked.

"So that you can get yours?" she answered back.

"If you're not going to be civil, Lucille," her mother said, "then you will leave the room. We made a deal and I expect you to stick by your side of the bargain."

"What kind of life is this?" Lucy asked. "When you have to bargain with your own parent. And her so-called friends."

She curled her lip. That was beyond the limit. "On your way, young lady."

"I'm all right to talk to when it's not convenient for him to be around," Lucy said. "Then I can stay up late, whether it's school night or not. But when he does deign to appear, because he can't think of any work to do, then no, it's 'Lucy off to bed,' even before the sun sets. Well, good night! And do enjoy yourselves!"

The living-room door closed firmly behind her.

"You look as if you're in shell shock," I said to my woman.

"How long does adolescence last?" she asked.

"A lifetime every day, I hear. Look, do you want me to go?"

"Certainly not."

"Thank heavens for that," I said.

"Not until you tell me what 'think like a woman' is supposed to mean."

"I told my landlord that the next stage on my job is to try to think what I would do if I were the woman I am trying to find. It was he who generalized the particular. You got the wrong Albert, lady. Or rather, you have the right one but you're pointing the finger of accusation at the wrong one."

She let me off. "Trying to find a woman, huh?"

Work was not a customary subject, but I hadn't been around for some time. And it was on my mind.

"I've even enlisted the help of the local law."

"Your friend Miller?"

"No. Guy in the Missing Persons called Powder."

"Leroy Powder?"

"The same. You know him?"

"From the same time that you know him," she said. "You found one of my girls who ran away, between you."

"Oh yes," I said, remembering.

"How is he?"

"Prickly, as usual."

"Yes," she said. After a while she said, "And he's helping you trace this woman you're hunting."

"Yes."

"Where are you looking for her?"

"Somewhere comparatively close by."

"Why? What's she doing?"

"We don't know. But we think she is in the state, more or less."

"What kind of work does she do?"

"What do you mean?"

"What sort of job qualifications does she have?"

"I don't know," I said. "She graduated from high school."

"College?"

"No. She went, but she blew it and dropped into the drug scene for a while."

"Is that the way she is likely to go again?"

"I wouldn't have thought so."

"And you don't think she has run off with anybody?"

"The only candidate got dead instead."

"So she's got to make a living somehow."

"Yes, I suppose so."

"Or is she the type to latch on to somebody?"

"She just cut loose," I said, "but I don't know."

"You don't really think she would, do you?"

"No. When I met her, she felt irredeemably alone."

"So she's trying to go it by herself. You say she went to college once. What were her high-school grades like?"

"She did well in high school."

"O.K.," she said. "You should look for her in colleges. That's where she's gone."

I thought about it. "She could have done that at home," I said. "More easily. Her husband worked at I.U."

My woman didn't say anything. She might have been asking me whether the husband would have encouraged that.

"But the husband wouldn't have encouraged that," I said.

She didn't even nod. She just sat looking wise.

"But if she goes to college," I said, "why not somewhere else? Why the risk of staying around here?"

"Money."

"What do you mean?"

"If she were just looking for a job, she could do that anyplace. But she's an Indiana resident, right? She can go to a state university a lot cheaper than she can go anywhere else."

I chewed on that one for a moment. It tasted good. Not wishy-washy at all.

30

Saturday morning was not, I felt, the best of times to turn out the records departments of the various state university campuses in Indiana. Not if you were Joe Citizen.

I called the Police Department. Powder was off duty.

"But he'll call later this morning," the officer on the Missing Persons extension said. "He always does, just to see what's happening."

"I'd like to talk to him now," I said. "Can you give me his home number?"

"No. Not allowed."

I left my name.

Then I picked up the phone book. Cops don't generally have their phone numbers listed. Unless maybe it's under their wife's name. But, being Powder . . .

It was there.

"Yeah?" he said when he answered.

"There was just this one and the Powder Puff Beauty Salon listed in the book," I said. "I had a hard time choosing the right number."

"Who's that?" he asked. No imagination.

I told him.

"Oh," he said. "I called you last night. But all I got was a goddamn machine. Why don't you get a secretary? I hate those machines. I won't talk to them. So what do you want?"

"I hope I interrupted something," I said. Then, before he could reply, I said, "No, I don't. What is it that makes me want to irritate you, Powder?"

"I don't know, but you're good at it," he said.

"I called to ask you to loosen up some police channels to get some information."

"What?" Quite a civilized question, considering.

"I think Priscilla Pynne has enrolled at one of the Indiana state universities. I figure you have a better chance of finding which one, quickly, than I do."

"What twinkie-bright idea makes you think she's gone to college, shamus?"

I explained.

"You think of this all by yourself?"

"No."

"You disappoint me."

"It seems a reasonable starting place," I said. "A little more specific than trying all the employment offices."

"I tried them," he said.

"Oh."

"I didn't have the broad's maiden name, though. Bound to use it. That's what I called about."

"Pitman," I said. "Priscilla Howell Donohue Pitman."

"I'll run out of ink writing all that down."

I gave him what little detail I had of her educational background.

"All right," he said. "I was just about to go out to my garden to clean it up for the winter. When I get back, I'll make a few calls."

"Come on!" I said. "What the hell's important around here? A garden, or getting a grip on this lady who may have killed a guy?"

"Pity you didn't call a few minutes earlier, gumshoe," he said sourly. "I already got my galoshes on." He hung up.

I sat and looked at the telephone for a minute. The guy irritated me. Maybe that was why I liked irritating him.

I went to the icebox and got some orange juice, and came back to the phone. I had one or two other calls to make.

I dialed Powder's number.

It was busy. Galoshes or not.

Then I called Kenneth Catherman in Springfield, Massachusetts. A man answered. "Hello?"

"Mr. Catherman?"

"I'll get him."

I heard the voice which answered the telephone say, "Some fella for you."

When Catherman came on, I identified myself.

"Ah, the man looking for the erstwhile Miss Pitman."

"I would appreciate a little help," I said. "I'd like the name and phone number of the person at your high school who would be responsible for sending out copies of high-school grade transcripts."

He was silent.

"Mr. Catherman?" Again, "Mr. Catherman? Are you there?"

Finally, he said, "Yes, I suppose I am."

"Is there a problem?"

"Is this still a matter of tracking Priscilla?"

"Yes," I said. "I think she may be attending a college hereabouts and she will have needed to produce her high-school records."

He hesitated again. "I suppose you could do this without my help anyway?"

"The name of the person in charge of transcripts? Yes. From the principal, and I can get that from the police or the board of education. I just thought it would save time to ask you."

"Then perhaps you would wish to know that I sent Priscilla a copy of her records."

"I thought you hadn't heard from her."

"If I recall correctly," he said, "you asked if I knew where she was, which I don't exactly, and when I had last spoken to her, which is more than nine years ago."

"Oh, for crying out loud," I said.

"She wrote asking if I could get her a transcript. One that didn't refer to the University of Bridgeport, but with an official school seal."

"And you did?"

"I did."

"And where did you send it?"

"To a hotel in your fair city. It was called the Penrod."

And he gave me the address of the hotel I had seen my client walk to near Union Station.

"And you sent it to her when?"

"She said it had to be in the mail by the first of June."

"What else did she say in her letter, Mr. Catherman?"

"Not much. That she hadn't forgotten me and hoped I hadn't forgotten her. That after an ill-fated marriage, she was planning to continue her education, though her husband would oppose her if he found out where she was. And she asked for my help."

"Which you gave. Without asking questions?"

"There was no one to ask. Just a short letter and a hotel address and a date."

"Where was the letter you got postmarked?"

"Memphis."

"Memphis, Tennessee?"

"I suppose so. I can't visualize the post imprint, but I remember clearly that it was Memphis. I remember thinking what a long way that girl must have gone in her life, from the last time I saw her."

"When did you get the letter?"

"Early May."

"Was there any indication of where she intended to continue her education?"

He paused. "No."

"Or any intimation that she might get in contact with you again?"

He sighed. "She asked whether, if it were necessary, I would be willing to write a reference for her."

"Was it necessary?"

Another sigh. "Yes."

"Where was it for, for God's sake."

"I would prefer not to tell you."

"I don't care what you prefer. I've got the police checking all the colleges around here now. They'll find her. And they will not be amused to find out how much money they've had to spend to tell us what you can tell us for free."

"Ball State University."

"Thank you so much," I said.

"My loyalty," he said, "is to the people I know, my respect for them and their wishes. If it were not plain to me that you would be able to find her from what you already know, then I would not have helped you at all."

"I am fascinated to hear about your loyalties, Mr. Catherman. The trouble is that the lady is involved in the kind of problem which will not just go away because people don't ask questions in the right way."

"My responsibility is to Priscilla, insofar as it exists at all."

"It's your responsibility to her that seems to have escaped you," I said. "It is in her interests to have this business settled. She'll have no future for education or otherwise until her past is dead and buried."

A poor choice of words.

31

Before leaving Indianapolis I called Powder's home again. The line was still busy, so I left a message for him at headquarters: "Memphis and Ball State."

Ball State began life as a teachers' college in Muncie, Indiana, about fifty miles northeast of Indianapolis. The Ball is of the Ball-jar Balls. The teachers' college became Ball State University in a rationalization of the mid-sixties, but the campus is still on the west side of the city, a cluster of new buildings among old.

I drove up on IS 69, to within eleven miles, where the IS turns north to find, more directly, Fort Wayne, and, eventually, Lansing. The morning drive gave me a chance to think about what I was expecting to find. I got as far as being able to frame alternatives. It was another way of saying to myself that I didn't know what I was getting into.

I followed signs to the Administration Center, which was a section of one of the sprawling cement structures built to celebrate universityhood. I could find what I was looking for without access to records, but it would be easier with it.

Inside, gaily painted cement-block walls tried to project the charm of construction techniques instead of just looking cheap. They got about halfway, far enough to show why the limestone industry was in decline.

There was a personnel index in the foyer, a ridged black menu board covered with a glass panel. Perhaps administrators were changed as fast as hot meals.

The directions to the student records office were clear enough, but when I got there, I found the door locked.

I walked along the hall trying handles. I found, finally, an open door, the bursar's office.

I walked right in.

There was no one in the outer room or behind a cashier's window. I could see an inner door ajar. I had the option of tapping on the counter to attract attention or lifting the passage flap myself and going through.

I went through. I did my tapping on the frame of the inner door.

A small man whose head was wreathed in fuzzy brown hair looked up slowly. He squinted at me, patted the papers on his desk top and found a pair of glasses. He put them on, pulled at the wire earpieces until they were comfortable.

"Do I know you?" he asked.

"No."

"Oh," he said. He worked it out. "Well, what do you want?"

"I am trying to locate one of your students," I said.

He shook his head immediately. "I don't know anything about students. I only deal in totals."

"Yours was the only office open," I said.

"Football game today," he said.

"Well, it's quite urgent that I find this student, but all I have is her name, and that she is here as a freshman."

He lifted his shoulders and looked around the room. "No freshmen here."

"Wouldn't you have her financial records? Tuition, accommodation?"

"No," he said, with diminishing patience. "That's all in the records section. All I have is the totals."

I persisted. "Wouldn't you have the key to the records section? It's very important."

"No, I wouldn't have the key to the records section. If I dealt with records I might, but I don't so I wouldn't."

"Well, could you suggest someone I might go to who could get me this information?"

"Come back on Monday," he said.

"I need it now," I said.

He sighed heavily and opened a desk drawer. He pulled out a stapled booklet with a red cover and pushed it across the desk top toward me. "The home addresses are in there," he said.

"Of the student body?"

"No! Of the faculty and staff. Maybe you can dredge up someone to come into the office to open up for you, if it's as urgent as all that. A matter of life and death, I suppose."

"Yes," I said.

I looked through the booklet, and the bursar took off his glasses and straightened the papers he had been working on. But he didn't start work.

After waiting a moment, he said, "Well, what's the problem now?"

"There are a lot of names in here. I'm trying to find the right job descriptions."

"Oh, give it here."

I passed the book to him and he leafed directly to the back. "Except for the bigwigs, administrators are always in the back," he said. "The ones who do the work. All right, ready?"

"Yes." And I wrote down the name and home address and telephone number of the head of records.

"All right?"

"What about a couple of others, in case I can't get in touch with—"

"Oh, for God's sake," he said. "President of the university? That do?"

"I was thinking more of someone in charge of undergraduates, or someone with special responsibility for freshmen or admissions."

He read me details of the dean of freshmen and the dean of intake. "All right?"

"Yes, thanks," I said.

He threw the booklet in the desk drawer and slammed it shut. He looked at his watch. Then he noticed that I wasn't leaving. He squinted at me again.

"Is there a telephone I can use?"

"Out in the office," he said with force. "Dial nine for an outside line. And close the door behind you!"

"Thank you," I said.

I closed the door behind me.

Make it easier for a bureaucrat to give you what you want than to refuse and you stand a chance.

The head of records didn't answer.

The dean of freshmen was away for the weekend. Her husband told me so.

The dean of intake was eating lunch. He told me that himself.

"I'm sorry to interrupt you," I said. "But I must locate a student at Ball State. I've just come up from Indianapolis and all I have is her name. It's urgent that I find her."

"More important than my lunch?" he asked stiffly.

"It is important," I said.

"Very well. What class is she in?"

"She would be a freshman."

"There are three freshman dormitories. Try there."

"She's older than most freshmen. Would that affect where she lives?"

"Older? How old?"

"Twenty-seven or so."

"A mature student," he said. He paused. "And what is the name?"

"Priscilla Pitman," I said.

"Oh God," he said. "You're not the husband, are you? Please don't tell me you're the husband."

. . .

Dean Caldwell opened the door before I knocked. His house was a small modern one-story building in a development to the north of the campus. The front yard sported two twenty-foot maple trees. I figured the house had been there getting on for ten years.

The dean was in his early forties and had a majestic profile but an extremely narrow face front, which matched a narrow body. He was clearly agitated, but making the best of it. We sat facing each other in the living room. I had already told him I was not the husband.

"She told me he was dead," he had said. "But I keep expecting him to turn up. It's a major source of my anxiety dreams."

Once seated, we began talking on a more formal basis. "Why are you looking for Miss Pitman?" he asked me.

"It's a police matter," I said.

"You're a policeman?" Shock.

"No, but they're not far behind."

He didn't say anything. I felt he was deciding whether he had the nerve to ask what it was about.

I said, "You clearly know her."

"I interview all mature students."

"You know her better than that," I said.

"I've taken a special interest," he said measuredly. It was clear that the interest was nearly proprietary. "I am not attached, and she's—"

"And she's separated from her husband," I interrupted. "That's not the question, or any of my business."

"Separated," he repeated.

"Yes."

"What kind of police matter?" he asked finally.

"It is necessary to talk to her about a murder case."

"Murder?" he asked. It was a word he'd probably never used in earnest before in his life.

"Yes."

"But, but you're not police."

I didn't answer. That had already been covered.

"So who are you?"

"I've been hired by the lawyer of a man who is suspected," I said, "but I've also been cooperating with the police."

"Hired?"

"I'm a private detective."

"She's in serious trouble?"

"She may be. I don't know. It depends entirely on what she has or hasn't done."

He stood up suddenly. "Hide her for me," he said. "Hide her."

"What?"

"I'll hire you. Hide her. Help me hide her."

I could have told him it was an offensive suggestion, or I could have punched him in the nose.

Instead I said, "Be sensible, man."

He bowed his head and put his hand over his eyes. He sat down again. "Of course. Always."

I waited.

"Life is so empty," he said. He paused. I didn't speak.

"She was desperate when she came into my office. I think she had been to the admissions office of every state university there is. It was not an easy situation, of course. She was late applying and had no money. The academic credentials seemed all right, but several years old. Mature students are always a risk. They either fail abysmally or succeed dramatically. The failures are so upsetting that we try to be very careful. But she was so needful, she wanted it so badly. I let her in despite everything, and since then, I've helped her. I think she's just about got herself settled, and against the odds she seems to be coping. I feel for her. And she's been manna for me. I've been constricted to dealing with pimply have-alls and racial quotas for years. Then she comes along. She makes me feel that a dean of intake can do something, once in a while. I don't know whether I could bear her not getting a chance to work it all out for herself. I have a kind of investment in her. I need to know how she's going to get on, how she will deal with problems she faces. I love her future, in that way. She doesn't know what she means to me, but I feel like a guardian angel and it makes me feel good. Worthwhile. I don't know whether I can stand for it not to have a chance to work itself out."

He stopped.

I said, "She will have no future until her past is straightened out."

"Did she kill someone?" he asked, simply.

"Do you think she's capable of it?"

"Certainly," he said. "As we all are, if there's nothing else we can do."

"Oh," I said.

"It's been one of my small pleasures to try to show her that extremes needn't be approached. That the world can be rational, helpful, can respond to an individual's needs."

"Where can I find her?" I asked finally.

"She has a part-time job as a waitress at the Campus Cookhouse. It's a restaurant on Uhle Street on the eastern edge of the campus. She'll be off duty at two. That's an hour earlier than usual because of the football game. But she's not going to it. She'll go to the library until five. She'll go back to her dorm, rest for a few minutes and then be back at the Cookhouse at six."

I raised my eyebrows.

"I know her every move," he said lightly. "I got her the job, although after this year I think I can get her some financial aid. She has a loan already, which I have underwritten, although she doesn't know that. She should get some scholarship money if her grades are as good as I think they will be. I see her on a weekly basis, sort of as a secular counselor. I also see her instructors from time to time."

"Dean Caldwell," I said, "I've got to insist that you don't warn her that I am coming."

He did not speak.

"I will call the police now and have her taken into custody if you can't make me believe that you will not tell her to run away."

"What good would that do?" he asked. "Her future is here. I don't want her to run away. I only hesitated just now because I was deciding whether there was some way I could keep you from getting to her."

"What did you decide?"

"I have a gun. I could shoot you. But that doesn't seem terribly sensible."

"I am relieved," I said. I intended to be sarcastic, but found that I felt it more than I expected.

"You said before that the police are not far behind you."

"That's right."

"So there wouldn't be time for her to get away effectively anyway."

"That sort of thing takes careful planning," I said. But his Priscilla could tell him more about that than I could.

32

Campus Cookhouse was one of a row of commercial premises on the public side of what appeared to be a boundary road separating the university from the rest of the world. All sorts of academically related services were provided and there were several eating places along the row, offering the cosmopolitan fast-food palate choice between Chinese, Mexican and Italian meals. The Cookhouse was your standard American. HAMBURGERS A SPECIALTY, a sign said. Pretty snappy.

I couldn't park on Uhle, but a big drugstore offered parking space around a corner.

It was about one-thirty.

I walked back to the Cookhouse and for a couple of minutes stood looking in the front window. There were two dozen booths and counter service for fifteen. It was about quarter full and at first I didn't see anyone who looked familiar. There was a waitress behind the counter and another on the floor, but both were too tall to be Priscilla Howell Donohue Pitman Pynne.

At least I thought they were. It was hard to remember, and harder still because I was looking for two different people. One a blonde bikinied beauty with a sulky face; the other a carefully downbeat brown-haired woman, who was a bit chubby.

I thought about the chubbiness while I watched. I pictured the woman eating calculatedly for two months, to help herself hide. It felt extreme to me. I began to feel stupid for having left Dean Caldwell. I visualized him meeting her somewhere not far from where I was standing. He would take her to her room for a quick pack-up, and then they would be off.

I would have to start the hunt all over again.

I grew uneasy and wondered if I should walk around the back before I went in.

A couple of minutes can be a long time.

Then she came out of the kitchen carrying a tray.

The woman I saw was a cross between the two I recalled. The hair was still brown, but longer than it had been when she came into my office in June with it cropped short to be undistinguishing.

She was also thin again.

But she was smiling, obviously comfortable and relaxed. That was new. Before, I'd seen a disapproving face in the picture and a tense face in my office. I'd never seen her really smile.

She carried the tray to a booth of four male students near my window. She distributed four different orders to the individuals without asking whose was which. Four different drinks; four different desserts. She was thriving in the situation, absorbing it. She chatted lightly, staying and swaying for a moment. She took an additional order for something, and went away again.

She didn't look like a murderer.

I went in.

I sat in an empty booth across the aisle from the four male students, on the assumption that it would be one of the tables which she was responsible for.

I took the menu from between napkin dispenser and condiment rack. I found that I was nervous.

I didn't have much time to worry about it. Priscilla Pitman Pynne reappeared through the swinging kitchen door with a plate of French fries. She brought it to the boys' table and noted in passing the new occupation of one of her booths.

She went to the end of the service counter and did some figuring. She got a glass of water. She returned to us all, the five men in her life.

She put the glass of water on my table and said, "Be with you in a sec."
She then distributed the four checks to the boys across the aisle.

Finally, she turned back, and looked at my face for the first time.
And stared.

"Doctor Staedtler, I presume," I said.

She stood, pen poised, motionless, for enough seconds for it to
seem like minutes.

I watched her face intently.

She swallowed. She breathed unevenly. She said, "I . . .
my . . . my heavens. What a surprise."

"I can imagine," I said.

"Is—? Are . . . you here by coincidence?"

"No," I said. "I'm pretty hungry. What would you recommend?"

"What?"

"To eat. What's good?"

"Special burger with the works," she said, but colorlessly. Her
voice, like her face, was suddenly wan.

"Sounds fine," I said. I snapped the menu closed. "And coffee
first," I said.

Mechanically the pen began to move. Then so did she.

She didn't even ask if I wanted anything else.

She walked back toward the kitchen. The coffee was near the end
of the counter, where the water was. She passed it without a look.

I was on my feet before she pushed through the kitchen doors. I
got to them before they stopped rocking.

There were small plastic windows in the doors. I paused to look
through, but saw only what I expected to see. Priscilla Pitman Pynne
pulling a coat on as she walked to the back of the kitchen.

I went in and got to the back door just after she disappeared
through it. I felt a moment of panic when I lost sight of her. I hadn't
quite realized how much of a stake I had in finding her. I wasn't
planning to let her slip away now.

She was walking along the alleyway behind the restaurant when I
got outside. She walked at a steady pace. I ran after her. I caught hold
of her arm. I swung her so I could see her face. I saw concentrated de-
termination, and anger, but no fear.

"Going my way?" I asked.

She said, "Leave me alone."

"No," I said.

"Please!"

33

I walked her to the end of the alley. It was the opposite end from the lot where I had parked my van. Instead of marching her along the sidewalk back in front of Campus Cookhouse, I took her across the street onto the university grounds. I could see some benches along a walkway between buildings and one of them was empty.

She didn't resist, but I kept a positive grip on her arm.

I sat her down.

"What do you want?" she said passively.

"You remember who I am?"

"Of course."

Then suddenly she put her hands to her eyes and said with rending mournfulness, "You're going to ruin it all, aren't you?"

"Ruin what?"

"My life. My nice new life."

"All I'm going to do is find out what it cost your old life to set you up in this one," I said.

"I don't know what that is supposed to mean," she said tiredly. She uncovered her face.

"I've been looking for you for quite a while," I said.

"But why? Who cares? Who could possibly care?"

"Technically, I'm working for your husband," I said.

"Frank?" she said, with all the pleasure of finding a fly in her mouth. "You're not telling me that Frank wants me back?"

"No."

"It's got to be the money, then," she said. But as a statement, rather than a question.

"Superficially, perhaps," I said. "But it's hardly enough to send someone looking for you the way I've been looking for you."

"Thirty-eight hundred dollars may not be much to you," she said, "but it's been the chance to live for me." Her voice was somber, factual.

"What thirty-eight hundred dollars?"

"That I took when I left," she said.

I had thought I was there to surprise her. "I don't know about any money except fifty dollars they say you took from Frank's wallet."

"Oh yes," she said.

I waited, but then said, "Tell me about this other money."

"I found it. It was all in cash and it was under a floorboard. I tipped over a floor lamp and saw the wood was cut underneath. I don't know why, but I picked at it. I never did that kind of thing before, messing with the house. But that time I did it and a floorboard came up and God, there was all that money. I cried I was so happy."

"Why were you so happy?"

"Because it meant I could get away. It meant I wouldn't have to have Frank's babies. It meant I could start over. It meant I could have my life back."

"But why did your husband report only the fifty dollars as missing?"

"He wouldn't want anybody to ask him where he got that kind of money in cash."

"Where did it come from?"

"I guess kickbacks from people he helped get I.U. contracts for and from selling things on the side. I didn't ask, though. I didn't want him to know I knew about it. I just organized my escape as fast as I could and got out."

"How did you go?"

"I got a ride with a student. They have this ride-and-rider system at the Union at I.U.

"I've seen it," I said. "How long was it between your finding the money and leaving?"

"The longest five days of my life," she said quietly. "And some of the other days of my life have been pretty long."

"That was more than a week after Billy Boyd's party," I said.

She was surprised that I mentioned it. "Yes," she said, shrugging, "I guess so. Why?"

"The business between Frank and Sharon Doans wasn't involved in your leaving?"

"If anything pushed me over the edge, it was my doctor giving me a lecture instead of the pills when I went in to renew my birth-control prescription. But . . . the whole thing . . . it trapped me, and had outlived its usefulness."

"Why did you go to Memphis?"

"It was the first place any distance away there was a ride to. And I thought with Elvis having lived there it would be one of those show-business towns with a lot of quacky doctors around so if I'd needed to, I could have got one to change what I looked like a lot."

"But after hiring me, you didn't think you needed to."

"That's right," she said. She lowered her eyes, and breathed in heavily. "I still don't know what you're doing here." Before I could tell her, she said, "God, I love this place. I've just spent nine years too long getting here."

She looked up and glanced around. Then started. "What's he doing here?" It was an unquerying question, a way of noticing.

"Who?"

"You wouldn't know him."

I turned and saw the slablike figure of Dean Caldwell standing by the gate to the campus. "Dean Caldwell, you mean?"

"Do you know everything?"

I watched the man. He watched us. It shouldn't have been a surprise to see him. I'd taken away his options of action, but not his hopes. He could have been expected to drive to town after me, to spectate at events he saw as affecting his future.

"A funny guy," she said.

"He thinks highly of you."

"I don't know about that," she said, "but he's helped me a lot. And he's never made a pass at me."

"You expect men to make passes at you?"

"I don't expect it. They do it."

She turned away, and glared at Caldwell. He saw this and straightened noticeably. She turned back.

I asked, "How has it been nine years too long getting here?"

"I should have been at college when I came out of high school."

"You were," I said.

"You know about that, too?"

I nodded.

"They don't know about it here."

"I talked to Elizabeth Staedtler. The real one."

"I always liked her."

"And I talked to Kenneth Catherman."

"Oh. Him." The resigned calm from which she'd been speaking to me began to waver for the first time.

"What about him?"

"A poof, that's what about him."

"So?"

"So? So!" she asked, with a raised pitch in her voice. "The first man, the only man I ever wanted to make a pass at me."

I didn't say anything. She was talking freely now.

"An innocent I was," she said, her voice, if not her mind, under control again. "I thought the world was like it was supposed to be. If you worked hard enough for something, you got it. I worked like hell in high school, for him. To please him. Then after I graduated I found out that I couldn't have him. I know it's a stupid thing, and kids are supposed to grow up knowing everything like that now, but I didn't and it blew my head. And it's taken me till now to find what I want to do again. Only, here you are and I only have to look at you to feel this terrible dread that you are going to ruin it all for me."

We looked at each other.

I asked, "Why did you kill Billy Boyd?"

She stood up like a shot. "What?"

I stood up with her. I grabbed at her arm instinctively, as if she were about to bolt from me.

"Let go of me!" she said.

Behind her a shadowy figure approached rapidly. He was a blur in the corner of my eye because I was struggling to keep the grip that I needed on this woman. I had listened to quite a bit, rather patiently. I had formed some opinions, but I had gone through too much finding her to let her get away from me without giving up answers to the hard questions.

"I said, 'Why did you kill Billy Boyd?' "

"Kill?" she said. "Kill?"

The shadow behind raised an arm. I didn't see anything at the end of it, but I heard him say, "Get out of the way. Get away!"

That made me pull at her, clutch at the coat. She pulled; I pulled back.

Just about then a pencil of flame shot out of the end of the dark arm. I felt the woman whose body I was clawing at convulse slightly. She turned to face the shadow, and she snatched at her side. She staggered, she fell.

Dean Caldwell stood and took this in. He followed the only honorable course. He turned his fire-spewing shadowy arm upon himself.

34

A campus cop saw it all. He happend to be on the walkway going to lunch. He called for assistance and ambulances on his radio, and what he said later made the difference in letting me get away from the Muncie police by evening.

My story was that I'd been tracing a runaway wife and that Caldwell was the new boyfriend. It would hold for a couple of days, while I worked on more important things.

From the Muncie police station I managed to call Powder. He helped too, by vouching for me on condition that I come and explain to him what had happened.

That was all right with me. Indianapolis is on the way from Muncie to Nashville.

Powder lived in an alternative life-style district on Vermont. He had the first-floor apartment of a three-floor frame house. He answered the door wearing his muddy boots, then made a show of taking them off after I came in. "Haven't had a chance before," he said.

He put on slippers which were sitting under the coatrack.

"Still warm?" I asked.

His living room was cluttered with papers. He waved at a chair, and sat on another himself.

"You couldn't have gotten yourself shot, instead of everybody else, I suppose?" he asked.

"The man was trying to shoot me."

"When he gets out, I'll arrange some target practice for him," he said. Then, "Why? Civic duty?"

"He had plans for the lady. He thought I might be busting them. He brought the gun to threaten me with, in case she wanted to run away with him."

"He tell you this before or after he pulled the trigger?"

"In the hospital," I said. "She jumped up suddenly while he was watching. I grabbed at her. He ran over and pulled the trigger. Only, he shot her instead of me. When he saw that, he shot himself. Which he did about as well as he'd done in the first place."

"Nice company you keep," Powder said.

"Yeah," I said.

"So why did she jump up? You pinch her?"

"I asked her why she had killed Billy Boyd."

He raised his eyebrows. "Subtle approach, huh?"

"I thought you were the one who wanted me to ask things instead of settling for good guesses."

"And why did she kill Billy Boyd?"

"She didn't," I said.

He rubbed his face with both hands. "Oh," he said. "She said so, huh?"

"No, she didn't get a chance to answer the question."

"Well," he said, "I'm glad we've got that all cleared up."

"I can tell you what I think happened," I said.

"No," he said. "You came to me to find the lady. You found the lady. Beyond that I'm not interested in what you 'think.' Maybe when you know."

"O.K."

"Unless you lost somebody else."

"Not lately."

"How is she?"

"She's got a couple of broken ribs. But she'll make it."

"She regain consciousness before you left?"

"Yes. I talked to her a few minutes."

"You're becoming a real go-getter, Samson. People get shot during an interview with you and they wake up in the hospital and you remind them of the sentence they were in the middle of. What do you do if someone dies on you?"

"I carry a life-support system in the truck."

"So what did the lady say?"

"She was worrying she was going to miss classes."

"That was all?"

"She said she never saw Billy Boyd the night of April twelfth."

"And you believe her?"

"Yes."

"Mmm," he said. "So where do you go from here, sleuth?"

"Back to Nashville," I said.

He looked at his watch. It was quarter to nine. "Now?"

"I'm not going to get much sleep anyway."

He rubbed his face. "Sleep," he said. "A wonderful thing."

"Yes."

"You're at the stage where you don't want to wait till morning, huh?"

"Yes," I said.

"Well, gumshoe, just watch your back."

35

Before I left Indianapolis, I stopped at home to change out of my blood-spattered clothes. But first I called Dave Hogue.

"David Hogue, Attorney-at-Law," Betty Weddle said.

"Hello," I said. "This is Albert Samson. I would like to speak to Mr. Hogue, please."

"He's not here, Mr. Samson."

"You're working late," I observed.

"David works late, so I really have to too."

On a Saturday night? Ah well.

"When will he be back?"

"It could be any time."

"I'm on my way down from Indianapolis and I'll want to talk to him."

"He will be tired when he comes in. He shouldn't do any more business until Monday."

"It is of the utmost importance that I speak to him tonight," I said. She heard the urgency in my voice. She didn't even offer tomorrow morning.

"What is it about?"

I settled for "You can tell him I talked to Priscilla Pynne today."

"Oh," Betty Weddle said.

"You'll tell him, then?"

"Yes."

"I'll be there—" I looked at my watch—"about ten-thirty or quarter to eleven."

It had already been a long day, but the end was not in sight. Before leaving, I washed myself thoroughly and felt fresher for it. As I was toweling off, the telephone rang.

"Yes?"

"Mr. Samson?"

"Yes."

"This is Betty Weddle again." Her voice was agitated.

"Is there a problem?"

"To tell the truth, David won't be coming back to his office to-night."

"He won't?"

"He will be coming to my place. It . . . it's a way for him to get away from things for a while. But if it's absolutely necessary for you to speak to him, you can see him there."

"It's necessary," I said.

She gave me directions.

Weddle's house was in a cul-de-sac off Hill Street, about three and a half blocks from Hogue's. A one-story brick structure, it was almost a vacation bungalow. She had told me to pull into the drive-way past the shrubs to help keep the turnaround at the dead end clear. There was a small Chevvy parked half on the grass, making space for my panel truck to pull up to the garage door. I'd never seen Hogue in a car. I didn't know whether the Chevvy was his or not.

Betty Weddle came outside as I got out of the car.

"David's not come back yet," she said. "Would you like some cof-fee?"

We sat in the kitchen at first. There was coffee already on.

"Cream and sugar?"

"No sugar," I said.

"Piece of cake?"

"No, thank you."

"Sandwich?"

"Thanks, no," I said.

She poured coffee into two mugs and added cream to both. She pushed one toward me and picked the other up. She stood for a mo-ment. "Let's go through to the living room," she said. "More comfort-able there."

"All right."

I followed her into a small immaculate front room. It had a couch and a leather armchair with an end table next to it. There was a small sideboard, a TV, some shelves. On the wall there were framed photographs of what seemed to be formal occasions, but the light was too dim for me to see clearly.

I made for the armchair, but Weddle moved suddenly to interpose herself.

"No! That's my chair," she said.

I stepped back from it.

"Oh, dear," she said. "I'm terribly sorry. It's very rude of me. But it was my father's and I like to sit there."

"Quite all right," I said.

"The couch is comfortable."

I sat on the couch.

"You found Priscilla Pynne, then?" she asked after she gulped a bit of coffee and put her mug on the table next to her chair.

"Yes," I said.

"Was Frank pleased or displeased?"

"I haven't told him yet."

"Do you think she'll be coming back?"

"No, I wouldn't think so."

I looked at my watch. It was ten past eleven.

"I don't know what's keeping David."

"That's all right."

"Oh, dear," she said. "I haven't offered you anything stronger than coffee."

"I'm fine, thanks."

"No, go on. I have some bourbon and some gin."

"No."

"And some wine. There's a vineyard near here, Possum Trot Vineyards, and they produce a nice red wine."

"Possum Trot?"

"It's really very nice." She got up quickly.

"I haven't finished my coffee yet," I said.

She went to the sideboard and opened a lower door. She took out a wineglass. I watched. Her hand seemed to shake slightly. She put the glass down, then went to another compartment for the wine. It was an unopened bottle.

"Please," I said. "Don't open a bottle."

"No, I want some too," she said. She found a corkscrew and opened the bottle. She filled the glass and brought it to me.

"And you?" I said.

"Oh God." She trotted back to the sideboard and took out another glass. She filled it, spilling some of the wine as she did.

She paused with her back to me.

"Are you all right?" I asked.

"Yes, oh yes," she said. She turned sharply back toward her chair, glass in hand, and spilled some more. "I just don't know where David can be."

"If I'm in your way, I can easily wait outside," I said.

"Oh no. Certainly not." She raised her wineglass to me. "Here's to your success," she said.

"What success?"

"Finding the Pynne woman, of course."

She waited.

I put my coffee down and took up the wineglass. I gestured toward her with it, and sipped.

Before I swallowed, I made sure she drank from her glass.

Better than its name, Possum Trot red.

"So what is finding Priscilla Pynne going to do to the case, Mr. Samson? Does it help, or does it make it all open and confusing?"

"Oh, it helps," I said. "It helps a lot."

"Oh?" I sensed she was trying to sound casual. "How?"

I hesitated, tempted to tell her what I thought. The fact that she wanted to know was interesting.

She said, "David will tell me anyway."

I said, "I think finding Priscilla Pynne will be the difference between finding out for sure who killed Boyd and maybe never knowing."

"Good heavens. Was she involved?"

"She had nothing to do with it at all."

"Oh," she said. Still straining to sound casually interested, rather than as if my words meant the world to her. "So how can that be so important?"

"Because Boyd was killed the same night she left."

"But—but you said she didn't have anything to do with it."

"That's right," I said.

I tried the wine again and waited to see if she would prod me to further explanation.

"What is the significance of that?" she said.

"The significance is in asking why Boyd should be killed that particular night. Why not some other night, if Priscilla Pynne herself had no knowledge of what was happening to him."

She didn't give me the answer.

"Because the killer wished it to be assumed that they disappeared together," I said.

I paused, but she didn't have anything to contribute.

"A distraction," I said. "A smoke screen. If Priscilla never returned or if Boyd's body was never found, then the questions could never be completely answered, whatever people might think."

She was still silent. Though, despite the dim light, I sensed that Betty Weddle was growing pale.

"But," I said, "that raises a new question. Who knew Priscilla Pynne had left home? And more precisely, who knew it early enough to use the fact? Who knew quickly enough to get to Billy Boyd and kill him?"

"Who?" she asked, but not as weakly as I expected. She put her wineglass down.

"Frank Pynne knew first," I said. "On the Sunday morning. But he called two people right away. One was Jeanna Dunlap. He called her at seven thirty-four a.m., according to the sheriff's log. But if Frank had killed Boyd, he wouldn't have called Jeanna so early, because he wouldn't want people on his wife's trail quickly enough to be able to find her."

"Yes," she said.

"So there's Jeanna. Frank also called David Hogue. And as far as I know, they were the only two people who knew that Priscilla Pynne was gone by, say, eight a.m."

Betty Weddle nodded. "Except for one thing," she said.

"What?"

"I knew Priscilla Pynne was gone," she said. "And I confess."

"What?"

"I killed Billy," she said. From a lacquered box on the table next to her chair she took a substantial automatic pistol. "There comes a time," she said, "when you have to stand up and be counted."

She pointed the pistol at my head.

36

I was fed up with people pointing guns at me. This made twice in one day. I decided to rush her. I thought if I acted immediately, she would be taken by surprise.

Before I made a move, she fired.

The bullet snicked my ear.

"I know how to use this thing," I heard her say when the crashing inside my head quieted down.

I looked at the blood on my hand after I took it away from my ear.

"I'm a little rusty. I wasn't aiming to hit you. I just wanted you to hear the bullet go past."

"I think you've made your point," I said. Despite myself, my will to control what part of the situation I could, I felt my heart accelerate. I felt my limbs go wobbly. All for the second time in the day.

I just wanted to be somewhere else. Forget it all, lady. Sorry I bothered you. Just let me go home and go to sleep and we'll call it quits. O.K.?

"I can't for the life of me see any way out of this except to kill you," she was saying.

I tried to think of something cogent to explain another option.

I managed "Don't," but the sound that came out had a kind of strangled quality.

"I don't want to!" she said emphatically. "But there's no other way. I've got to protect my interests. What I've got to decide is how best to do it."

We sat for a few minutes.

As my head cleared, I began to see that she was nearly as agitated by all this as I was. Which puzzled me.

"Is it all right if I have my drink?" I asked.

She nodded. Her head moved, but the gun didn't.

I had a choice between coffee and wine. I took the coffee. I watched her nervousness. It calmed me.

"Why did you kill Boyd?" I asked.

She chuckled. "There comes a time when you have to stand up and be counted."

She had said that before.

"I thought you were friendly with him."

She stared at me.

"The will," I said. "It includes you."

"Oh yes." As if remembering something terribly distant. "That—that wasn't quite what it seemed. It was . . . I don't know what it was."

"A way to make David Hogue jealous?"

"Leave David out of it," she snapped.

"You started seeing Billy around the time Dave was planning to marry Billy's mother, didn't you?"

"What of it?"

"Or was your relationship with Billy a way to gain access to Ida Boyd? I'd have thought you a far more likely candidate to murder her."

Everyone had concentrated on the one coincidence of Billy's

mother dying just before she drew up her will. But she had also died before getting a chance to marry Dave Hogue.

But the woman holding the gun on me began to shake with anger. "No! I didn't do that!"

She glared. She glowered. Her cheeks grew pink.

"But maybe I should have," she said, almost as if she thought of killing for the first time. "She was no way good enough for David. He was going to sacrifice himself to save that land. It mattered that much to him. It mattered . . ." She paused to think. "It mattered more than anything."

I watched her now, nearly interested enough to forget my own predicament.

"Maybe I should have," she mused. Then, more harshly, "Except that Billy saved me the trouble."

"Billy did?"

"He killed her. Yes."

"How do you know?"

Belittlingly she said, "Has it occurred to you to ask how Billy knew his mother was going to make her will?"

"Yes. I asked Dave. He thought Ida might have told him."

"I told Billy," Betty Weddle said. "My intention was for him to talk her out of it. I thought he could stop it that way. But instead, he killed her."

"You presume," I said.

"I presume nothing! I saw him," Weddle said.

"You saw him kill his mother?"

"I didn't see him *do* it," she said. "But from my desk, the same day I told him, I saw him walk up to the house when he claimed he was with Sharon Doans. He wore a navy-blue anorak with the hood up."

"If that's all, it might have been somebody else," I said.

She sneered. "There aren't two men his size around here. And he opened the door with a key. And he didn't want to be seen going in, and I know that because he didn't just drive up to the house. He drove Sharon's car and parked it around the corner. Because I saw that there too."

I absorbed this. "Dave didn't tell me about your seeing Boyd," I said.

"He doesn't know."

"Why not?"

"He was so angry with Billy when Ida died, I thought if I told him he might do something rash. David gets terribly involved. All these things matter so much to him, and afterward Sharon swore Billy was at her place the whole time. There'd have been no conviction."

"You could have tried."

"It worked out. And Billy deserved what he got."

I asked, "Do I deserve what I'm going to get?"

For a moment she felt some sympathy for me. "There's nothing else I can do. Please believe me when I say I'm sorry about that."

"I don't believe you at all," I said.

"It's true."

"You're a cold-blooded murderer. You like killing. You're going to enjoy killing me."

"No, I'm not."

"Like you enjoyed killing Billy."

She paused for a moment before saying, "I didn't enjoy killing Billy. He had to die."

"There was no other way with him either, I suppose."

"That's right," she said, suddenly forceful, venomous. She bolted out of her chair.

I thought I was all over. I nearly died of shock.

But she was only going to get something. She went to the mantelpiece over a mock fireplace. She took the lid off a ceramic jar which looked like an urn. She took out some folded sheets of paper.

All the time she was moving, she kept the gun accurately trained on me. I believed she knew how to use it.

She stood by the mock hearth.

"There was no other way with Billy," she said. "No other way."

I heard an energy in her voice, a vocal gleam.

"I can tell you why," she said.

She shook out the papers she had taken from the urn. She flattened them against her body with one hand and then began to read.

"One. Ida's wishes for the land were unequivocal. Billy is equally specific that he will ignore them. Two. It is unrealistically unlikely that Billy had nothing to do with Ida's death. Three. My own life will be significantly diminished if Ida's forest is destroyed. Four. There comes a time when one must stand up and be counted. Are beliefs worth having? Is life worth having without them? Five. I—"

There was a knock at the door.

Betty Weddle's voice faded dramatically as she heard it while saying, " . . . have little to lose."

Instinctively we were both silent for a moment.

The knock repeated.

Weddle dropped to one knee, training the gun at my head.

"If you make a sound, it will be your last."

I stared at the gun. I thought, If she fires it, then the sound will be sure to bring whoever it is into the house. That person will see what's happened and she will have to kill him or her too. That kind of chain of killings means she is sure to be caught. Therefore there is no point in her shooting me. I decided to explain this to her.

It came out as a scream for help. And I dived forward.

Again there was that horrible huge loud long hurtful harmful noise of the firing of a gun pointing at me.

37

When I reached the floor, I scrambled forward and found a little solace by crouching beside the leather chair. The back of my head hurt, but I was otherwise whole and conscious.

I hadn't seen him come in, but Dave Hogue stood in the middle of the room. Betty Weddle stood facing him.

"What in God's name is happening, Betty?"

"Why did you come here, David?"

They asked these questions at the same time.

Then they both looked at me.

I edged toward the back of the chair, not secure enough in the probability of my heart's continued beating to overlook any opportunity to make myself less visible to them.

"You weren't meant to come here," Weddle said. "You never come here."

"You sounded so upset on the phone," he said.

"I just said I was going home. I left notes of all your messages."

"You sounded strange," he said, making it clear that she hadn't sounded half so strange as things looked.

Hogue surveyed the room. Weddle's eyes followed his and I began to feel more present. Not a comfortable feeling, among the limited feelings I had to choose from.

"What are you doing, Betty?" he asked.

She didn't answer at first, but then his eyes fell upon the sheets of paper she had been reading from.

"I'm killing him," Betty Weddle said. I saw her look for me again with the big black eye in her hand. I drew back behind the chair, wishing the leather were steel.

"Stop it! Stop it!" a voice said. I didn't think it was mine.

I couldn't see Weddle from my hiding place but I saw Hogue moving toward her. The goddamn gun went off again. Beside my face I saw a hole open up in the back of the leather chair. It just flowered, petals of leather pulsing out momentarily, then sagging back to stillness. A complete lifeless cycle.

I didn't see the bullet as it went past. I must have blinked.

I uncoiled then.

My sprung fear and tension and sense of injustice that I—I!—should be the object of this absurd violent attention opened into action. It wasn't much, but I pushed the leather chair forward, toward the death dispenser, as fast and hard and straight and hard as I could. I wished to push it through her. Through her and through the wall and into the next county and country and world. If I was to be killed, I wished to kill back.

But all my effort didn't stop the banging noises. Bang. I couldn't bear it.

I stretched myself to full length behind the chair.

It hit something. Bang. There were shatterings, crashings, smashings. Bang. Explodings, screamings. Bang. I didn't know if I was dreaming. Bang.

And then the heaviest weight in the whole world crushed me and I went to sleep for a while.

38

I didn't know how long I had been unconscious when I realized that I was still breathing. I wasn't thinking about time. I was too aware that breathing was difficult. Terribly difficult.

I didn't understand why until it occurred to me that the chair was on top of me, pinning me at the shoulder blades and down my back.

But it seemed too heavy.

Then I figured it out.

I push chair. Chair hits Betty. Betty falls forward. Chair and Betty tip over. Albert underneath.

Poor Albert.

What I didn't understand was why she didn't get up. It's not very nice to stay seated when your chair is crushing your houseguest.

Maybe she didn't know I was there.

I tried to squirm, but all I managed to wiggle was my toes.

She wouldn't notice that, but I found it hard to do more because breathing was so hard.

I moaned a little, but that tired me out.

I tried to take a deep breath, but I couldn't.

Suddenly I felt I wasn't going to get another breath. I panicked. I heaved with every heaving muscle I owned, and the chair rocked, and toppled sideways, thudding off me.

I rolled onto my side and rested again.

I had no sense of passing time, but while I lay there I thought to wonder were Dave Hogue was.

Nobody was moving in the room. It was very quiet.

It was a small room. I decided I would have heard him breathing if he was there, even if I couldn't see him. I seemed preoccupied with breathing.

I listened. Nobody besides me was breathing.

No body was breathing.

When I found the strength to sit up and look to the floor on the other side of the chair, I saw Betty Weddle dead.

There was a small hole under her jaw on the right side. Her right eye socket was filled with blood and juice, from the pulping shock wave of the bullet passing up. There was a big hole above her forehead on the right.

Dave Hogue was not in the room.

I could understand that. She was a sickening sight.

I looked around. Everything was in chaos, broken lamps, bullet holes in the walls.

I saw the telephone across near the door, and went to it.

I dialed the operator. I told him I wanted to talk to the law about a killing but I couldn't remember the number I was supposed to dial. He put me through to the state police.

I said where I was and that there was a dead person and that they should send someone over. They asked me how the person had become dead. I said gunshot. They asked whether I had touched the gun. I said I hadn't.

They told me to stay put.

I said I had no intentions of going anywhere.

When I put the phone down, I looked around the room again.

I saw both of Betty Weddle's hands but I didn't see the gun.

I looked from all angles and then elsewhere in the room. But I still couldn't see the gun. It was possible that it had happened to fall just where the body now would cover it.

It was also possible that it had been taken.

By the fireplace, three sheets of paper caught my eye. The papers Weddle had been reading from when Dave Hogue interrupted her.

I picked them up and now read for myself.

They were all typed, clearly set out and centered on the pages. The first was headed "Reasons for Killing William Boyd, March 29, 1980."

Weddle had read me the five reasons listed.

The second was headed "Risks of Detection, March 29, 1980."

One. The best chance is if the body is not found.

Two. The best time would be one when his absence is not considered suspicious.

Three. It is safer to hide the body well in territory I know than to hide it less carefully under pressure of time in unfamiliar territory.

Four. There is no point in trying to disguise the body by removal of fingers, teeth, etc. Any male that size found here will be identified as Boyd.

Five. I retain the option of confession to protect an alternate suspect.

The third sheet was laid out like the others, although it was dated December 18, 1979. It was headed "Reasons for Marrying Ida Boyd."

39

As I got in my van, my head began to throb. At the back I found hair matted with blood, and a wet hurty streak.

I sat for a minute.

It was not a particularly smart thing to do. The police were on their way and if I was still around when they arrived I would be tied up for hours, if not days.

I didn't want that.

I wanted to find Dave Hogue.

But I sat anyway. It felt too much for me. If I were more liberated, I would have cried. It was because my head hurt. It was because of the familiarity of the interior of my van. It was because I had a woman I cared for. It was because I had a neon sign outside my office. It was because I still had a parent, and a child, and, despite opportunities to stop, was still breathing myself.

It made me shudder, the jump I had made in this last day.

I'd spent days prancing around, place to place, talking about murder. Speculating on factors behind murder. Building guesses about murder.

Nice cozy exercises of the mind. Think about this, work out that.

All safe, because it was done in the head.

Then suddenly, harshly, cruelly, I had been thrust through the barrier between mind games and body death.

I walked in ready for more chatter. I walked out lucky to be alive.

It had become suddenly real.

Murder is not a game. Murder is about pulpy eyes, and broken necks and not breathing. People who do murder are ugly, and wicked.

Dave Hogue had committed murder.

I needed, worse than I needed anything, to find him, to scream at him, "No! You were wrong! You were bad!"

I got out of Weddle's cul-de-sac without passing a police car, but as I turned off Hill Street farther on, I heard the screeching of tires somewhere behind me.

I didn't look. Not even in my rearview mirror.

I went to Hogue's office. There were no lights visible from the front. I parked, and walked around to the back.

No lights visible there either.

I looked in the double garage, but couldn't make out whether there was a car in it or not. I tried the garage side door. It was locked.

I didn't feel like going back to my van for a flashlight.

I took off a shoe and smashed the little window. I unlocked the door and went in. I felt for a light switch. The sudden light was temporarily blinding.

One bay of the garage was empty, as before. But I was more interested now in the pile filling the other space.

I went to it and pulled off pieces of scrap wood, cloth, iron.

Eventually I came to a fender and the hood of a white Datsun.

Not long before, I would have given a lot to find that car, but now I was looking for something else.

I dug through the junk pile on it only as far as a window. The light was good enough to show me that there was no one inside.

Not that I expected otherwise, but Dave Hogue had to be somewhere.

I went back to my van. I drove to the center of town. I stopped by a phone box. The operator put me through to the state police. Again.

I told them that the man they were looking for was Dave Hogue. That there was a chance he had run for it.

I didn't want him to have a chance.

The duty officer had taken my last call.

"You said you were staying at the scene," he said. "But they've just called through that you aren't there. Where are you?"

"I'm getting medical attention," I said. "There were a lot of bullets whizzing around the place. A couple of them grazed me."

I jiggled the lever in the receiver's cradle to make some static on the line.

The state cop said, "Where are you?"

"Something's wrong with the line," I said. "I can't hear you."

"The hell you can't."

"I can't hear you," I said, louder. "Can you hear me? Can you hear me?"

I drove out State 46, to the east.

A mile or so on this side of Gnaw Bone.

By the roadside edge of Ida Boyd's tract of land I found a car. It was pulled into the space where I'd met the Mappes family frolicking.

I was worried about walking in the woods. I'd become disoriented last time. In daylight.

But . . .

I drove at the woods head on. Put my headlights on high beam shining into the shadowy trees. Took my flashlight out of the glove compartment.

And went in at about the same place I had come out some days before.

My headlights helped for a little while, though I had left them on more as a help to get me out.

If, when, I managed to get out.

But they were bright enough for me to notice the last of the blazes which my Boy Scout had casually chopped into some of the trees as he passed them.

I'd thought him stupid and destructive at the time.

I thanked him now. They led me, with the help of my flashlight, exactly where I wanted to go.

The hollow which had been Billy Boyd's grave.

I saw Hogue first when my light picked up his white shirt.

He was lying on the ground, his feet in the center of the disturbed earth from which Boyd's body had been reclaimed, his head near some rocks.

I stopped where I was. Hogue didn't move. I approached him cautiously.

As I shined the light over his body, I located the gun. In his right hand, pointing nowhere in particular.

I saw no blood.

I bent down and put my ear near his mouth to listen for breath.

"Come to hear the last words of a dying man?" he asked.

I jerked back, stood up. Hogue pulled himself to a sitting position against the rocks.

For the third time in less than a life, I found myself at the wrong end of a gun.

He said, "I listened to you get closer, just as I've been watching you get closer to . . . what happened."

"You surprised me."

"It's dangerous to walk alone in the woods at night unless you know them well."

I thought of a lot of things to say. I said, "I suppose so." I turned my light out and sat down, facing him.

"There are wild animals in the woods," Hogue continued. "Not that they usually are dangerous to people. Only when they're cornered, only when you don't leave them alone."

"Are you threatening me?" I asked.

He shrugged. "Not really. It's just that I have been lying here trying to die and I haven't managed it yet." He sounded almost dreamy.

"How are you trying to do it?"

"My heart," he said. "I've been on the edge since I was thirty-two. I've taken care of it pretty well, so you would think that in a time of crisis, it would take care of me." He exhaled hard, a throaty half-laugh.

"And if it doesn't?"

"The weather might get worse. A touch of exposure would do nicely. But if I wake up in the morning, and I'm not dead, I will just shoot myself. It's messy and I don't like the idea of disturbing this nice little place again, but it may have to be."

"Why die at all?" I asked.

"Natural justice," he said. "I killed someone intentionally. And that led to someone else dying. I didn't intend that, but it is the direct consequence of my actions. And I don't want to live with the consequences of my actions." He stopped talking for a moment, then said, "It feels different to have killed than I thought it would. Less important, yet more wrong."

There was much I wanted to know, but I couldn't find words to ask.

He said, "You saw the sheets of paper I left at Betty's?"

"Yes."

"She must have found them at the office," he said sadly. "Poor Betty." Then he asked, "Was she really trying to kill you?"

"Yes."

"Why?" He seemed genuinely puzzled and curious.

"She knew I knew you had killed Boyd. She was going to kill me to protect you."

"What an extraordinary thing to do."

"She was accustomed to protecting you," I said. "And it was a last chance to win your affection."

"My affection?" He considered it, as if it were a point of law.

"What a blind and arid bastard you are," I said.

"I don't think it's up to you to make judgments like that," he said sharply. He shifted his position leaning against the rocks. "You don't know what it's like being me."

"You're breaking my heart," I said.

"The heart," he said. "That's the rub." Hogue began to speak loudly, aggressively. "By nature I am an active person," he said. In the night light I saw him wave his right hand at me, to emphasize his point. I don't think he remembered that he had a gun in it.

"After Korea, I was a social worker in Detroit," he said. "Did you know that?"

"No."

"Do you know what it's like to be a social worker in Detroit?"

"No."

"One who cares? One who gets involved?"

I didn't speak.

"It's hell," he said. "Hell on wheels, that's Detroit. And too involved, that's my problem. Not arid. Not detached. I was swamped with the utter unsolvability and injustice of it all. It became too much for me, and I had to get out."

He shifted again, bringing a hand to his head.

"So I went to law school," he said. "I thought the law might give me some perspective on the same problems. But it nearly killed me instead. I was in the city and . . . Oh hell. It doesn't matter. I had a heart attack. I was thirty-two and I was on death's string. I had to read-just my whole life, my whole way of thinking. While I was recu-perating, I saw a painting, a landscape of what I know now is a hill-side near Story, on Route 135. That picture meant a lot to me. It looked like a nice place to come, to be, to survive. So I moved here. And instead of becoming too involved with desperate people, I've be-come involved with the land."

"Involved enough to kill," I said.

"Involved enough to kill," he said. "I killed in Korea, to defend democracy. A matter of principle. Things are either important to you or they're not. Billy's destruction of this quiet little forest would have been something that could never be put right. I watched him working at his mother to get control of the land, and I knew I had to prevent it from happening. I was ready to marry the woman if I had to. But Billy saw fit to prevent that. I spent days among these trees, walking this soil, afterward. In the end I had no other effective option. I had to de-cide what was important to me; what life, including my life, was worth. I tried to talk seriously to him at his party, but he only joked and taunted. That was the watershed for me. I went home and worked out what I had to do, and why."

"What did you do?"

"I gave myself two months. I started preparing this grave site and looking for an opportunity. But then early one Sunday morning Frank Pynne called to say his wife had absconded. He didn't care about her, but she'd taken a lot of money, nearly four thousand dollars that he'd made in off-the-record deals. And he wanted to know what he could do, without having to explain where the cash came from. I was his lawyer—he could tell me—but he didn't want to tell the sheriff. Any-way, I talked to him about it and then I nearly went back to bed. But I saw it was a chance. She was a pretty enough little thing that people wouldn't worry about the idea that Billy had run away with her. It was a matter of whether I could kill him in time. So I walked across to his house, and let myself in."

"The door was open?"

"I had a key from Ida," Hogue said. "I went in. I found him alone. He was even sleeping on his stomach. I put my knee on the back of his neck and I strangled him with a wire. It was terribly easy. And very humane. He never knew what happened. I wrapped him in the sheet and put a fresh one on the bed. I packed some of his clothes and carried him downstairs. I put him in his car and locked the garage with his keys. Then I went home. In the middle of Sunday night, I walked back to the house and drove him across the street and into my garage. I put him into my car and drove him out and buried him. His car is still in my garage."

"I found it tonight."

"If anybody saw me coming or going, they didn't register it as important. And I was lucky for a while. I had Billy gone and the rest of my remaining life intact too. But these things catch up with you eventually. There was always that chance. I have no complaints."

"Betty Weddle might," I said.

"If I were going to live, I would feel very bad about that," he said. "But I won't have much time."

"You will if I have anything to do with it," I said.

"You feel aggrieved about what I've done?" he asked lightly.

"Yes," I said.

"On what grounds? An argument based on philosophical foundations of the law?"

"Right and wrong," I said, sounding more righteous than I expected. "You're the kind of person who gives having principles a bad name."

"Oh, I don't know," he said dismissively. "Action and reaction. Consequences. I've always thought that there was a utility for someone like me. Living on borrowed time, as they say. And without attachments. I live without fear of death, so I can administer it without fear. The world is a better place without Billy Boyd. He would have died one day anyway. I just hastened it a little, in exchange for hastening my own a little. You can tell I'm going to die soon anyway."

"I can?"

"The way I've been talking about all these things. They say one's life passes before one's eyes. You—"

He was interrupted by a sound we both heard.

A muted kind of rattling.

"What's that?" he asked.

We listened again. It seemed to come from near him.

I turned my flashlight on.

The rattle came again. Hogue twisted away from the rocks he had been leaning against. "A snake!" he shouted. "Oh God, I hate them!"

Near his side, on his left, I saw a gray coil. My light picked up two vertical lines above it. The tail, rattling, and the head.

"Aaaaah!" Hogue screamed, and as he twisted, he aimed his gun at the thing and pulled the trigger half a dozen times. There was only one shot.

A shock seemed to snatch at the rattling shadow.

I sat stunned. For one thing, I had been getting ready to bet, if necessary, that Weddle's gun didn't have any bullets left in it. For another, as a reflex action, to fire and hit a small shadowy line was impressive shooting.

If it came to that, the appearance of the snake at all at night was surprising. Though Hogue had been leaning on and disturbing the pile of stones which the snake presumably lived in. Billy Boyd's body had been found in the first place because the campers had chased a snake around those stones.

Hogue had drawn himself into a ball behind his gun. He was pulling the trigger again and again. Scared almost to death.

But not quite.

40

I made my way back toward the roadside. I saw my dimming headlights from well inside the woods.

I also saw someone walk in front of one of them, a momentary human eclipse.

"Hello!" I called.

My voice seemed to reverberate through the night, and suddenly there was the return sound of feet running and car doors slamming.

A voice came through a bullhorn. "Whoever you are, come out slowly and with your hands above your head."

As I walked into the glare of the lights, I made out three police cars and a number of figures.

There were people pointing guns at me again.

But I was tired. I couldn't have cared less.

"Get your hands up!" the voice from the bullhorn shouted.

"Go away," I said.

They either didn't hear me or were naturally contrary. Two men rushed at me and each grabbed an arm.

"Oh, cut it out," I said.

They twisted my arms behind my back and brought me out of the glare into comparative dark. From behind an open car door, a figure rose, and I saw the bullhorn in his hand. A sound-gun. I had guns on the mind.

Then there was an unamplified sound. "Do you know who it is, Sheriff?"

I recognized the voice. Darrow Junkersfield.

A powerful flashlight blinded me.

"Turn it off!"

"Ah," Junkersfield said. "The private detective."

"My head hurts. I want a doctor."

"None of my men laid a finger on you," he said sharply.

"Your paranoia is showing," I said. "I got shot earlier this evening. I want treatment."

"You look all right to me," he said.

"By God, I'll die if you don't get me to a doctor," I said. I felt like throwing a tantrum. "Look at the back of my head." I turned it to him. "Go on, look."

"Some blood," he said. "So maybe you cut yourself shaving."

"I demand medical attention."

"Is there a hospital around here?" he asked Jeanna Dunlap.

"Nearest is in Columbus. About fifteen miles."

"That's that," Junkersfield said, expecting me to be unwilling to travel as far as fifteen miles.

"I don't want a hospital. Take me to Andrew Kubiak in Nashville. He's the coroner there. You've already got him out of bed to deal with the body. He might as well fix me up too."

"As soon as you tell me why you killed the lady there," he said.

"Aren't you supposed to read me my rights first?"

"I already did."

"And you have witnesses to prove it. Just as well I don't need them. But don't take my word for it. You go into the woods and get yourself a real witness to what happened. Even though the angle the bullet went in should have told you, unless you think a gunman hid in her bra until he got a chance to plug her under the chin."

"What's he talking about?" one of Junkersfield's flunkies asked.

"What witness?" Junkersfield asked.

"David Hogue," I said. "He's in there shooting snakes. I bit pieces out of the trees on the way in. All you have to do is follow the trail."

"And he saw what happened to the woman?"

"With his own two eyes. He also killed Billy Boyd. He is also trying to work out a way to shoot himself with a gun that has no bullets. The gun is the one that killed the woman and made all the holes around her house."

There was a rush of activity which led to a party of state policemen taking a walk in the woods.

"It is also the gun that wounded me," I said. But people didn't seem to care very much.

I was left in the tender care of Jeanna Dunlap. Almost as an afterthought, Junkersfield told her to get me some medical attention. She led me to her car woodenly, silent.

Junkersfield hadn't noticed the effect on her of my identifying Dave Hogue as Boyd's murderer. But I had.

I was also adequately *compos mentis* to turn my van's lights out. If I left them on and drained the battery, you could be sure none of this platoon of cops would be around to help push it. They're never there when you want one.

Jeanna Dunlap remained silent as we pulled onto the main road. But when we got up to cruising speed she spoke, without taking her eyes off the road ahead. "I suppose you're sure."

"About Dave Hogue? Yes," I said.

She was quiet only for a moment. "I want to apologize to you," she said.

"What?"

"I've disgraced the honorable office I hold. And at no time worse than when I broke the glass in my door."

"You were suffering then far more than I have about it since," I said.

"Yes," she said meditatively.

I didn't ask what it was all about. But, proving that Leroy Powder's was not the only way to learn things, she volunteered, "I always thought I was a special person for Billy. Not just another entry on a list. It hit me where I am vulnerable."

We were silent the rest of the way into Nashville. We both had things to think about.

There were lights on downstairs at the Kubiaks' house.

Mrs. Kubiak answered the door. She wore an embroidered bathrobe, and she didn't seem surprised to have people on her doorstep.

"What's the problem, Jeanna?" she asked.

"He says he was shot."

She peered at me in the porch light. "Do I know you, mister?"

"We met several months ago," I said.

"Don't quite place you," she said. "And I can't see no holes in you."

"I was grazed twice. Once on the ear. Once on the back of the head. They need cleaning up, mostly."

"No point in waiting for the doctor for cleaning up," she said.

She took me to the doctor's office and had a look at my wounds. Jeanna Dunlap waited on the front porch.

"Your head's kind of flat back there," she said. "Good thing too, 'cause if it stuck out more you'd have lost a piece of it."

"Oh," I said.

"You already lost a piece of ear."

"Stitch it, please," I said.

She did so and then went to the back of my head.

After cutting the hair away, and daubing with cotton doused with antiseptic, she said, "I can stitch this too. Or if you don't mind a scar, I'll leave it like it is."

"Leave it," I said. "It'll give me character when I go bald."

She came around the front of me again.

"How do you feel?"

"Bad enough to know I'll live," I said.

"What is it? Touch of shock?"

"Maybe. But I also want to ask your husband about something else."

"What?"

"Ida Boyd."

"Oh," she said, clearly surprised that I should pull that name out of the evening air. "What about her?"

"Your husband examined the body."

"That's right."

"I keep hearing reasons to think that her death wasn't an accident."

"Sounds like you've been talking to that David Hogue," she said.

"He was the first who raised it."

She shook her head. "He made Andy look at her again, and all Andy found was pretty much what he found the first time. Her head was broke bad, and it broke on the edge of her bathtub. It's the sort of thing that could happen to anyone, and my Andy was absolutely certain that's what happened to her."

"There was nothing funny or unusual at all?"

"The only thing he said was that her skull seemed a little brittle."

"What made him say that?"

"There were a few more small pieces of bone than there might have been. But folks' bones get brittle as they get older."

"So they do," I said.

"You can wait for him if you want," she said.

"I don't suppose he'd tell me much more."

"Not about Ida," she said. She seemed to study me and a worried configuration came across her face. "Are you all right?"

"I'm terribly terribly tired."

She said, "I can fix you up a bed here."

"Thank you, Mrs. Kubiak," I said, "but the kind of tired that I am is not the kind of tired that sleep can fix."

I returned to the sheriff's custody on the porch. We walked down the stairs and got into her patrol car. I leaned back to relax a moment.

"Ow," I said. I'd forgotten about my head.

"You've had a rough time down here," Sheriff Dunlap said.

"All traffic on life's one-way street," I said.

"And all part of the job?"

"The job's not over," I said.

She looked at me.

"What time is it?" I asked.

"Getting on for one a.m."

"How do people round here take to folks dropping in this time of night?"

She said nothing.

"It's just they're likely to be at home, see?"

She listened attentively to what I had to say.

We drove out of town to the west.

With all Jeanna Dunlap's flashable lights flashing, we turned into Sharon Doans' driveway. I was not pleased to see Frank Pynne's Fiesta parked comfortably next to Doans' VW. But I had planned for that contingency.

A dull illumination showed through the front window.

I got out of the patrol car and walked to the front door.

I pounded on it.

And I kept pounding until a tousled Sharon Doans opened it a fraction and said, "Who the hell is that?"

"I'm terribly sorry to disturb you, Miss Doans," I said. "But I've got an urgent message for Frank Pynne and I've been helping the sheriff here to try to find him."

I stepped aside, just in case she hadn't noticed that I was accompanied.

It certainly concentrated her attention. "Oh," she said. She thought for a moment. "Hang on."

She closed the door and it took some time before it was opened again.

Frank Pynne, looking decidedly displeased with life, stood before me. "What's so goddamned urgent?" he asked.

"Your wife," I said. "She's been shot."

"So?" he asked. Still waiting for the urgent bit. Nice people I mix with.

"She's been asking for you. It's about something she wants to give back to you."

He thought about this.

"Shot, huh?"

"Yes."

"Bad?"

"Yes."

"She going to make it?"

"I don't know about all that. I only wanted to make sure you got the message. She's in the Columbus hospital. I don't know exactly where it is, but when you get there, I'm sure you'll find it easily."

"O.K.," he said. He closed the door again.

I gave the thumbs up to Jeanna Dunlap. She began the maneuvers to turn around and when Pynne came out of Doans' house, the patrol car drove up the driveway.

Pynne offered no further words before he jumped into his car and spun it away.

Doans and I stood watching as he left.

"Hey," she said, suddenly realizing. "Where'd Jeanna go?"

"Back to wherever Jeannas go," I lied.

"But you haven't got a ride."

"Christ! I forgot about that. Oh well. Doesn't matter, I can walk. It's not a problem. Don't even think about driving me."

She thought about it.

"Just as well she did leave," I said.

"What do you mean?"

One whiff of the air in there, and I think she would have called out to invite some friends."

"Yeah, maybe," she said thoughtfully. "We don't usually have trouble with Jeanna about that kind of thing, but with the state police around so thick, that's a new ball game."

I nodded.

"Hey, before you start, you want a drink or something?"

"I thought you'd never ask," I said.

She paused. "Oh hell. Why not?"

Though I hadn't really smelled it from the door, the atmosphere inside was overwhelmingly aromatic. If I wasn't careful, I would get happy.

I said, "I don't mean to waste valuable fragrances, but could you open the window a little?"

"It's good for you, you know."

"Old dog. New tricks," I said.

"Yeah, O.K.," she said. She opened the window near her wicker chairs. I settled in one of them.

She got two bottles of beer and gave me one. I sipped from it. She sat down opposite me.

"Whew," she said. "That was a bit of a shake-up, the heavy knock on the door in the middle of the night."

"Not middle," I said.

"Right, right," she said. "Lots of night left. Hey, what happened to your ear?"

"It got shot."

Her eyes opened wide, then narrowed. "For true?"

"A lady was aiming to miss it, but missed and hit it."

"What's the matter? She come home early and find you with her husband?" Doans snickered and didn't seem consumed with further curiosity.

I sipped from my beer again, and then said, "I've been thinking about you."

She smiled. "You have?"

"I have," I said.

"Hey, that's sweet." She looked at me. "Is that sweet?"

I said, "People have been telling me things that have made me think about you."

"What sort of things?"

"They've been calling you a liar."

She pulled herself out of a slouch on the wicker chair. "Who? About what?"

"It's about the time Billy was here when his mother was dying."

She became rigid.

"People have been saying he wasn't here all that time. They're saying that he went back to the house."

"Well, it's not so!" she said emphatically. "He was here every single minute from—from four-fifteen till nearly nine."

"I believe you," I said.

She sat angry, for a moment or two.

"I do," I said.

She relaxed a little. "Oh." She didn't know quite what to say.

"Well, nearly. You've shaded the time he arrived a little. It would have been later, because he didn't come here until his mother had slipped in the bathroom in the first place. And he would have wanted to be covered over the whole period she might have died in."

"That's not so," she said.

"And now that Billy's will is out, and people know you were more than just a friend of his, they won't be nearly so ready to believe about the time just because you say it."

"I wrote it down," she said.

"Oh?"

"I have a book I write things in, things that happen to me, and I wrote it down what time Billy got here that day and it says four-fifteen."

"Show it to me."

"I . . . I don't want to. It's personal, full of private things, you know."

"Just show me where it says Billy came at four-fifteen. If you show me that part now, then I can be a witness to say that you didn't change it, if somebody asks later."

She thought about it. "I'll cover up the rest of it," she said.

"O.K. Fine," I said.

She got up and went to a bookcase by her bed. I watched as she took one from a row of red books.

She leafed through.

"It would be the beginning of March," I said.

"I know, I know."

She found the part she was looking for, and read it, and came over to me.

Before she bent down, she said, "Now, promise if I hold my hand over part of it, you won't knock it away and try to read under."

"I promise."

She put the book on my lap, holding both her hands over a section beneath the first two lines. The lines read, "Billy came over about quarter past four. He stayed till nearly nine and we made . . . "

"O.K.?"

"I've read them," I said.

She closed the book, and lifted it off.

"I'm dying to know what you and Billy made," I said.

"Nosy."

She took the book back to the bookcase.

"You're not shy, are you?" I asked as she returned.

"A little bit." She sat down. "So see? He was here when I said and he stayed the whole time."

"I said that I believed he was here the whole time," I said.

"But now you know."

"I know that you are a little bit shy, and that you are a little bit unlucky."

She frowned. "Unlucky? What do you mean?"

"I mean that Billy may have been here the whole time, but you weren't."

She sat.

"And I say you were unlucky, because somebody saw you."

Still silent.

I repeated, "Somebody saw you."

"They couldn't have," she said.

"Oh, but they did."

She frowned harder. "They couldn't have seen me," she said again, emphatically.

"Why not? You mean because you were dressed up like a man?"

Her face went suddenly blank.

"Let me try this out on you," I said. "Billy is told his mother is about to make a will to his disadvantage. He goes to the house to talk to her. He is in the house when his mother slips in the bathroom. Maybe he made that happen. Maybe he didn't. But he definitely knows it's happened and he knows she is hurt and he comes here instead of getting help for her. He comes here because he thinks she is going to die and wants to make sure he has an alibi, in case people accuse him. But while he's here, he thinks maybe she isn't going to die after all. And if she lives, she'll know he hasn't sent for help for her. Maybe if she lives she will even be able to incriminate him. He decides to ask you to go to the house to see how badly hurt she is. Maybe you're willing or maybe you have to be pressured into going, but you agree."

I sipped from my beer. Doans stared at me, her eyes and her mouth a little bit open.

I said, "You decide that if you have to go, you're better off dressed up some way or another. Maybe you're just more comfortable that way or maybe you think anybody seeing you go to the house would wonder what you were doing there, since you never go there. Anyway, you dress up. You drive your own car, but you park out of the way, and, dressed up, you walk to the house. Billy has given you a key. But you're a little bit unlucky because someone sees your car, sees you and sees you go into the house with the key."

"I don't want to hear crap like this," she said.

"You go into the house and you find Ida Boyd. Maybe she is still unconscious, but she is still breathing. You see she is going to live after all. But she is weak, and she is vulnerable. And I think you take her head in your hands and line it up and take aim and I think you hit her head on the tub again, as hard as you can."

Sharon Doans inhaled sharply. The memory of Ida's last breath.

"Now, I don't think you knew that a pathologist can tell the difference between one blow and several blows. I don't think you banged her head just once because of that. You did crack off some of the rough edges which the first break left, but you lined her head up so well and hit it so hard that I think she must have died right away and obviously, so you didn't feel you needed to hit her again. So," I said, "so I believe

what you say about Billy. It's what you say about you that I don't believe."

"It's horrible," she said.

"I agree."

"You can't prove anything," she said, raging and fearful at once.

"Well," I said, "I'm not so sure about that. We've got quite a lot of
bits and pieces. You were seen. And I'm particularly interested to
have the forensic scientists go over the clothes you wore. Navy-blue
anorak with a hood, wasn't it? I'd be very surprised if we don't find a
little blood or hair or something on it."

Inadvertently her eyes darted to a closet.

"There we are," I said. "In the closet. And on top of that, we have
whatever oblique references you might have made about it in your
book. Got to be a big event for you and you're bound to have referred
to it. What you wrote might not mean much by itself, but it likely
wouldn't sound too good read out in court at the trial of someone
accused of murder. Especially the main beneficiary of the victim's
main beneficiary. And then we can start looking for other people who
might have seen you. When we tell the story to the papers and get
everybody in the county thinking about it, who knows what we
will turn up."

She flew at me, screaming. "You're horrible! Horrible!" She
swung her beer bottle, overturned the table. Clawed at me. Bit.
Kneed. Spat. Pulled at my ear.

I just tried to protect myself until she was spent. I tried to feel
lucky that at least she didn't have a gun in hand to point at me, to shoot
me with. It made a change.

I would have been safe enough anyway. Once the screaming
started, Jeanna Dunlap left her listening position to come full face into
the window. We had arranged that she would come back, quietly, as
soon as Pynne left. And she had her gun out.

When I sensed a little of Doans' energy subsiding, I tried to sur-
round her, wrap my arms around to pin hers.

She suddenly gave up.

She said, "She was probably dying anyway."

It was said in as cold and clear and feelingless a way as anything I have ever heard. I let her go. We stood limp for a moment, leaning on one another. Then she drew away.

I didn't know what the hell was going through her head, or what she was doing. I didn't care. In a matter of an hour, I had faced two different murderers who felt no guilt.

I was thinking that, of the two, I preferred neither.

I preferred not to have known about any of it. I preferred to have stayed an indigent anachronism, getting ready to explain my unemployability to a welfare office somewhere in the security of a murky gray-green government office due for repainting when the inflation rate dropped. I preferred to have been anywhere and anything else. I preferred to have hung up my gumshoes and learned a dishonest trade.

I preferred not to see a crazy-eyed little woman hurtling toward me like a fastball.

I wished all such ugly things, all such visions, to go away.

I swung at this one with the back of my doubled-up hand. And I hit it for a home run. I've never hit a pitch so hard in my life. The sweet solid contact felt good and felt like the first good thing I'd felt since I could remember.

At first I thought the crack was her neck breaking. I thought I'd killed her.

But I hadn't.

Jeanna Dunlap had. She shot her dead.

41

There was a lot of commotion after that. Shouting voices, some scuffling.

But I didn't make it out at the time.

I just kind of decided to sit down, on the floor.

Then I lay down.

The noise, I learned later, was because Frank Pynne had reappeared outside Doans' house.

He hadn't been supposed to do that.

He'd been meant to be speeding toward Columbus in the full flush of thinking he would get his money back.

Only he'd gone home, instead, to call the hospital.

I guess he'd suspected that I, Albert R. Samson, bonded private detective of this state, wouldn't drop a wounded lady into a visit from the likes of him. In the course of the legal shakeout he would inevitably locate his wife, but it wasn't my job to help him. Not part of what he was paying me for. His lawyer's secretary had told me as much.

And when he did find his wife, when she was stronger, he'd have to decide whether he could afford to try to get his cash repaid. What with the cloud over where it came from.

Naw. He never would.

I don't know why I lay down just when I did.

Jeanna said later she'd been afraid Sharon Doans' sewing shears had got to me. That I was dead too.

I hadn't seen the scissors.

Naw. I wasn't dead. Just tired, I guess.

I stayed tired a long time.

Fatigue is a funny business. Which doesn't always have much to do with sleep. In the Second World War scientists tried to define it, determine the chemical components or the fundamental conditions which make people "tired." The idea was maybe to find a pill for it. They didn't do very well. Not even on the definition. The closest they got was to say that if someone was tired, he must be kind of bored. No pills for that.

For my tiredness I rested. Guarding the glass.

And at first I spent a lot of time abusing myself about my way of life. It was not because of the financial precariousness this time. It was because of the ugliness it got me into.

I couldn't stop ugliness happening in the world. But I didn't have to volunteer to take part in it.

I bought a set of paints.

I guarded the glass well.

But gradually I was drawn back into the world.

First it was through Hogue's trial. He made it as simple for them as it could be, and stood without expression as he drew a sentence for life.

By that time, he had decided it was just as well that his heart was still working, because he got it in mind to start a fund to raise enough money to buy Ida Boyd's land for the B.C.T.

I know this because he sent me a letter with the money I was owed for my rendered services on behalf of Frank Pynne. In it he said that he would be administering the fund appeal from prison and that he had sold all his own assets to launch it with. He even suggested that I might want to donate my check for the noble purpose of saving this land for posterity.

I cashed my check the same day.

I guess when you're tired you just don't feel noble.

The second thing that brought me back into the world was a visit from Glass Albert.

It was December and there was snow. I suspected right away that he hadn't stopped to see if I could come out to play.

"I'm calling in a few of the days you owe me," he announced.

I was at my easel at the time.

"Oh, yeah? Someone finally wants to marry your daughter?"

"Not exactly."

I put my brush behind my ear. "What, then?"

"It's my wife," he said.

"Someone finally wants to marry your wife?"

"She's lost a lot of weight," he said. "It's not medical—I talked to her doctor—and she's not on a diet, because those never work for her. So I want her followed around for a while."

"Suspicious mind you have."

"I find myself asking questions. And if you can't have them answered, what's the point of being rich?"

"Something I ask myself often," I said.

"So when can you start?"

"As soon as I finish this painting," I said.

He walked over to have a look.

It was the first time I had known him to be speechless.

And while I was waiting for him to find words, I felt the first inklings of curiosity that I'd felt in a long time.

I thought about Priscilla Pynne. Her putting on weight, taking it off. I wondered about her post-gunshot career. I didn't see why she shouldn't carry on at college. She'd wanted it badly enough to overcome a lot of other things.

I made the decision to make the effort, to find out for sure.

Curiosity is the pill for fatigue.

"Wife's been losing weight, eh?" I asked, giving Glass Albert the chance to be relieved of the tiredness of looking at the outpourings of my undiscovered primitive genius.

Perhaps I was only undiscovered and primitive. But I was suddenly more willing to settle for two out of three. Not a bad percentage in most things life has to offer.

THE PERENNIAL LIBRARY MYSTERY SERIES

Ted Allbeury

THE OTHER SIDE OF SILENCE   P 669, $2.84
"In the best le Carré tradition . . . an ingenious and readable book."
      —New York Times Book Review

PALOMINO BLONDE   P 670, $2.84
"Fast-moving, splendidly technocratic intercontinental espionage tale
. . . you'll love it."   *—The Times* (London)

SNOWBALL   P 671, $2.84
"A novel of byzantine intrigue. . . ."*—New York Times Book Review*

Delano Ames

CORPSE DIPLOMATIQUE   P 637, $2.84
"Sprightly and intelligent."

      —New York Herald Tribune Book Review

FOR OLD CRIME'S SAKE   P 629, $2.84

MURDER, MAESTRO, PLEASE   P 630, $2.84
"If there is a more engaging couple in modern fiction than Jane and
Dagobert Brown, we have not met them."   *—Scotsman*

SHE SHALL HAVE MURDER   P 638, $2.84
"Combines the merit of both the English and American schools in the
new mystery. It's as breezy as the best of the American ones, and has
the sophistication and wit of any top-notch Britisher."
      —New York Herald Tribune Book Review

E. C. Bentley

TRENT'S LAST CASE   P 440, $2.50
"One of the three best detective stories ever written."
      —Agatha Christie

TRENT'S OWN CASE   P 516, $2.25
"I won't waste time saying that the plot is sound and the detection
satisfying. Trent has not altered a scrap and reappears with all his old
humor and charm."   —Dorothy L. Sayers

Andrew Bergman

THE BIG KISS-OFF OF 1944   P 673, $2.84

"It is without doubt the nearest thing to genuine Chandler I've ever come across. . . . Tough, witty—very witty—and a beautiful eye for period detail. . . ."
—Jack Higgins

HOLLYWOOD AND LEVINE   P 674, $2.84

"Fast-paced private-eye fiction."
—San Francisco Chronicle

Gavin Black

A DRAGON FOR CHRISTMAS   P 473, $1.95

"Potent excitement!"
—New York Herald Tribune

THE EYES AROUND ME   P 485, $1.95

"I stayed up until all hours last night reading The Eyes Around Me, which is something I do not do very often, but I was so intrigued by the ingeniousness of Mr. Black's plotting and the witty way in which he spins his mystery. I can only say that I enjoyed the book enormously."
—F. van Wyck Mason

YOU WANT TO DIE, JOHNNY?   P 472, $1.95

"Gavin Black doesn't just develop a pressure plot in suspense, he adds uninfected wit, character, charm, and sharp knowledge of the Far East to make rereading as keen as the first race-through."   —Book Week

Nicholas Blake

THE CORPSE IN THE SNOWMAN   P 427, $1.95

"If there is a distinction between the novel and the detective story (which we do not admit), then this book deserves a high place in both categories."
—New York Times

END OF CHAPTER   P 397, $1.95

". . . admirably solid . . . an adroit formal detective puzzle backed up by firm characterization and a knowing picture of London publishing."
—New York Times

HEAD OF A TRAVELER   P 398, $2.25

"Another grade A detective story of the right old jigsaw persuasion."
—New York Herald Tribune Book Review

MINUTE FOR MURDER   P 419, $1.95

"An outstanding mystery novel. Mr. Blake's writing is a delight in itself."
—New York Times

THE MORNING AFTER DEATH   P 520, $1.95

"One of Blake's best."
—Rex Warner

A PENKNIFE IN MY HEART　　　　　　　P 521, $2.25
"Style brilliant . . . and suspenseful."　　　—*San Francisco Chronicle*

THE PRIVATE WOUND　　　　　　　　　P 531, $2.25
"[Blake's] best novel in a dozen years . . . . An intensely penetrating study
of sexual passion. . . . A powerful story of murder and its aftermath."
　　　　　　　　　　　　　—Anthony Boucher, *New York Times*

A QUESTION OF PROOF　　　　　　　　P 494, $1.95
"The characters in this story are unusually well drawn, and the suspense
is well sustained."　　　　　　　　　　　—*New York Times*

THE SAD VARIETY　　　　　　　　　　P 495, $2.25
"It is a stunner. I read it instead of eating, instead of sleeping."
　　　　　　　　　　　　　　—Dorothy Salisbury Davis

THERE'S TROUBLE BREWING　　　　　　P 569, $3.37
"Nigel Strangeways is a puzzling mixture of simplicity and penetration,
but all the more real for that."
　　　　　　　　　　　—*The Times* (London) *Literary Supplement*

THOU SHELL OF DEATH　　　　　　　　P 428, $1.95
"It has all the virtues of culture, intelligence and sensibility that the most
exacting connoisseur could ask of detective fiction."
　　　　　　　　　　　—*The Times* (London) *Literary Supplement*

THE WIDOW'S CRUISE　　　　　　　　　P 399, $2.25
"A stirring suspense. . . . The thrilling tale leaves nothing to be desired."
　　　　　　　　　　　　　　　—*Springfield Republican*

Oliver Bleeck

THE BRASS GO-BETWEEN　　　　　　　P 645, $2.84
"Fiction with a flair, well above the norm for thrillers."
　　　　　　　　　　　　　　　　—*Associated Press*

THE PROCANE CHRONICLE　　　　　　P 647, $2.84
"Without peer in American suspense."　　—*Los Angeles Times*

PROTOCOL FOR A KIDNAPPING　　　　P 646, $2.84
"The zigzags of plot are electric; the characters sharp; but it is the wit
and irony and touches of plain fun which make the whole a standout."
　　　　　　　　　　　　　　　　—*Los Angeles Times*

John & Emery Bonett

A BANNER FOR PEGASUS   P 554, $2.40
"A gem! Beautifully plotted and set. . . . Not only is the murder adroit and deserved, and the detection competent, but the love story is charming."   —Jacques Barzun and Wendell Hertig Taylor

DEAD LION   P 563, $2.40
"A clever plot, authentic background and interesting characters highly recommended this one."   —*New Republic*

THE SOUND OF MURDER   P 642, $2.84
The suspects are many, the clues few, but the gentle Inspector ferrets out the truth and pursues the case to its bitter and shocking end.

Christianna Brand

GREEN FOR DANGER   P 551, $2.50
"You have to reach for the greatest of Great Names (Christie, Carr, Queen . . .) to find Brand's rivals in the devious subtleties of the trade."
       —Anthony Boucher

TOUR DE FORCE   P 572, $2.40
"Complete with traps for the over-ingenious, a double-reverse surprise ending and a key clue planted so fairly and obviously that you completely overlook it. If that's your idea of perfect entertainment, then seize at once upon *Tour de Force.*"   —Anthony Boucher, *New York Times*

James Byrom

OR BE HE DEAD   P 585, $2.84
"A very original tale . . . Well written and steadily entertaining."
—Jacques Barzun and Wendell Hertig Taylor, *A Catalogue of Crime*

Henry Calvin

IT'S DIFFERENT ABROAD   P 640, $2.84
"What is remarkable and delightful, Mr. Calvin imparts a flavor of satire to what he renovates and compels us to take straight."
       —Jacques Barzun

Marjorie Carleton

VANISHED   P 559, $2.40
"Exceptional . . . a minor triumph."
—Jacques Barzun and Wendell Hertig Taylor, *A Catalogue of Crime*

George Harmon Coxe

MURDER WITH PICTURES P 527, $2.25

"[Coxe] has hit the bull's-eye with his first shot."

—*New York Times*

Edmund Crispin

BURIED FOR PLEASURE P 506, $2.50

"Absolute and unalloyed delight."

—Anthony Boucher, *New York Times*

Lionel Davidson

THE MENORAH MEN P 592, $2.84

"Of his fellow thriller writers, only John Le Carré shows the same instinct for the viscera." —*Chicago Tribune*

NIGHT OF WENCESLAS P 595, $2.84

"A most ingenious thriller, so enriched with style, wit, and a sense of serious comedy that it all but transcends its kind."

—*The New Yorker*

THE ROSE OF TIBET P 593, $2.84

"I hadn't realized how much I missed the genuine Adventure story . . . until I read *The Rose of Tibet*." —Graham Greene

D. M. Devine

MY BROTHER'S KILLER P 558, $2.40

"A most enjoyable crime story which I enjoyed reading down to the last moment." —Agatha Christie

Kenneth Fearing

THE BIG CLOCK P 500, $1.95

"It will be some time before chill-hungry clients meet again so rare a compound of irony, satire, and icy-fingered narrative. *The Big Clock* is . . . a psychothriller you won't put down." —*Weekly Book Review*

Andrew Garve

THE ASHES OF LODA P 430, $1.50

"Garve . . . embellishes a fine fast adventure story with a more credible picture of the U.S.S.R. than is offered in most thrillers."

—*New York Times Book Review*

THE CUCKOO LINE AFFAIR P 451, $1.95

". . . an agreeable and ingenious piece of work." —*The New Yorker*

A HERO FOR LEANDA P 429, $1.50
"One can trust Mr. Garve to put a fresh twist to any situation, and the
ending is really a lovely surprise." —*Manchester Guardian*

MURDER THROUGH THE LOOKING GLASS P 449, $1.95
". . . refreshingly out-of-the-way and enjoyable . . . highly recommended
to all comers." —*Saturday Review*

NO TEARS FOR HILDA P 441, $1.95
"It starts fine and finishes finer. I got behind on breathing watching Max
get not only his man but his woman, too." —Rex Stout

THE RIDDLE OF SAMSON P 450, $1.95
"The story is an excellent one, the people are quite likable, and the
writing is superior." —*Springfield Republican*

Michael Gilbert

BLOOD AND JUDGMENT P 446, $1.95
"Gilbert readers need scarcely be told that the characters all come alive
at first sight, and that his surpassing talent for narration enhances any
plot. . . . Don't miss." —*San Francisco Chronicle*

THE BODY OF A GIRL P 459, $1.95
"Does what a good mystery should do: open up into all kinds of ramifica-
tions, with untold menace behind the action. At the end, there is a
bang-up climax, and it is a pleasure to see how skilfully Gilbert wraps
everything up." —*New York Times Book Review*

FEAR TO TREAD P 458, $1.95
"Merits serious consideration as a work of art." —*New York Times*

Joe Gores

HAMMETT P 631, $2.84
"Joe Gores at his very best. Terse, powerful writing—with the master,
Dashiell Hammett, as the protagonist in a novel I think he would have
been proud to call his own." —*Robert Ludlum*

C. W. Grafton

BEYOND A REASONABLE DOUBT P 519, $1.95
"A very ingenious tale of murder . . . a brilliant and gripping narrative."
—*Jacques Barzun and Wendell Hertig Taylor*

S. B. Hough

DEAR DAUGHTER DEAD   P 661, $2.84

"A highly intelligent and sophisticated story of police detection . . . not to be missed on any account."   —Francis Iles, *The Guardian*

SWEET SISTER SEDUCED   P 662, $2.84

In the course of a nightlong conversation between the Inspector and the suspect, the complex emotions of a very strange marriage are revealed.

P. M. Hubbard

HIGH TIDE   P 571, $2.40

"A smooth elaboration of mounting horror and danger."

—*Library Journal*

Elspeth Huxley

THE AFRICAN POISON MURDERS   P 540, $2.25

"Obscure venom, manical mutilations, deadly bush fire, thrilling climax compose major opus.... Top-flight."

—*Saturday Review of Literature*

MURDER ON SAFARI   P 587, $2.84

"Right now we'd call Mrs. Huxley a dangerous rival to Agatha Christie."   —*Books*

Francis Iles

BEFORE THE FACT   P 517, $2.50

"Not many 'serious' novelists have produced character studies to compare with Iles's internally terrifying portrait of the murderer in *Before the Fact,* his masterpiece and a work truly deserving the appellation of unique and beyond price."   —Howard Haycraft

MALICE AFORETHOUGHT   P 532, $1.95

"It is a long time since I have read anything so good as *Malice Aforethought,* with its cynical humour, acute criminology, plausible detail and rapid movement. It makes you hug yourself with pleasure."

—H. C. Harwood, *Saturday Review*

Michael Innes

APPLEBY ON ARARAT   P 648, $2.84

"Superbly plotted and humorously written."   —*The New Yorker*

APPLEBY'S END   P 649, $2.84

"Most amusing."   —*Boston Globe*

THE CASE OF THE JOURNEYING BOY   P 632, $3.12
"I could see no faults in it. There is no one to compare with him."
— *Illustrated London News*

DEATH ON A QUIET DAY   P 677, $2.84
"Delightfully witty."   — *Chicago Sunday Tribune*

DEATH BY WATER   P 574, $2.40
"The amount of ironic social criticism and deft characterization of scenes and people would serve another author for six books."
— Jacques Barzun and Wendell Hertig Taylor

HARE SITTING UP   P 590, $2.84
"There is hardly anyone (in mysteries or mainstream) more exquisitely literate, allusive and Jamesian—and hardly anyone with a firmer sense of melodramatic plot or a more vigorous gift of storytelling."
— Anthony Boucher, *New York Times*

THE LONG FAREWELL   P 575, $2.40
"A model of the deft, classic detective story, told in the most wittily diverting prose."   — *New York Times*

THE MAN FROM THE SEA   P 591, $2.84
"The pace is brisk, the adventures exciting and excitingly told, and above all he keeps to the very end the interesting ambiguity of the man from the sea."   — *New Statesman*

ONE MAN SHOW   P 672, $2.84
"Exciting, amusingly written . . . very good enjoyment it is."
— *The Spectator*

THE SECRET VANGUARD   P 584, $2.84
"Innes . . . has mastered the art of swift, exciting and well-organized narrative."   — *New York Times*

THE WEIGHT OF THE EVIDENCE   P 633, $2.84
"First-class puzzle, deftly solved. University background interesting and amusing."   — *Saturday Review of Literature*

Mary Kelly

THE SPOILT KILL   P 565, $2.40
"Mary Kelly is a new Dorothy Sayers. . . . [An] exciting new novel."
— *Evening News*

Lange Lewis

THE BIRTHDAY MURDER P 518, $1.95
"Almost perfect in its playlike purity and delightful prose."
—Jacques Barzun and Wendell Hertig Taylor

Allan MacKinnon

HOUSE OF DARKNESS P 582, $2.84
"His best . . . a perfect compendium."
—Jacques Barzun and Wendell Hertig Taylor, *A Catalogue of Crime*

Frank Parrish

FIRE IN THE BARLEY P 651, $2.84
"A remarkable and brilliant first novel. . . . entrancing."
—*The Spectator*

SNARE IN THE DARK P 650, $2.84
The wily English poacher Dan Mallett is framed for murder and has to confront unknown enemies to clear himself.

STING OF THE HONEYBEE P 652, $2.84
"Terrorism and murder visit a sleepy English village in this witty, offbeat thriller." —*Chicago Sun-Times*

Austin Ripley

MINUTE MYSTERIES P 387, $2.50
More than one hundred of the world's shortest detective stories. Only one possible solution to each case!

Thomas Sterling

THE EVIL OF THE DAY P 529, $2.50
"Prose as witty and subtle as it is sharp and clear. . .characters unconventionally conceived and richly bodied forth . . . . In short, a novel to be treasured." —Anthony Boucher, *New York Times*

Julian Symons

THE BELTING INHERITANCE P 468, $1.95
"A superb whodunit in the best tradition of the detective story."
—August Derleth, *Madison Capital Times*

BOGUE'S FORTUNE P 481, $1.95
"There's a touch of the old sardonic humour, and more than a touch of style." —*The Spectator*

Henry Kitchell Webster

WHO IS THE NEXT?   P 539, $2.25
"A double murder, private-plane piloting, a neat impersonation, and a delicate courtship are adroitly combined by a writer who knows how to use the language."   —Jacques Barzun and Wendell Hertig Taylor

John Welcome

GO FOR BROKE   P 663, $2.84
A rich financier chases Richard Graham half 'round Europe in a desperate attempt to prevent the truth getting out.

RUN FOR COVER   P 664, $2.84
"I can think of few writers in the international intrigue game with such a gift for fast and vivid storytelling."
                                  —*New York Times Book Review*

STOP AT NOTHING   P 665, $2.84
"Mr. Welcome is lively, vivid and highly readable."
                                  —*New York Times Book Review*

Anna Mary Wells

MURDERER'S CHOICE   P 534, $2.50
"Good writing, ample action, and excellent character work."
                                  —*Saturday Review of Literature*

A TALENT FOR MURDER   P 535, $2.25
"The discovery of the villain is a decided shock."   —*Books*

Charles Williams

DEAD CALM   P 655, $2.84
"A brilliant tour de force of inventive plotting, fine manipulation of a small cast and breathtaking sequences of spectacular navigation."
                                  —*New York Times Book Review*

THE SAILCLOTH SHROUD   P 654, $2.84
"A fine novel of excitement, spirited, fresh and satisfying."
                                  —*New York Times*

THE WRONG VENUS   P 656, $2.84
Swindler Lawrence Colby and the lovely Martine create a story of romance, larceny, and very blunt homicide.

Edward Young

THE FIFTH PASSENGER   P 544, $2.25
"Clever and adroit . . . excellent thriller. . . ."   —*Library Journal*

If you enjoyed this book you'll want to know about THE PERENNIAL LIBRARY MYSTERY SERIES

Buy them at your local bookstore or use this coupon for ordering:

Qty	P number	Price
——	————	——
——	————	——
——	————	——
——	————	——
——	————	——
——	————	——
——	————	——
——	————	——
——	————	——
——	————	——
——	————	——
——	————	——
——	————	——
——	————	——
——	————	——

postage and handling charge $1.00
———— book(s) @ $0.25   ————

TOTAL ☐

Prices contained in this coupon are Harper & Row invoice prices only. They are subject to change without notice, and in no way reflect the prices at which these books may be sold by other suppliers.

HARPER & ROW, Mail Order Dept. #PMS, 10 East 53rd St., New York, N.Y. 10022.

Please send me the books I have checked above. I am enclosing $_____ which includes a postage and handling charge of $1.00 for the first book and 25¢ for each additional book. Send check or money order. No cash or C.O.D.s please

Name_____

Address_____

City_____ State_____ Zip_____

Please allow 4 weeks for delivery. USA only. This offer expires 7/31/85
Please add applicable sales tax.